DARKNESS RISING

DARKNESS RISING

A CONTEMPORARY FANTASY TIME TRAVEL
ADVENTURE

SHADOW SLAYERS STORIES
BOOK FIVE

NELLIE H. STEELE

CHAPTER 1

eline's lower lip trembled as she stared at the newest arrival in the bar. Her muscles tensed and her heart thudded loudly enough against her ribs to drown out the din of the crowd around her. A shiver ran up her spine as sweat beaded on her brow.

The woman sashayed to the bartender, dressed head-to-toe in black. She flicked her long, dark hair over her shoulder and leaned onto the bar, speaking a few words to the man. Her cropped leather jacket inched up her back, revealing her porcelain skin and the tail of a dragon tattoo.

Celine recognized the woman immediately. And she knew what trouble would sweep into the sleepy town of Bucksville in her wake. Trouble powerful enough to change the town forever. Trouble powerful enough to destroy them all.

Panic swept through her, and she swallowed hard. She needed an escape. And she needed one fast.

* * *

Damien furrowed his brow as he studied Celine's severe reaction to some unknown stimulus. He waved his hand in front of her unwavering eyes. She seemed frozen.

He glanced around, expecting to find Marcus Northcott looming in a corner of the bar, but he did not spot the man. Other patrons continued to enjoy their drinks, chattering and laughing as though nothing had happened. Though the expression on Celine's face suggested something was very, very wrong.

Damien glanced at Michael before his eyes scanned the bar again. Celine's warm hand slipped around his and the world turned black.

One moment he sat at the round wooden table, next to Celine and across from Michael in the dimly lit local bar, The Thirsty Seal. In the next, cool evening air caressed his cheek and the smell of salt hung in the foggy atmosphere.

With his chair no longer supporting him, he toppled backward, landing hard on his backside. A stunned Michael sat across from him on the ground. Celine straightened from a squat to stand, recovering without trouble.

Ocean waves crashed against the rocky shore and the harbor bell clanged in the distance, announcing the tiny port town to ships passing in the night.

"What the hell just happened?" Michael asked. He groaned as he climbed to his feet and dusted his pants. "Oh, no." His eyes went wide, and his gaze darted around to take in their surroundings. "Please tell me we didn't just end up in a parallel universe."

"Ohhhh," Damien grumbled. "Not again." He pushed himself up to standing. "At least Celine's with us this time. You can get us back right?"

All eyes turned to Celine. She ran a trembling hand through her blonde curls. "We have to get back to the house."

"Wait, what?" Damien said as Celine stalked toward the glowing facade of the Buckley house on the hill. He hurried behind her. "That's it? We just randomly landed in parallel time and that's all you have to say?"

Michael shoved his hands in his pockets and trailed behind them, happy to let them sort out the details.

"We're not in a parallel time," Celine huffed. She shot a glance at Damien. "Though you may wish we were."

Damien stopped walking for a beat. Celine continued to storm toward the property line, hanging a right at the winding driveway on the outskirts of town and disappearing into the trees that surrounded it.

Michael caught up to him. "What's going on?"

"I have no idea. But it can't be good."

"Does she not know how to get us out of parallel time? We did it once before, I'm sure we can figure it out again."

Damien shook his head. "She says we're not in parallel time."

"What? Then what the hell just happened?"

"I don't know. But the way Celine's acting, I can't imagine it's anything good."

The two men pushed forward, following Celine on her trek back to the Buckley house. Moonlight glowed through the leaves, bathing the surroundings in an eerie light. Ahead of them, Celine's blonde locks gleamed with an almost ethereal glow.

Damien kept his gaze fixed on her. His stomach somersaulted as he considered her odd behavior and her chilling last words to him. Why would they wish they were in a parallel universe?

They'd visited one once before, accidentally sent there by a radiating electrical pulse created during an epic battle between Celine and Marcus. The experience created a lasting effect, physically and emotionally. Damien still woke up in a sweat from nightmares of the alternate reality. One in which Celine had married Marcus Northcott and had become nearly as vicious as he was.

He shivered as he recalled the details. They may not be in an alternate universe now, but given the trouble Celine hinted at, he had no desire to fight whatever they were facing without her. He quickened his pace, determined to reach the house when she did. He hoped she'd provide a better explanation then.

* * *

Celine hurried up the winding driveway. Her thoughts jumbled in her brain, and she struggled to sort them out. She fought the panic lacing every one of them as it threatened to manifest itself in physical form.

With her hands shoved tightly into the pocket of her hoodie to stop them from trembling, she worked to keep her breathing calm and measured. The hard pace she'd set as she climbed the hill to the Buckley house made it all the more difficult.

She glanced behind her. Michael and Damien trailed her by several yards, snippets of moonlight shining down on them through the trees. As she emerged on the hilltop, the twinkling lights of the town glowed below her.

Her mind twisted them from warm, pleasant signs of a lively small town into a burning, forsaken wasteland. The sparkling luminescence spiraled into flames that engulfed the people and the town.

Celine bit her lower lip and twisted to face the house ahead of her. Warm lights glowed from within the rambling, gothic structure. Its gray walls, foreboding to most, represented a safe haven to her. For now.

Would it also perish along with her beloved town?

She shook her head. Not if she could help it.

With a renewed determination, she pushed forward across the front lawn. The front doors blew open as she approached. The muddled thoughts in her mind manipulated the world around her, manifesting themselves through her powers.

"Gray!" she shouted as she stormed into the massive entryway.

The heels of her boots clicked against the gray stone floor echoing off the room's second-story ceiling. Celine scanned the gallery hallway above in search of her husband of two centuries.

"Gray!" she called again.

Damien and Michael hastened through the open doors behind her.

"Maybe now you can tell us what's going on," Michael said as they skirted around her.

Celine ran her fingers through her hair again with a sigh. Gray and Alexander appeared in the doorway to the sitting room.

"Celine?" Gray questioned. "I didn't expect you back this early."

"We have a problem," was her response.

He raised his eyebrows at her statement.

"So, what else is new," Damien said.

Celine's jaw tightened and she flicked her gaze to him. She tilted her head, giving it a slight shake. "This is nothing like you've seen before."

Damien's eyes shot side to side. "Worse than the time we dealt with two Dukes?"

Celine's head bobbed up and down as she squeezed her eyes closed. "Much worse."

"Celine," Alexander chimed in, "what is it that has you so on edge?"

She squeezed her lips together as she sucked in a deep breath, her chest rising high. The wrinkles on her forehead deepened as she considered the statement she was about to make.

She studied each of their faces, her eyes darting from Damien's loyal innocence to Michael's shrewd and discerning eyes. Her human companions would not be prepared for this. Even making them understand would be difficult.

Her eyes slid sideways to Gray, standing tall in the doorway. The concern on his face would exponentiate with her answer. She shifted her glance from his face to his cousin's. Alexander waited to assess the situation and help create a solution.

What she would say would shock them both. She lowered her eyes to the stone floor, her delicate features distorting with upset.

"It's Dominique. She's back." Thunder boomed overhead and lightning flashed in the sky, punctuating Celine's statement.

Damien ducked and winced. "Seriously?"

Gray's eyes widened at the admission. "What?" he shouted.

Celine nodded to confirm it, her palm pressing against her forehead.

"Where did you see her?" Alexander questioned.

"The Thirsty Seal."

"Did you speak with her?" Alexander asked.

Celine shook her head as she stalked toward the sitting room. "No. I got us out of there."

"I'm surprised she didn't spot you," Alexander said.

"I used a location hop."

She stalked to the brandy decanter and poured herself a

generous glass. The barely perceptible shake of her hand as she lifted the glass to her lips did not escape Damien.

Gray lifted his eyebrows in surprise at her statement. "You used a location hop and left Michael and Damien in the bar with her?"

"No, I used a location hop and took Michael and Damien with me."

Gray collapsed onto the sofa behind him, an expression of shock etched into his features.

"Sorry, but could someone clue in the two humans about what's going on?" Michael asked.

Alexander expounded on the concept. "A location hop is a tricky maneuver in which one projects themselves from one location to another. It takes a good deal of doing. I cannot imagine the stamina it would take to convey oneself *and* two humans to another location. Celine, how are you still standing?"

Celine sipped at the brandy. "Adrenaline," she claimed. "I didn't think much about it. I saw her and realized we needed to get out fast. It was all I could think to do."

Alexander raised his eyebrows, sucking in a deep breath. "Your power still amazes me at times."

"I'm sorry," Michael said, waving his hand in the air before he placed both on his hips, "I'm still not getting it."

"Location hops–" Alexander began.

Michael waved his hand around again. "No, no, not that. I get that." He paused for a moment, his forehead wrinkling. "Weirdly, I get that part. Who is this Dominique and why is everyone reacting like the Devil himself just walked into The Thirsty Seal?"

"Because he did. Or rather, she did," Gray answered.

Damien studied Gray and then Celine before he focused his attention on Alexander. The man seemed rattled. They all did. What was he missing? Who was Dominique?

"We have to do something," Celine said.

"What?" Gray shot back, leaping from the couch and pacing the floor.

"Leave?" Celine suggested, phrasing it as a question.

Alexander motioned to the humans in the room. "Michael and Damien should at the very least."

"Whoa, whoa, wait a minute," Michael shot back, "Michael and Damien aren't going anywhere. We're not slinking away with our tails between our legs over some woman showing up in town. We didn't back down from the Duke. We're not going to back down from some girl."

Celine wrinkled her nose. "Seriously? That's a bit sexist."

"You'll do what we tell you," Gray snapped.

"She's not just some woman," Alexander added.

"Come on. Aren't you being just a tad dramatic here? I mean we've faced down Marcus Northcott more than once. Hell, we defeated a soul eater," Michael said.

"And I survived a run-in with an adjudicator," Damien added.

"You don't understand," Celine said.

"Then tell us!" Michael said. "How bad can this really be?"

"She makes Marcus Northcott look like a cuddly kitten," Gray barked.

"Declawed," Alexander added.

"With its eyes still closed," Celine said. She flicked her gaze to Gray. "This is what Marcus meant by his warning in the In-between. He knew. He knew she was coming."

"That bastard," Gray yelled.

"He did try to warn me," Celine responded. "I didn't listen."

"Wait a minute," Damien said. "All this time the story has been the Duke is the boogeyman. Now you're telling me he's nothing to worry about compared to this Dominique person?"

"Yeah, how can that be? He's evil," Michael said.

"She's worse," Gray said.

Michael's eyes raised to the ceiling as he pondered the statement. "I'm sorry, I'm just trying to figure out how she's more evil than the Duke and worse than the nearly undefeatable soul eater we just destroyed."

"With Marcus's help," Celine reminded them.

"Do you think he'd help us again?" Damien inquired.

"Fat chance," Gray snarked.

"He's in league with her," Alexander explained.

"And if she's here–" Celine began.

"They're planning something big," Gray finished.

Alexander nodded at their assessment. "Big enough to destroy us all."

CHAPTER 2

ominique downed her bourbon in one swallow, slamming the glass onto the bar. She signaled the bartender for another. He poured it and she snatched the glass from the wooden counter and spun to take in the room.

With her elbows propped against the bar, she crossed one ankle over the other. The leather of her high-heeled boots squeaked as they rubbed together.

Her eyes peeked over the rim of her glass as she slowly sipped her bourbon and scanned the space. Her lips curled at the edges when she noted the empty table in the back corner.

Three seats. Three drinks. A blonde woman had sat there moments ago with two men. Celine.

Dominique narrowed her eyes at the table as she enjoyed another sip of the amber liquid, hints of vanilla and caramel tickling her tongue. Who were the men with her? Not Gray nor Alexander.

She cocked her head as she considered it. They could prove useful. Or, at the very least, entertaining playthings.

Celine had fled. Quickly, too. Typical of her cowardly cousin. How had she managed to pull off her quick getaway, though? She must have learned a few new tricks since the last time they'd met.

She had also taken both men with her. That indicated a level of caring for them. A deep level. Useful information. More baggage for Celine. And more people to apply pressure to in order to make her snap.

She puckered her lips and stared into the glass's contents as she swirled it. No matter. Celine would be no match for her this time. The thought brought a smile to her face.

Her cell phone vibrated in her jacket pocket. She pulled the device from inside and toggled on the display.

A text preview flashed across the screen with a one-word message: *Report.*

With her bourbon in one hand and the phone in the other, she tapped the keyboard with one thumb. *Arrived.*

Another one-word response: *Celine?*

Dominique heaved a sigh as she responded. *Located.*

The response came within seconds. *Did you engage?*

Dominique arched a perfectly-shaped eyebrow as she typed back. *No. She fled. Typical.*

The next message caused her to frown. *I didn't ask for your opinion. Do what you were tasked. Report back when you have more information.*

Another message popped on the screen as she read the first. *Don't dally. I expect results.*

Dominique clicked off the phone without answering. "And you shall have them," she murmured aloud. She downed another sip of the bourbon before twisting to request another from the bartender.

With a raised eyebrow, he poured her third. She resisted rolling her eyes at him as she scarfed the glass from the bar. Her gaze ran over the others in the bar. Humans. Toys. They would suffer, too. They would all suffer. And she would take immense pleasure in watching them squirm.

As devious ideas flitted at the edges of her brain, a man approached her. He hovered at her right on the edge of her peripheral vision. She ignored him, too tantalized by her own notions of destruction and suffering.

The man cleared his throat. Dominique's eyes narrowed and her jaw clenched. The idiot wasn't going away. She slid her eyes sideways and let them roam from his head to his feet. A typical townie. His middle-class attire was as off-putting as the hairy growth on his face, which he probably assumed made him look dashing.

Her lips puckered before turning into a Cheshire Cat grin. She tilted her head and faced him.

He offered her a coy grin. "Hello, pretty girl."

Dominique arched an eyebrow. It couldn't get any more predictable. She resisted the urge to zap him right in the middle of the crowded bar. Instead, she forced a smile onto her face.

She leaned a shoulder toward him, curving her hip. "Hello."

He wiggled his eyebrows at her and struck a pose, leaning against the bar with one outstretched arm, his other hand hanging by his thumb from the loop of his jeans.

"So, what's a pretty girl like you doing drinking alone?"

She flicked a brown curl over her shoulder. "I'm new in town."

"Ohhhh," he said, flashing that ridiculous grin again, "well, you'll need someone to show you around then."

Doubtful, Dominique thought. Instead of voicing her response, though, she flicked her eyebrows up and down and cocked her head.

The idiot continued with his offer. "Someone local who knows the place."

"Are you offering?"

He squared his shoulders and eyed her like a wolf. "Are you accepting?"

Dominique downed the last swallow of her bourbon. "What do you say we get out of here?"

A look of delightful surprise shone on the man's face. *Truly an idiot*, she reflected. The simpleton assumed she was interested in him.

"Your place or mine?" he purred at her.

She offered him an amused glance, tossing a few bills onto the bar. As she turned, the man caught her wrist, twisted it, and tugged up her sleeve. His finger traced the outline of one of her tattoos: an upside-down pentagram inside a triangle.

"Mmm," he murmured, "I love a girl with ink."

Dominique resisted the urge to wrench her wrist from his grasp and punish him for touching her. Instead, she leaned forward and whispered in his ear, "I've got plenty more."

She pulled back and eyed him. Her comment had had the intended effect. His breath quickened just slightly, and he flushed. His eyes sparkled as they traveled up and down her body, imagining where else she may have been inked. As he met her gaze again, his lips curled in a predator-like grin.

Dominique matched his smile. Little did he know the predator would soon become the prey.

"Shall we?" he questioned, motioning to the door.

She pranced toward it, her victim following behind her. Eager and willing now, he'd soon regret the moment he'd approached her with every fiber in his being. She'd enjoy that.

The corners of her mouth lifted in a wicked smile as she pushed into the cool Maine night air.

* * *

Damien's forehead wrinkled as he considered the information about the newcomer. His fuzzy understanding of the world around them made the task more difficult. Was Dominique a soul eater or some similar entity? How did she make Marcus Northcott, one of the most frightening people he'd ever met, seem tame?

And if she and Marcus Northcott were in league–a terrifying thought in and of itself–why would he warn Celine?

Questions bombarded his beleaguered mind faster than he could process them. Celine, Gray, and Alexander discussed options for escaping, vetting plans and their downsides. Their voices faded into the background as his mind worked overtime.

Words turned to gibberish as he struggled to understand their concern.

"Wait a minute. Wait, wait, wait," he finally said, waving his arms in the air.

All eyes turned to him. He swallowed hard and found his voice.

"I still don't understand. Who is this person? Is she some kind of soul eater? Or some other entity with crazy power?"

"No," Gray snapped. "Suffice it to say she's extremely dangerous. We wouldn't be discussing plans to hightail it out of here or trying to determine a place to keep you and Michael safe if she wasn't."

Michael stood with his hands on his hips and shrugged. "I already told you, we're not going anywhere."

Gray stalked to within inches of the man, his arms crossed tightly over his chest. "And I already told you, you'll do what we tell you. Your lives depend on it."

"Yeah, I still don't get that part," Damien said. "Is she some sort of special witch or something?"

"She's my cousin," Celine said. "Dominique Laurent."

"Identical cousin, I might add," Gray said. "Making this trickier to navigate than you may think."

"Well, identical outside of the brown hair," Alexander chimed in.

"Which can be changed in an instant," Gray said, snapping his fingers. "She's dangerous. And she'll use whatever tricks she can to do as much damage as possible."

"Okay, so, this Dominique is your lookalike cousin," Damien said, processing his thoughts aloud. "And she's super powerful like you?"

"Super powerful, yes, though, I would venture to say Celine is the more powerful of the two," Alexander answered.

"Oh, so we're good then. Why are we all worrying about this? Toss a fireball at her and be done with it," Michael suggested.

"It's not that simple," Celine said.

"Why?" Michael inquired.

Damien lifted a shoulder. "Yeah, if you're more powerful than her, why all the concern?"

"What she lacks in raw power she makes up for in many other ways," Alexander said.

Damien bit his lower lip. "Such as?"

Gray expounded on his cousin's comment. "Knowledge for one thing. She has vast amounts of it. She has studied under some of the best and most ruthless witches, warlocks, and other creatures on and off this planet."

Damien winced.

"On top of that," Celine added, "she has a variety of nefarious connections."

Alexander nodded, shoving his hands into his pockets. "All of which are extremely useful in coercing others to join her or do her bidding."

"In short," Celine said, "she's an extremely dangerous adversary."

"And combined with Northcott, that makes this situation even worse."

"I don't get that part either," Damien said, scratching his head.

"Me either. Surely these two have been in cahoots before," Michael said. "Obviously, it worked out in your favor. You're all still here."

Celine sucked in a breath before she explained. "Dominique and Marcus have what you may call a tenuous alliance. They rarely see eye-to-eye."

"Oh, perfect. So, we'll let them fight amongst themselves again," Michael said.

Celine shook her head. "Bad idea."

"I agree," Alexander said.

"Why?"

Celine finished her brandy before replying. "Because Marcus knew she was coming. That implies they've communicated."

"Right. He expected her," Alexander said.

Gray flung his hands in the air. "Of course the bastard did. It's his latest attempt to crush us. The last few haven't gone so well, have they?"

Damien narrowed his eyes at the statement. "That's the part that doesn't make sense to me."

Gray snapped his head at him. "Makes perfect sense to me. He's probably called her for backup."

Damien shook his head in disagreement. "Why warn Celine then?"

Celine lifted her eyebrows and flicked her gaze to Gray. "He has a point."

"I don't buy it. They're in league."

"I'm not disagreeing, but Damien makes a good point.

Why warn me if he knew she was coming? He tried to stop me from coming back to this time band. He said it was the biggest mistake of my life. What if I agreed with him?"

"He knew you wouldn't. He's twisting the knife."

"Perhaps it's a plan he doesn't agree with," Celine suggested. "Marcus does prefer to work alone and control things."

Gray offered a sarcastic laugh. "An evil plan he doesn't approve of? That would be a first."

"Damien may have a point," Alexander agreed.

"Not enough of one to change anything. The fact is," Gray said, ceasing his pacing for a moment, "Dominique is here. The second fact is that spells serious trouble for us."

Celine shot Alexander a glance and shrugged. "He's right. No matter who knew what, Dominique's arrival is not a good thing. The turmoil we've been living in since I've returned has been only the warmup."

* * *

Dominique eyed the limp form on the ground in front of her. She arched an eyebrow as she nudged his body with her foot. Nothing. Her full lips formed a frown, and she tilted her head, studying him.

A trickle of blood ran from the corner of his mouth. One of his legs stuck out at an awkward angle. A purplish-black bruise covered a wrist swollen to the size of a softball. Blood pooled in his jugular notch from a gash on his chin.

Had she killed him? It hadn't been her intention. Not yet, anyway. She'd only been warming up. Toying with him. Maybe she'd been too rough, though. Like a cat when it accidentally kills its prey.

Dominique poked at him again with the pointy tip of her knee-high leather boot. She wrinkled her nose at the lack of reaction. With a huff, she placed the boot's spiked heel onto his chest and dug in. A groan emanated from him, providing the only indication that he remained alive.

A smile formed on her features. "Oh, good. You're alive. Get up."

The man's eyes fluttered open. His face scrunched into a mask of pain as he stared up at her.

"No, please."

"Spare me your begging. Get up."

The man blubbered on the ground, his head rocking back and forth. A few tears leaked from the corners of his eyes, rolling toward his hairline. Spit flew from his mouth as he continued his mewling. "Just let me go."

"Let you go?" Dominique questioned. "But you were so interested in me. So willing to leave the bar with me. You promised me a night of fun. I'm having fun. Aren't you?"

He thrashed his head back and forth in answer.

"Such a pity. I'm having a lovely time."

"Let me go," he requested of her again.

"I would very much like to. But you refuse to get up."

"You broke my leg."

She eyed the limb sticking out at an awkward angle and clicked her tongue. With a wince and a wrinkled nose, she returned her gaze to his face. "Yes, it appears I did. Do you think you'll need it?"

"My wrist. My ribs and my nose."

She laced her fingers together and stretched them out in front of her. "And I was only warming up!"

"Haven't you done enough damage?"

"Do you always whine this much?"

"You bitch," he spat at her.

Her top lip curled in a snarl, and she flew on top of him, hovering above him. Her hand clamped around his throat.

Her nostrils flared as she reached her other hand down to his swollen wrist.

He moaned in pain as she wrapped her fingers around the bruised appendage and squeezed.

"Stop," he cried.

"That's not what you said a moment ago, is it?"

He didn't respond. Her snarl intensified as she began to twist his wrist.

He screamed in pain. "Stop!"

The request did little to cease her actions.

"I'm sorry," he squeaked.

Dominique's dark eyebrows raised. She flipped back onto her feet and placed her heel onto his chest again. She drilled her heel further into his chest as she leaned closer to him, tilting her ear to his lips. "I didn't quite catch that."

"I'm sorry," he whispered again.

She straightened and stared down at him. "So meek. I can barely hear you."

"I'm sorry!" he screamed before another sob wracked him.

"How interesting. What exactly are you sorry for?"

"Everything," he said. "Anything. I shouldn't have said that. I shouldn't have even spoken to you."

"Apology accepted," Dominique said, crossing her arms over her chest. "Now, get up."

"No," he groaned. "Just leave me here to die."

Dominique straightened, dropping her arms to her sides. "Die? No, that simply won't do. I need you alive."

"Why?" he gasped.

"I require your services."

"I can't do anything. My leg is broken. My ribs are broken. I need a hospital."

"Oh, that's right. How silly of me. You won't be able to do much in this state, will you?"

His forehead scrunched as he shook his head. Dominique studied him, puckering her lips as she considered her next move. With a shrug, she said, "I suppose I'll have to kill you then."

The man's eyes widened as she reached for his throat again. He screamed in agony as she lifted him from the ground with one hand. His shrieks bounced off the buildings surrounding them in the tiny alleyway as Dominique snuffed out another life.

CHAPTER 3

"I don't understand," Michael said. "If Celine is way more powerful than this Dominique person, why are we so concerned? Surely, she can be defeated."

"I am marginally more powerful than her," Celine explained. "And again, we're talking about raw talent. Dominique makes up for whatever deficiency she has with other talents."

"But surely with all of us together, we can outmaneuver her," Damien said. "We've done it before. In really, really dire situations."

Gray stared into the flames leaping inside the room's massive fireplace. "You've never faced Dominique."

Michael's forehead crinkled and he shook his head.

Damien bit his lower lip before speaking. "We thought all was lost when we faced Tobias Greene. But we came together, and we beat him. We can deal with this."

Celine shook her head. "You're not dealing with anything. Alexander is right. Both you and Michael need to leave."

"No," Michael said as Damien said, "No way."

"We're not leaving you," Damien added.

"D–" Celine said with a shake of her head.

"Celine, no!" Damien shouted. "We're family, right?" Damien's eyes pleaded with her.

Celine's chest deflated as his words hit her. She read deeper into the source of his comments. He'd just learned about his adoption. He was reeling. They had no information on his birth family or where he'd come from. He felt lost. Sending him away now would deliver another blow. But she couldn't see a way around it.

"I'm sorry, D. I know the timing is bad with your recent news, but I won't take a chance with your life."

"Perhaps this will provide you some time to focus on finding your family," Alexander suggested.

Damien's lower lip bobbed up and down, but no sound emerged. He licked his lips as he stared at the floor.

Celine recognized the crushing hurt. She flexed her jaw as she considered their situation. Fury burned through her soul at their predicament.

Silence filled the space between them. After a moment, Damien sucked in a deep breath. He rubbed the back of his neck before he lifted his chin. With a shake of his head, he announced, "I'm not leaving."

Michael snapped his head in Damien's direction. He widened his stance and crossed his arms over his chest. "Me either.'

"You'll regret that," Gray said.

"D, we may all be leaving."

"Then we'll go together," he said with a curt nod of his head.

Alexander shook his head. "If we leave, she'll track us down."

"It buys us some time, though," Gray said.

"No matter what, we stick together," Michael said.

"Yeah. There's no way I'm leaving without you, Celine. As

far as I'm concerned, this is no different than any other situation we've been in since the start of this whole mess."

"D, it is *very* different."

"I don't see it that way."

"You will," Gray warned.

"Until I do, I'll–"

His words were interrupted as the doors in the foyer blew open, slamming off the stone walls on either side. Thunder boomed overhead. Lightning tore through the sky.

"Dude, careful what you ask for," Michael whispered to him.

An icy wind gusted through the open doors and blasted past them. Celine stared into it, her eyes narrowing and her hair blowing back.

"What the hell?" Michael questioned.

The whistling of the wind died down, replaced by a thumping sound.

"What is that?" Damien whispered.

"Shh," Gray warned, skirting around them to peek into the foyer.

The thudding sound continued. A scraping noise followed every thwack. The smacking and dragging reverberated in the large space for several seconds before the source revealed itself.

The blood drained from Damien's face and his knees wobbled as he stared at the sight. He stumbled back a step as he blinked rapidly, certain his eyes were deceiving him. Michael's eyes widened and his jaw dropped open.

Gray grimaced and Alexander narrowed his eyes at the scene. Celine stepped forward and shoved Damien behind her, retreating back several steps.

A specter of a man stumbled toward them. White as a sheet, his glazed eyes focused straight ahead. Dried blood created a stain from the corner of his mouth to his jawline.

From his broken nose, black bruises stretched under both his eyes.

One arm dangled limply at his side. The scraping noise emanated from him as he dragged a seemingly broken leg with each step, tugging it forward as he lumbered slowly toward them.

"What the hell?" Michael breathed.

Gray screwed up his face at the sight. "Stay back from him."

"What the hell is he?" Damien questioned.

"My best guess is some form of zombie," Alexander answered.

Damien swallowed hard. "Zombie?" He choked on the words as they came out.

Michael shot Alexander a glance. "Are you serious?"

"Yes," Celine answered. "Stay back. We don't know how dangerous he is."

"Are zombies usually dangerous?" Damien whispered.

"They can be," Gray answered as the man dragged himself through the doors leading to the foyer.

"This one appears rather slow-moving, though," Celine assessed, her arms outstretched to shield Damien. "He looks fairly battered."

"I wonder how long he has been dead," Gray said.

As he entered the room, ceasing his difficult ambling, Celine studied him, narrowing her eyes as she stared at his damaged face. "Less than four hours."

Alexander flicked his gaze to Celine then back to the zombified man. "How do you know?"

"He was in the bar earlier."

Alexander's eyebrows shot up at her response.

Celine kept her eyes trained on the dead man. "I would bet anything he tangled with Dominique."

Michael winced. "Looks like he lost."

"No doubt," Gray answered.

"Why is he here? Does he need help or something?" Damien questioned.

Celine shook her head in response as she continued to keep her gaze trained on the zombie. Her eyes narrowed as a hissing sound filled the room.

"What's that?" Damien whispered as he grabbed Celine's arm and squeezed.

"Sounds like a snake. He has a snake," Michael breathed.

"Shh, quiet," Alexander hushed them. "He's trying to speak."

"Zombies can speak?" Damien questioned.

"Sssssssssssss," the man continued to attempt to push a word out of his mouth.

"What's he trying to say?" Michael inquired.

"Save me?" Damien suggested.

"Stuck?" Michael guessed.

Damien snapped his fingers. "Skull."

The gray-faced man blinked his blackened eyes once. "Cccccccceline."

"Oh, Celine," Damien said, throwing his arms out. "Why didn't we guess that?"

"Totally obvious," Michael said.

"Will you two stop babbling?" Gray hissed.

"Celine," the zombie repeated.

Celine arched an eyebrow and stepped forward. "I'm Celine."

"Careful, Celine," Gray warned.

She nodded in response, keeping her focus on the zombie.

His frosted eyes slowly moved to stare at her. "Celine," he repeated, his jaw clenched tightly, the words sticking on his bruised lips.

"I have a warning," he slurred.

"Of course, he does," Michael said.

"Come…" He stopped, his glassy eyes sliding shut for a moment before popping back open. "C-Come…"

Celine tilted her head as he stammered. Gray's head slid forward as he narrowed his eyes.

"Come with me?" Damien tried.

"Come here?" Michael suggested.

"Come," the man spat out again before his eyes rolled back in his head. He flopped forward, landing hard in a heap on the floor. His broken leg stuck out at a horrid angle and his jaw slid to one side, offset from his upper teeth. His eyes remained half-open, staring blankly ahead.

"Whoa!" Michael and Damien exclaimed as they leapt away from the grotesque corpse sprawling in front of them.

"Is he dead?" Michael questioned.

"He's been dead," Gray answered. "Haven't you been listening?"

"No, I mean like dead dead this time. Is he like done? No longer working? Completely dead?"

Celine leaned over him, studying the battered body. Alexander joined her, crouching down as he tilted his head to study the man.

"What do you think?" Celine inquired.

"Hard to say with zombies," Alexander answered. He reached toward the man's eyes when thunder clapped overhead. Celine's eyes wandered upward as the sound reverberated in the sky, grumbling for several more seconds.

"Why is it always storming at the worst moments here?" Damien groaned.

Another loud crash of rumbling thunder sounded as the wind picked up again. It swirled around them, racing in from the still-open front doors.

The clicking of a woman's high heels echoed across the foyer. A leather-clad female sashayed through the front doors. She swung her head in their direction, facing them fully. Damien's eyes widened and he shot a glance at Michael. Michael's slack-jawed expression clearly conveyed his shock over the woman's appearance. She was a dead-ringer for Celine outside of the brunette hair and the hardened expression.

Her eyes searched the sitting room, focusing on the body sprawled across the area rug. Her shoulders slumped as she spotted it, and she squashed her lips. With a click of her tongue, she tossed her arms out to the side.

"Ugh," she groaned with a shake of her head, "sorry about that." She stomped her way into the sitting room. "It's so hard to get good help these days. I'm sure you understand."

Celine backed up, shoving Damien back further. "Get out of here, Dominique."

"I'd love to. I just need to retrieve what's mine." She reached the man and hauled him up by the collar. His limbs dangled as she lifted him with ease. Dominique studied him, wincing. "Yeesh, he's got a bit of damage, hasn't he?"

"Get out!" Celine screamed.

The woman fixed her icy blue eyes on her cousin and arched a dark eyebrow. "Tsk, tsk, Celine. You don't need to get so bent out of shape. I could have been a real you-know-what and left a disabled zombie on your living room floor, you know? Show a little gratitude."

"You need to leave," Gray retorted. "And take him with you."

Dominique snapped her head in his direction and offered him a grin. "Aww, look, Gray's still alive. After all this time. Good to see you, buddy. Say, this fella here didn't happen to give you a warning, did he?" She pounded against his chest as his head and body hung limply from her one hand.

Silence met her question. "Hello? Did no one hear me? Did he give you the warning or not?"

"Leave, Dominique. Now," Celine ordered.

"Again, I'd love to, but I had a really important warning to pass along. Now, for the third time, did he manage to spit it out before he collapsed or not?"

She raised her thick eyebrows and scanned the room. "Anyone?" Her eyes landed on Michael. She offered him a coy glance with a half-smile. "How about you, hot stuff? Do you know?"

"Don't answer her," Celine said.

"Aw, don't be such a spoilsport, Celine. He looks fun. I'm very interested in these newbies, who by the smell of things–" Her nostrils flared as she took a sniff of the air. "–are human. Interesting."

She craned her neck to glance around Celine at Damien. "Who's the one hiding behind Mommy's skirts?"

Celine cocked her head in warning at Dominique.

"Ohhh, touchy about that one, are we?" She sucked in a breath. "Oh well, they are beside the point at the moment. We were trying to establish if the warning has been voiced." Her head snapped toward Alexander. "Maybe good old Alexander can answer. You were always quick on the uptake, Al. Did he make it through the warning?"

"Stop playing, Dominique. You know very well he didn't," Celine snapped.

"Ah, finally, an answer. Thank you, Celine. I really appreciate that." She pursed her lips and glanced at the dead man drooping from her fingers. "Really a shame he failed."

She slapped his cheeks. "Come on, wakey, wakey, Brendan. You've still got work to do!"

Celine chewed the inside of her lower lip as she squeezed her eyes closed. With a clenched jaw, she growled, "Stop this game and say what you came to say, Dominique."

Dominique shot Celine a baffled glance. "Where's the fun in that?" The man in her grasp groaned. "Oh, here we go.

He's back!" She tapped his cheeks again. "That's it. Come on."

The man's eyelids fluttered, and he glanced around. His shoulders slumped, and he moaned. His lower lip trembled. "Oh, no."

"Oh, yes!" Dominique said. "You died again before you could finish your task. That's the second time I had to revive you. You're really becoming quite a pain."

"Please, just let me die."

Dominique lowered him toward the floor. "I have. Twice."

The man blubbered as his toes brushed against the thick carpet.

"Come on, now. Stop your whining. Everyone's waiting for your message."

Dominique propped him up on his feet. His legs wobbled and he grimaced in pain. His chest heaved as he sobbed, covering his face with his hands in a pitiful display.

Celine's jaw tensed with disgust at the scene. She circled her hand, whipping a fireball into existence and launching it at the weeping man. He collapsed in a heap on the floor.

Dominque's jaw dropped and she snapped her gaze to Celine. "Now, Celine, that was uncalled for and just plain rude."

"It was disgusting, Dominique. And pitiful. But you never have been very good at not crossing lines."

Dominique pulled the listless form from the floor again. "Now, I'll have to revive him again." She slapped her palm against her thigh. "And look, you've charred him a bit. Just there. See?" She shook her head at the damage Celine's fireball left behind.

She snapped her fingers in the man's ear before she squashed her lips together. "Oh, this is going to take some work. You've really done some damage. Well, I suppose we should be going."

Still grasping the dead man's collar, she let her arm drop and stalked from the room, dragging his slack form along with her.

She reached the middle of the foyer when she stopped and snapped her fingers. She released her grasp on his collar. He hit the stone floor with a sickening smack.

Dominique spun on her heel and hurried across the foyer, waving a finger in the air. She offered them an amused grin. "The message. Silly me. I almost forgot."

She paused, hovering in the doorway, and held her hands out to both sides. "Celine, come to our side or I'll personally kill all of your friends and family." She clicked her tongue and winked at Celine.

"TTFN!" Her hair flicked outward as she spun again and sauntered across the foyer. She snapped her fingers in the air over her head as she passed the dead body. "Come on, loser, let's go."

A wheezing groan sounded as the man reanimated and struggled to his feet, limping his way behind her as she left the house.

As the sounds of his broken leg dragging against the stone floor receded, the doors banged shut and the lights flickered. Thunder boomed again overhead, punctuating the ominous threat.

CHAPTER 4

$\mathcal{S}$ilence filled the room for a moment as each of them considered the most recent events. Celine blew out a long breath and collapsed on the couch, covering her face with her hands.

"What the hell was that?" Michael asked.

"That," Gray answered, "was Dominique Laurent."

"Did she send a dead guy in here who died again? And then she revived him and he died again? And then–" Damien shook his head as he attempted to piece together the number of deaths and revivals he'd just witnessed, his fingers splayed as he counted them.

"Yes, it's what she considers a spot of fun," Alexander said as he hurried across the room and closed the doors to the foyer.

Michael poured himself a brandy as he processed the events. "The guy seemed really upset."

Gray stared into the dancing flames in the fireplace. "He was likely in a tremendous amount of pain. I'm sure she didn't fix whatever she broke when she revived him. She wouldn't waste her time."

"So," Michael said, running his fingers through his dirty blonde hair, "you can still feel pain even after you're dead."

"Yes," Alexander answered, "if you are revived, you can. And judging by the looks of him, he was extremely battered when she brought him back."

"Likely the result of her toying with him before he died," Gray added.

Celine blew out another long breath. "We need to get them out of here." She jabbed a finger in the direction of Michael and Damien.

Gray nodded. "I agree. Where?"

"Wait a minute, I thought we established that we are sticking this thing out together," Michael said.

"You established that. We continued to believe you should go," Gray corrected.

"Come on!" Damien shouted. "If you send us away, we're easy pickings for her if she finds us."

"We'll make sure she doesn't," Alexander chimed in.

"D, you've got to go. It's far too dangerous with her here."

"But–"

"No buts." Celine leapt from her seat and flung her arm toward the closed doors. "Did you just see what happened here? Did you see the condition he was in? I don't want that happening to either of you. I don't want you delivering the next message to me. Or trying to."

Celine bit her lower lip as she pressed her palms against her cheeks.

Gray approached her, wrapping her in his arms. "It'll be okay, Celine. We'll get them somewhere safe."

"Maybe we should all go," Damien suggested.

"The risk in that plan is Dominique finding you while she searches for me. Whether we go to two different places or stick together. It's too risky," Celine answered.

"Well, we have to figure something out. I'm not leaving you here and running away," Damien said.

"Neither am I," Michael added.

"I'll give it some thought but right now, you two should pack, because one way or another you'll be leaving soon."

"But–"

"I said no buts, D!" Celine shouted at him. She squeezed her eyes closed. "Sorry. I'm sorry. I'm just... stressed. Dominique has that effect on people."

Damien approached her and grabbed her hand, squeezing it. She broke from Gray's embrace, and circled her arms around Damien's neck, pulling him close. When she pulled back, tears streaked her cheeks.

"I just don't want to see anything happen to you," she cried. "And Dominique is too much of a wild card to take a chance with."

Damien's shoulders slumped and he pulled Celine closer to him. "I feel the same way about you. But we're a team. All of us. We stick together. Through thick and thin."

Michael nodded behind Damien. "And we've faced some pretty tough adversaries before. We're not afraid."

"You should be," Gray snapped.

"Marcus Northcott has the ability to snuff us out and doesn't. So–"

"The problem is, gentlemen," Alexander said, "Marcus Northcott has enough sense to realize snuffing you out gains him nothing with Celine. Dominique simply does not care."

"Are you actually trying to tell us Marcus Northcott has a conscience?" Michael questioned.

"I'm trying to tell you Dominique does not."

"Nor any morals," Gray said.

Alexander continued where Gray left off. "No scruples. No shame. Nothing that would prevent her from killing you outright. She will not care what it does to you or to Celine. In fact, she will likely relish in it."

"She will kill you *because* it will bother Celine. Your presence here makes this one thousand times worse for Celine because Dominique will do what she can to get at her. Including use you or kill you," Gray added.

Michael licked his lips as he considered the warning. "I just don't like to run away."

Gray stalked toward him, confronting him nose to nose. "This isn't a test of your ego."

"He's right," Celine said. "They both are. And I don't want to take any chances. I also don't want you somewhere unprotected where she can get to you."

Gray returned to her side and slipped an arm around her waist. "We'll figure something out." He kissed her golden hair as she leaned into him.

Silence fell over the group for several moments. Celine sniffled as she chewed her thumbnail.

"I–I guess we'll head up for the night," Damien said. "I'll throw some clothes in a duffel, but I'm not okay with this. Not by a longshot."

"Me either," Michael agreed. "Let's take the night to think about it and discuss it in the morning. Sound like a plan?"

Celine nodded in response, refusing to make eye contact with either of them.

Michael strode to her and squeezed her arm. "We'll be fine. You know me. I always come out on top. I never lose a fight."

Celine forced a weak smile onto her face at his words, squeezing his hand. Damien followed behind him and pulled her into another hug. She wrapped her arms around his waist and squeezed him tight.

"We'll get through this, Celine," he promised.

She nodded and, after one last hug, he and Michael headed into the foyer, pulling the doors shut behind them.

The second the latch clicked, Celine flicked her gaze to Gray. "They have to go."

"I know that. Try to convince them of that."

"We have to do whatever it takes," Celine said. "They can't be pawns in Dominique's game."

"I agree, Celine, but there's only so much we can do. The last time you wanted them both to go it didn't happen."

"But this time it has to. No ifs, ands, or buts. Michael and Damien must leave Bucksville."

* * *

Damien and Michael shuffled across the foyer after leaving the rest of the group behind in the sitting room. Michael lifted his chin at Damien as they reached the stairs. "We need to talk," he murmured in a low voice.

"No kidding," Damien agreed. He raked his fingers through his hair as they mounted the stairs and climbed to the second floor. They navigated to their bedrooms in silence.

Damien blew out a long breath as he pushed through the door to his room. Michael followed him, slamming the door shut.

"Okay, I don't know about you, but I'm not leaving."

"Me either!" Damien exclaimed as he stalked across the room and pushed open the window. The sound of the ocean crashing on the rocks below wafted into the room. He took a deep inhale of the salty sea air.

"I don't care what Celine says."

Damien stared out over the choppy waves in the distance. "She's just worried about us. But she's always worried about us."

"Yeah, she says the same stuff every time. It's too danger-ous. We could get hurt or worse."

Damien pressed his lips together as he stared out to the dusky sky.

"What?" Michael asked when he failed to respond.

Damien shook his head and pried his eyes from the hori-zon. "Nothing. I just– Do you ever worry our luck's going to run out?"

Michael's eyebrows squeezed together. "No?"

Damien nodded, lowering his eyes to the hardwood floor below.

"Are you considering leaving?"

"No, definitely not," Damien answered. "But… well, you saw that guy. Battered and bruised. Dead like three times or something. And she just kept toying with him."

"Celine's not going to let that happen to us," Michael said.

"What if Celine can't stop it? She's powerful, Michael. But she's not all-powerful."

"Come on, this is Celine being jittery like she always is. She doesn't want to be the reason something happens to us. I get that. But you heard Gray and Alexander. She's more powerful than Dominique."

"Dominique looks pretty darn powerful. She raised a guy from the dead twice in front of us."

"Okay, but to use your own words: she's powerful, but she's not all-powerful. And Celine has an edge. I trust that if push comes to shove, Celine can manage to keep us safe."

Damien nodded, his brows pinching in thought.

"And another thing. The reason I don't worry our luck's going to run out is that we aren't surviving in this world on sheer luck. We're surviving because we're smart and savvy. We have each other's backs. And we need to keep it that way. We can't split up."

"I totally agree."

"She can't make us leave, Damien."

"I don't want to leave her. Especially now."

Michael sighed. "I get it. She's your only connection to your family after finding out you were adopted."

Damien snorted a laugh. "I meant because she's really upset over Dominique, but yeah, there's that, too. Though that's the least of our problems."

"Look, man, it's okay if you're still reeling from that. It's a huge thing to find out. And we'll find your family. It just might take a little longer while we focus on this Dominique woman."

Damien shivered as he recalled the encounter with her. "She's kind of creepy, huh?"

"Do you mean because she's a dark-haired dead-ringer for Celine or just in general?"

Damien considered the question, his eyes staring in the air as he thought. "Both. It's super creepy that she looks just like Celine but acts nothing like her. It's even worse that she's so evil."

"Well, we've made it through an alternate-reality version of Celine, so I know we can cope with that."

"That one still gives me nightmares. Just saying'."

"And we've dealt with the dark side of things before, too. Marcus Northcott, Tobias Greene. Even Celeste can be a little dark."

Damien heaved a sigh and shook his head. "This is different."

"How?"

"I believe Alexander when he says Marcus has a boundary and there are lines he won't cross."

"Oh, come on, really? That guy wouldn't know a boundary if it smacked him in his pompous face. He's chased Celine around for centuries with no regard for anyone but himself."

Damien cocked his head. "Mmm, I'm not quite sure that's true."

"What are you saying? That he has a conscience? That he suddenly grew one? Because he literally just kidnapped Celine while we were busy stealing her painting back and made no apologies about it."

"He also saved her life and mine."

"Because he needed you. His own words," Michael reminded him.

"When he had Celine prisoner, he came to me."

"Yeah, I remember. And if this Dominique character ever does that, tell someone, okay? Do *not* run off on your own again."

Damien waved the comment away. "Fine, whatever, that wasn't what I was getting at. When he had Celine, he came to me and asked me to meet him. I did and when I questioned him about why he said it was because I was important to Celine."

Michael flicked his eyes sideways and shrugged, sticking his hands on his hips. "Okay, so?"

"And when I told him Celine was dying, he didn't hesitate to save her life."

"I'm not following you."

Damien's head fell toward his shoulder, and he offered Michael an unimpressed stare. "Come on, man. He wanted to make her happy."

Michael chortled at the notion. "What are you saying? That he loves her? Marcus Northcott wouldn't know love if Cupid himself beat him over the head with his bow and arrow."

"I'm telling you," Damien said. "Alexander is correct. In all likelihood, he won't kill me because if he did, Celine would never forgive him."

"I wouldn't bank on that, Damien."

"I'm not. And I'm not suggesting we trust Marcus North-cott. I'm just saying I think we have an advantage with him we may not have with Dominique. Which makes her all the more dangerous."

"Okay, fine. But we didn't have that advantage with Tobias Greene, and we beat him."

Damien pointed a finger at Michael. "With Marcus's help."

"Which we won't have this time, according to the Buckleys."

"Right."

"Are we sure about that?"

"That he won't help?" Damien asked.

"Yeah. I mean, if you're right, and he has some feelings for Celine like you think he does, will he really go along with Dominique?"

Damien ruminated on the question for a few moments. "Possibly. He's nearly destroyed Celine's family before. And with Dominique in the mix, he can blame her and–"

"Still have things work out to his advantage," Michael finished. "Yeah, I get it. This is stacking up to be another humdinger of a battle."

Damien winced. "Yep." He shook his head. "We need some kind of protection, so Celine won't send us away. She's going to need the help."

"What are you suggesting?"

Damien bit his lower lip. "Nothing. I don't know. I'll do some research and see what I can find. There has to be some-thing to help."

"Want me to help you hunt something down?"

Damien plopped onto this bed and dragged his laptop toward him. "No, you go ahead to your room. I'll just spend an hour or so digging into some resources and then I'm going to try to get some sleep."

"You sure?"

"Yeah. If I can't find anything, maybe I'll ask Alexander. He's pretty open-minded. He may see our side of it."

"Okay. Well, if you need more help, just give me a holler."

"Will do," Damien said with a salute.

Michael offered a wave back before he disappeared through the door to their shared bathroom. The door to Michael's room clicked closed seconds later.

Damien flipped open his laptop and stared at it as the display sparked to life. Thoughts raced through his brain faster than he could process them. Worry consumed him as it always did at the start of trouble.

His conversation with Michael replayed in his head. The image of the tears staining Celine's cheeks rattled around in his mind. The flippant nature of Celine's lookalike cousin shoved forward for attention.

He rolled his shoulders back and pulled the laptop toward him again. He performed a search on Dominique Laurent. He found nothing. Unsurprising. He figured she, like the other immortals around him, had precious few records providing clues to their real identities, birth dates, and so on.

He tried a few ill-fated searches for talismans to protect against the supernatural, warlocks, or witches. After falling down a few rabbit holes of odd information that led mostly to dangerous sites filled with questionable theories, he slammed the laptop shut.

He'd have to ask Alexander tomorrow about the possibility of using some sort of object or spell to protect them from any ill effects Dominique may bring.

He tossed the laptop aside and nestled under his covers. Cool air blew in from the open window across the room. He closed his eyes and listened to the sounds of the ocean crashing against the jagged coastline.

Damien gulped in deep breaths of the salty air as he

attempted to focus on anything but the trouble looming over them. Michael's statement about his recent finding of being adopted jumped to the forefront of his mind.

Who was he? Why had his parents never said anything? He had a tenuous connection to Celine before that news, now he had none. Would she use that to force him to leave? Would she claim he wasn't her family anyway and shouldn't be here?

His mind turned to her real cousin. The daughter of her mother's sibling since she carried the Laurent surname, Celine's mother's maiden name.

Images from the earlier encounter with her shot across his brain. He struggled to stop them, but he couldn't. Replay after replay of the man with his gray skin, his broken leg, swollen wrist, and broken nose forced their way to the front of his mind.

He recalled the sound of the dead man hitting the floor and his jaw dislocating as he smashed into the thick carpet covering the stone floor below. He recalled how roughly Dominique had picked him up and dragged him around, as though he was nothing more than a doll.

And then her final words rang in his mind. "Come to our side or I'll personally kill your family and friends."

He grimaced as he recalled the amused grin on her face as she uttered them. He scrubbed at his face as he considered for a moment being a zombie at the beck and call of Dominique Laurent. The idea held no charm for him.

He shook his head and blew out a breath into the darkened room. He couldn't let that happen. He wouldn't let that happen. He also wouldn't fail his newfound family. These people may not be his blood, but they were as important to him as if they were. He'd stay and he'd help. They had to beat this, too. And they would. At least, he hoped they would.

CHAPTER 5

$\mathcal{C}$eline stared at her bedroom ceiling, making out only blurry details in the blackness of the room. Her mind whirled, replaying the encounter earlier in the evening with Dominique.

The sudden arrival of her cousin did not bode well. Then again, Celine ruminated, was the arrival really sudden? Marcus had warned her months ago, telling her returning to this time band would mark the worst mistake of her life.

She hadn't listened. Perhaps she should have. Celine rolled onto her side, eyeing the golden jewelry box on her night table. She popped it open. Music floated through the air. This time, though, the music couldn't soothe her frayed nerves.

She flopped onto her other side, wondering if Michael and Damien were busy packing or if they had stubbornly ignored her request.

Would they have to force them to leave? And if they did, would they be safe? Dominique spotted them earlier this evening, her interest in them keen. Would she track them down?

Perhaps sending them away would draw more attention to how vulnerable and important to Celine they were. With a deep sigh, Celine rolled onto her back, facing the ceiling again.

She squeezed her eyes closed, trying to shut out the world. As silence consumed the room, she drifted off to sleep.

Visions of Bucksville burning haunted her dreams. She stood on the Buckley estate, staring down at the town. An orange glow lit the sky as building after building blazed in the night sky. Despite the raging fires below, a chill swept past Celine. She shivered and pulled her cardigan tighter around her.

The acrid smell of burning materials filled the air. Flecks of ash fluttered upward toward the moonlit sky.

The wind whipped again, tossing her blonde curls across her face. A voice whispered in the wind.

Celine twisted and studied the landscape behind her. Tall trees swayed in the breeze, their branches bending toward the earth. The voice sounded again, this time resembling a groan.

"Celine," the unearthly voice moaned through the branches of the coniferous and deciduous trees.

Celine narrowed her eyes into the strong wind as she spun fully to face the sound. Leaves blew past her, rustling in swirling eddies at her feet.

"Celine," the voice called again.

Celine stalked toward the tree line, ducking underneath the thick canopy. Moonlight filtered down through the branches, creating moving shadows along the ground.

She followed the path through the forest. Wind swept past her, carrying the voice with it again.

A whooshing sound blasted her from above. Instinctively,

she ducked, searching the sky, shielded by a thick layer of foliage, for the source. She found nothing.

As she continued along the path, the noise overhead swished past again. Celine froze, peering upward through the branches. The moon beamed through an opening in the canopy. Its blue-white glow bathed her in ethereal light.

Celine studied the round object, full and bright. The noise tore through the sky again. For a moment, the moon blackened, obliterated by a massive object.

Her heart thudded as the monstrous object sailed by overhead, blotting out the moon again. It darted past the opening in the canopy, temporarily blackening the landscape.

Something splattered on her upturned face, smacking against her fair skin in thick drops. Celine swallowed hard and wiped at the wet spots on her face. She studied her fingertips in the pale moonlight.

Crimson streaks covered her hand. Blood. Blood rained from the skies. Celine's breathing turned ragged and she raced through the trees, branches tearing at her hair and skin.

She skidded to a halt as she raced into the open area beyond the forest. Gravestones poked from the mossy ground.

An owl hooted in the distance and a wolf howled. Celine sucked in breaths as she threaded between gravestones, searching for what flew overhead. She backed into a cold, hard object. She twisted to identify the source.

A large stone angel rose behind her. With slumping wings, the angel buried her face in her stone hands in a perpetual state of weeping. Stone curls framed her face, falling to her shoulders. Celine reached out and ran her fingers along the rough surface. Blood from her fingers stained the gray stone.

Celine's brow furrowed as she gulped in a breath. In the distance, the wolf howled again, this time closer than before. She turned away from the weeping angel and stepped forward, tripping over a gravestone.

Celine glanced down at it before she stumbled back several steps, falling onto her backside. Her bloody hands trembled. She covered her gaping jaw with her shaky hand. Her lower lip shook and tears formed in her eyes as she read the name etched on the grave marker.

Damien Sherwood
Loyal cousin and friend

Celine gasped as she opened her eyes, springing up to sit. Her pulse still raced from the name she'd seen carved into the tombstone. Her chest heaved as she wiped at a tear that escaped onto her cheek.

She sucked in deep breaths, attempting to calm herself. After a moment, she swung her legs over the side of the bed, sliding her bare feet to the cold floor below. She hurried across the room, pulling her robe on as she padded toward the door.

She flung open the door and stared down the hall. Damien's door lay several feet down the hall. She studied it. No light shone from underneath.

Celine strode down the hall, the plush runner softening her steps. She reached his door, her fingers wrapped around the door handle.

Clinging to the cold metal, she pressed her ear against the wood. No sound reached her ears.

She depressed the handle, wincing as the latch bolt clicked as it slid free. She inched the door open and peered into the darkened room.

The smell of sea air wafted to her nostrils. Moonlight streamed through the open window, illuminating a sliver of the dark floorboards and the bed. A lump lay buried under the covers. Next to him, a laptop sat open, its screen long since in sleep mode.

Celine crept into the room and approached the bed. She stared down at Damien's sleeping form. His chest rose and fell in an easy rhythm. She smiled down at him before she lifted the laptop from the bed.

The display blinked to life, basking the room in a blue glow. Celine started to push the top closed when she caught sight of the material displayed on the open window. A mix of emotions surged through her as she noted the last topic Damien had researched on his laptop.

How to protect yourself from an evil witch sat in the search box, a list of results displayed below it. She stared at the luminous glow of the screen and shook her head. Half of her wanted to chuckle at Damien's search. The other half realized the situation was more dangerous than anything a Google search may help with. While she wanted to smile at his innocence, she also worried it may cost both of them.

Celine pursed her lips as she snapped the laptop closed and slid it onto the night table. She stalked to the window and leaned against the sill. The full moon illuminated the rocky coastline outside the window. Celine stared out at the rolling ocean, the crashing waves lulling her into a more relaxed state.

The moon's light reflected in the choppy waters. The ocean glowed under the bright orb. It painted the trees in a supernatural light. Celine shivered as she recalled her dream. She reached for the handle and began to pull the window shut.

Outside, the moonlight dimmed, plunging the world into temporary darkness. Celine froze, her fingers still clasping the brass handle. The divot between her eyebrows deepened as she scanned the sky.

She searched for a cloud that may have blotted out the moon seconds ago but found nothing. Stars sparkled in the clear night sky.

Her pulse quickened as she twisted to eye Damien. His chest still rose and fell in an easy rhythm. She licked her lips as she flicked her gaze outside again, giving one final suspicious glance around before she pulled the window closed and latched it tightly.

She sucked in a deep breath as she shuffled to the armchair and collapsed into it. She fixed her gaze on her sleeping cousin. Her dream had rattled her. She didn't trust Dominique. She'd stay here through the night to ensure his safety.

She propped her elbow on the arm and rested her cheek against her palm. Visions of Damien's gravestone taunted her. She had to find a way to convince him to leave. She had to do whatever it took to keep him alive.

* * *

Dominique kicked her feet up onto the wooden coffee table as she lounged in the wing-backed leather chair. Darkness surrounded her as she sat in the sitting room of the seaside house. Only the ticking of the grandfather clock indicated the passage of time.

She took a sip of the whiskey she'd helped herself to, swallowing down its sweet caramel flavor. She lifted the glass to her nose and breathed in its aroma. This blend was much better than the bourbon at the town's popular drinking establishment. She'd expect nothing less from the man who stocked it.

She studied her fingernails using her ability to see in the

dark, a trick she'd picked up in the South American jungle. She twisted her wrist, curling her fingers toward her palm.

Her tattoo stood starkly against her milky white skin. An upside-down pentagram trapped in a triangle. A symbol of who she was. A symbol of who she belonged to. Of where her loyalties lay.

She narrowed her eyes at it as she squeezed her fingers into a fist. She rolled her shoulders back to ease the tension in her neck.

Her mind turned toward her cousin. She arched an eyebrow as she recalled the encounter earlier in the evening. She hadn't changed. Even despite her twenty-five-year absence, her cousin maintained her rosy countenance and her heavenly glow.

Her twin in every way except hair color and personality, Celine always managed to find adoring fans to follow her to the ends of the earth. Dominique did not understand how. The woman was a dullard. Sickly sweet. If she possessed the powers Celine had, she would not waste them the way Celine did, languishing her days away with nearly powerless Grayson Buckley.

Her mind turned to the others she'd encountered. Who were the two humans who had suddenly appeared in the Buckley household? They weren't Buckleys, of that much she was certain.

Celine seemed to favor the darker-haired one. Dominique arched an eyebrow as she considered the blonde. He looked fun. She may have to get to know him better.

A sound outside interrupted her rambling mind. A wicked smile formed on her lips.

The front door creaked open. Footsteps sounded on the hardwood floor. A cane tapped alongside them. Dominique flared her nostrils, breathing in the musky scent of cologne and brandy.

The steps proceeded toward the darkened room in which she waited. As the shadowy figure stepped into the doorway, Dominique reached up and flicked on the table lamp. Warm light flooded the room, startling the newest arrival.

Dominique wiggled her eyebrows and cocked her head as her smile spread across her face.

"Hello, Marcus."

Marcus Northcott set his jaw as his eyes focused on Dominique. She downed another swallow of her whiskey as he strode across the room. Without a word, he poured himself a brandy. After a sip, he inhaled deeply then said, "Dominique, to what do I owe the displeasure?"

Dominique approached him at the drink cart, brandishing her empty glass. "Aren't you going to offer me a drink?"

Marcus side-eyed her, his eyes flicking to the empty glass clutched in her hand before he snapped them back to her icy blue eyes.

"It seems you have already helped yourself."

"Still, you could be a gracious host and pour me another."

Marcus's features settled into an unimpressed glare, and he snatched the glass from her grasp.

"Brandy?" he inquired.

"Whiskey," she answered.

His eyebrows twitched and his jaw wiggled in disapproval as he grasped the whiskey decanter. "Of course," he muttered through clenched teeth. "How could I have forgotten?"

"I'm surprised, too," she answered as he offered her the glance. She grasped it and took a sip. "So, how have you been?"

"You cannot honestly expect me to believe you've come for a pleasant chat."

She offered him a coy glance. "Is it really that hard to believe?"

"Yes. Whatever you've come to say, Dominique, say it and get out."

Dominique winced. "Oh, so touchy. Though I can imagine you would be given your most recent failures."

"Is there a point to this?"

"Don't say I didn't warn you. I was perfectly happy to engage in pleasantries, but you insisted we cut to the chase."

"I'd prefer not to be around you longer than necessary."

"Afraid I have cooties?"

"Something like that," Marcus answered.

Dominique narrowed her eyes at him. "Why have you not converted Celine to our side yet?"

Marcus made a quarter turn as he sipped his brandy, staring at the fireplace. "I told you, she's stubborn. Though I have made progress."

Dominique's eyebrows shot to her hairline. "Not enough. I just saw her. She's still warmly wrapped up in that farce she considers family. Gray is still very much alive as is his only slightly smarter cousin. And she's got two new playmates."

Marcus sighed. "Dominique, these things take time."

"We don't have time. This should have been ended centuries ago. Instead, she's paraded around the globe evading you at every turn for over two hundred years. She even did a stint as a human only to return right back to the fold and still elude you."

"There have been some… setbacks, I admit."

Dominique swallowed the last of her whiskey, pouring herself another glass. "Such as?"

"Various things. Nothing to concern you."

She slammed the glass down on the drink cart, sending the whiskey sloshing dangerously close to the brim. "That is where you are wrong, Marcus. This very much concerns me. It concerns all of us."

Marcus's jaw twitched as he weighed her words. "Give me more time and I shall deliver Celine as promised."

"Promises, promises. Though I suspect you cannot deliver on any of them."

"With you in the mix, I'd wager that is correct," Marcus said, shooting a sideways glance at her. "You'll do nothing but muddy the already dirty waters. You should leave and allow me to continue to pursue my goal alone."

Dominique puckered her lips in a faux display of consideration. "Hmmm." She tapped her lips with her index finger as she paced around the floor. "No."

"Dominique–"

"No, Marcus. You've bungled this for far too long. Celine will be ours. And I shall be here to ensure that happens."

"Oh? And where do you suggest we begin? This war has raged for centuries. And now, when I am closest to gaining her trust, you suggest we change course."

"Closest to gaining her trust?" Dominique let out a harsh laugh. "You must be joking."

Marcus narrowed his eyes at her as she continued to cackle.

"Oh, come now, Marcus. Do you really expect me to believe she is nearly within your clutches? Because I don't. Not after what I witnessed earlier."

"Which was?"

"Which was Celine happily ensconced in that monstrosity on the hill. No, she is no closer to joining us than she was before. It's time we applied more pressure. And since you seem to lack the constitution for it, I will do it."

"I cannot do it."

"That is obvious," Dominique said, tossing a lock of her hair over her shoulder.

Marcus shook his head. "You misunderstand my meaning. I cannot do it for a reason. I told you. There have been setbacks."

Dominique cocked her head at him. "Care to enlighten me?"

"I do not."

Her features turned icy. "I wasn't asking so much as demanding."

Marcus sipped his brandy, returning his gaze to the fireplace.

"You may as well tell me now. I will find out."

He stared into the amber liquid. His lips twitched with displeasure before he opened his mouth to explain. "Celine has my soul marker."

Dominique's eyes widened and she clenched her hands into fists at her sides. "What?"

"It was unavoidable."

She stormed to the drink cart and poured herself another whiskey. "How did it happen?"

"Celine and I engaged in a rather substantial battle. The effects of our machinations hurled us into the Shadow World realm where our adjudicator was on repose. It was none too pleased and ordered me to stay in Shadow World while Celine returned here."

Dominique's eyes traveled up and down him. "Yet here you stand."

"Celine had me released."

Dominique raised her eyebrows in disbelief. "Celine had you released? Celine. Celine Devereaux."

"Yes."

"Why?"

"She required my help to cross to an Alterra and retrieve someone. In the process of securing my release, she somehow managed to convince the adjudicator to give her my soul marker as a temporary peacekeeping measure. It agreed."

Dominique's bottom lip squeezed toward her top and her jaw flexed as she considered the tale. "So, you not only helped Celine, you allowed her to keep your soul marker?"

"I did not realize she held the marker until the help had been provided."

Dominique shut her eyes for a moment before she opened them and focused on Marcus. Her nose wrinkled in annoyance. With a slight shake of her head, she downed the last of her whiskey and lunged forward.

Her fingers tightened around Marcus's throat. She drove him back against the wall, lifting him from his feet. He dangled in the air, smashed against the wood paneling. The brandy glass dropped from his hand, shattering on the floor below him.

"You're slipping, Marcus," she growled.

Marcus gasped for breath as her fingers tightened.

"Fix this or I will destroy you, too."

"I–I–" Marcus choked out.

Dominique's eyes glowed red. "I don't want to hear your excuses. Get your soul marker back or I'll kill you before I destroy Celine's so-called family."

Dominique gave his throat one final squeeze before she dropped him in heap on the floor and stalked from the room. The door slammed behind her.

Marcus swallowed hard and sucked in a deep breath, coughing as he climbed to his feet. Dominique's arrival was a problem. A problem he'd have to face, sooner rather than later.

He stalked to the drink cart and poured himself another brandy. He took a sip as he considered the latest demand she'd issued. Celine would never trade the soul marker back to him willingly. Could he steal it? Could he force her to give it to him?

He needed a plan quickly before Dominique made good on her threat. They had a dubious alliance. Would she violate it? The powers above them supported him. Did they still? Even if they did, Dominique was a loose enough cannon that he couldn't guarantee his own safety.

He needed his soul marker back. Quickly.

CHAPTER 6

Dominique stormed from Marcus Northcott's seaside home. She pounded down the steps to the pathway leading from the home. Her hands balled into fists as she squeezed her eyes shut.

The fool. Marcus Northcott had bumbled the claiming of Celine for centuries and he continued to prove his ineptitude. The powers above her would not be pleased. No wonder she'd been sent to pick up the shattered pieces of the plan.

Dominique pounded down the pathway toward the tree line. Did they realize the extent of his failure? Perhaps. Perhaps not. Either way, it would be up to her to solve the issue. And she would.

As much as she despised the need for Celine, it remained a fact. She'd love nothing more than to fill Celine's role, but she couldn't. The notion bothered her more than she preferred to admit.

Her mind turned from her annoyance to her plan. Given the latest turn of events, she needed all her resources. She'd call in a few markers. Or she'd use another persuasive technique. Either way, she'd solve the problem.

Dominique ducked into the canopy of trees. The scent of pine needles filled the air. Her nostrils flared as she detected another smell mixing with them. Her eyes lifted skyward, and she peered through the thick foliage toward the moon.

A black streak blotted it from her view for a moment before it reappeared, beaming at her. She smiled. Time to call in one of those markers.

She hurried along the winding path toward the cliffs. Somewhere along the edge a cave opening led down to the beach. She scanned with her night vision, unable to find it.

Annoyed, she approached the cliff's edge and peered over it. Jagged rocks littered the bottom. Dangerous, she thought. A half-smiled turned one corner of her mouth up. "Just the way I like it," she murmured as she took a step back and then leapt forward.

She sailed through the air and down toward the craggy rocks below. With the grace of a cat, she landed in a crouched position on the slick, wet rock.

The ocean rushed toward her, smacking off the stone and sending a spray high in the air.

Dominique rose to stand and hopped off the boulder to the pebbled beach below. She stalked toward the sheer cliff. As she rounded a large outcropping, the entrance to the cave became visible.

Moonlight streamed across the rocky beach as she approached the black hole. Her heels ground against the rocks as she picked her way toward the opening.

Two hulking creatures stepped from within the safety of the cave's darkness. Their webbed feet slapped across the stones as the moonlight shone down on their leathery skin.

"Oh, good, you got my message," Dominique called.

The larger of the two spoke, his voice a deep-throaty growl. "Why did you summon us?"

"Because I require your assistance."

"To enter the Sangmond realm?"

Dominique scoffed. "I don't need your help for that."

The creature turned his massive head, his snake-like eyes narrowing at her.

"I need an army."

The creature glanced at his companion before returning his yellow eyes to Dominique. "We have no war here."

Dominique raised her eyebrows and licked her lips. "You have sworn allegiance to me. And I require your army."

"What will you do with it?"

"Bring a war the likes of which these humans have never seen before."

The creature's head swiveled back and forth. "I told you. We have no war with the humans."

"And I told you I don't care. We have an alliance. You listen to my command."

"Then the alliance must end now." The creature raised its claw-like hands and dusted them to dismiss her request.

"I don't think so." Dominique swung her arm forward, a long blade sliding out from within the sleeve of her leather jacket. She slashed at the creature's thick, leathery skin. Her sharp knife tore through its flesh, sending a spray of blood across the rocks as she severed an artery.

The creature grabbed at its throat, gurgling as it stumbled backward and sprawled at the mouth of the cave's entrance.

Dominique pulled a handkerchief from her pocket and wiped at the gooey syrup covering her blade. As she worked, she spoke to the remaining creature. "Now, go back to Sangmond and gather your army. I expect them here in two weeks."

The second creature stood motionless for a moment.

Dominique flew toward it, squeezing its thick jaw between her thumb and forefinger. "And if you think for a moment of betraying me, I will personally see to it that your realm burns." She shoved the creature away. "Now go."

Without responding, the creature shot skyward. Dominique stared after him, replacing her knife as she listened to the ocean's surf pound against the rocks. The sky above reflected a bright red ring of fire as the creature crossed realms.

Dominique returned her attention to the rolling ocean and considered her last statement. It brought a smile to her face. One way or the other, she'd watch someone's home burn.

* * *

Celine stared out over the steep cliffs leading to the rocky shore below. She tugged her sweater tighter around her, despite there being no chill in the air. The sun had risen over an hour ago. The bright fiery ball painted the calm waters below it a blinding yellow. The gentle sea lapped at the rocks below.

She'd left Damien still asleep as the horizon had turned pink, changed her clothes, and made her way into the crisp morning air and to the cliffs.

She'd spent most of the night awake, worrying. Dominique's arrival endangered so many of them, herself included. She needed to find a way to protect her family. And get rid of Dominique.

A rustling noise interrupted her meandering thoughts. She twisted, glancing over her shoulder. Damien emerged from the trees, pushing back a thick branch as he stepped onto the path that wound next to the cliffs.

"Good morning," he called as he closed the distance between them.

Celine gave him a tight-lipped smile before returning her attention to the calm waters. The sight of him caused her emotions to well up and the same worry that consumed her after her nightmare bubbled to the surface.

Damien sidled up to her, gazing out over the sparkling water. "Were you in my room last night?"

She nodded. "Yes. Just checking on you."

"I thought someone moved my laptop. I started to worry I did it and forgot. Or maybe I was sleepwalking. Either way, I'm glad it wasn't me." He waited for a beat then added, "By the way, thanks, but you don't need to worry about me. I was okay."

She flicked her gaze to him before returning it to the rocks below with a heavy sigh. "I had a nightmare. Figured I would check to settle my own nerves."

"Nightmare? You mean the one with you in the cave and the book and all that?"

"No," she said with a shake of her head. "No, another nightmare."

"Care to share?"

"I'd rather not," Celine admitted.

Damien winced. "That sounds ominous."

Celine let the comment go, waiting a few moments before changing the subject. "Have you packed yet?"

Damien frowned and kicked a pebble around with his foot. Celine inferred the answer to be no.

She turned to face him. "D–"

"No," he said. "Okay? No. I haven't packed and I'm not going to."

She flicked her gaze to the tree line, clamping her jaw together as she let the frustration waft over her. She shook her head and huffed.

"You need to pack."

"I said no!" he insisted.

Celine raised her eyebrows, drawing her chin back in surprise.

"Sorry," he said, his shoulders slumping. "I just… I don't want to leave. And it's not like it's a fool-proof plan. Can't this Dominique person just find us wherever we go?"

"I'd just prefer you to be out of her immediate reach. Out of sight, out of mind, right?"

"Wrong. If she's looking for a way to get at you, she's going to come after us. We're already all over her radar. She mentioned both of us last night. Do you think if we both disappear she's just going to say, 'Oh well, guess I can't kill them!' I doubt it."

Celine held her hand out to temper her response. "I get what you're saying, D, I do. But the simple fact is you are in *way* more danger here than not. While I don't expect Dominique to simply forget about you and Michael, I do expect her to take advantage of attacking those closest to me and easily accessible to her."

"If she's as brutal as you say, she'll come after me and Michael no matter what you do."

"And I want you to be far, far away so it's much harder to do that!"

Damien shook his head. "I don't think we should rush into any decisions. Let's just take a day to see what shakes out."

"We need a proactive approach this time, D. This is not a sit-and-wait situation. Believe me, Dominique is already making her moves. I don't want to react too late."

"I'm not saying sit on our hands, but let's not panic just yet."

Celine massaged her temples. "I'm not panicking. This is

that serious. Dominique is like nothing you've ever encountered before. She's smart and she's savvy."

"But you're more powerful than her."

"We can't depend on sheer power this time. She knows how to play this game. She's been around a long time–"

"So have you."

"But she's spent her time in pursuit of as much power, influence and expertise as she can."

"All the more reason to have the entire team here."

"Not if it means your lives."

"Oh, so it's okay to risk your life but not for me to risk mine?"

"My life is much harder to take than yours."

Damien sighed. "I just think we need to explore other options before we make an extreme decision."

"It's hardly an extreme decision," Celine argued. "Though I'm on my way to gather more information now. We'll see what I find and go from there."

"That sounds like a plan."

Celine shot him a glance as she stepped around him to continue down the path. "This doesn't mean I'll agree that you should stay. You should pack a bag and be ready."

Damien scrunched his lips together at the statement.

Celine twisted to continue away from the cliffs and toward her sister's seaside cottage. Her mind parsed through questions as she wandered toward the house. Did Celeste know about Dominique's arrival? Did she have a role in it?

Her sister's previous loyalties had laid with Dominique. Did they still? She's repaired her tattered relationship with Celeste after centuries of warring. Was the fragile truce about to be torn apart?

The house loomed in the distance, perched on the edge of the cliff. Celine paused for a moment before striding toward it. She climbed the steps to the covered porch and knocked at the thick wooden door.

Her brother-in-law, Teddy, pulled it open. He arched a graying eyebrow. "Celine! Come in! Are you here to see Celeste?"

"Both of you, if you don't mind," Celine said as she stepped into the hallway-like foyer. Her eyes rose up the wide wooden staircase in search of her sister.

"Celeste is upstairs. One moment, I'll retrieve her." Teddy signaled for Celine to wait in the sitting room across from the stairs.

Celine shuffled into the generous, square room and wandered to the window. Her nerves did not allow her to sit. Instead, her eyes darted over the landscape, expecting to see Dominique pop up at any moment.

"Celine!" Celeste greeted her. "How lovely to see you."

Celine spun to face her sister. A smile graced her full lips, sending her high cheekbones even higher on her heart-shaped face.

"How are you feeling?" Celeste inquired.

"Not so well," Celine admitted.

Teddy scrunched his eyebrows. "Are you still unwell from the experience with Tobias? Celeste filled me in. How terrible of an ordeal it must have been."

Celine lowered her eyes to the area rug below her feet and shook her head. "No, it's not that."

"Please, sit down and explain it to us," Celeste prompted.

Celine didn't budge. She flicked her gaze to her sister, now seated on the sofa. The woman patted the seat next to her.

Celine studied her. "Dominique blew into town last night."

Celeste's eyes widened and her jaw fell slack. Celine glanced at Teddy. The man's posture stiffened. Their initial reactions suggested they were unaware of Dominique's arrival. Though, in the past, her sister had proved a fantastic liar. Was she lying now?

"You didn't know?" Celine pressed.

"No!" Celeste answered. She shot a pleading glance to Teddy.

"I knew nothing of this. Though I am unsurprised. I doubt Dominique would run her plans past us. Particularly given the ongoings of late."

"You haven't heard from her?"

"No," Celeste answered. "Have you?"

Celine nodded as the memory of the previous evening's encounter flitted through her mind. "Unfortunately, yes."

Celeste raised her eyebrows and cocked her head, signaling Celine to continue.

"I saw her at the bar in town. I managed to escape without a confrontation. The same cannot be said for the rest of the evening. She showed up at the house, a new plaything in tow, and threatened me and everyone else."

"What did she say?" Teddy inquired.

"Come to her side or she'll destroy all my family and friends."

Celeste leapt from the couch, crossing her arms as she stalked across the room. "As pleasant as always, I see."

"I'm surprised she hasn't contacted either of you," Celine said.

Celeste spun to face her. "Don't be. I cannot imagine she would. I'm certain she's well aware that we assisted you out of that tricky business with Marcus recently."

"Still, Dominique likes to control everything."

"She has no reason to come here," Celeste answered.

"Yet, I'm certain she will. If not to demand your allegiance, to make you pay for the lack of it," Celine answered.

"She will not have it. I did not like Dominique even when we were aligned, Celine. You do believe that, don't you?"

Celine stared into her sister's crystal blue eyes, so very like her own. After a moment, she blinked and let her eyes wander. "I believe you." She flicked her gaze back to her sister. "But you'll tell me if and when she appears on your doorstep?"

"Of course, we will, Celine," Celeste said.

Celine nodded and cocked her head. "Well, consider yourselves warned. And let me know if you hear from her."

Celeste crossed the room and pulled Celine into a tight embrace. "I will, sister dear." She leaned back and studied Celine's face. "I love you."

Celine squeezed her sister's hands. "I love you, too."

She spent another moment with Celeste's hands clutched in hers before she tore herself away. Satisfied neither of them knew anything about Dominique's arrival or plans, she left the seaside cottage behind in search of another seaside home.

As she wound along the path, she pondered her decision. Would she learn anything? Would it settle her mind or further agitate her? Perhaps she should return home instead.

She reached the edge of the trees and stared up at the house. No, she decided, she needed to know as much as possible. She pressed her lips together and stepped forward toward the home of Marcus Northcott.

<h1 style="text-align:center">CHAPTER 7</h1>

Celine strode down the path away from Damien. Her words rattled through his brain as he watched her depart. He kicked at the little pebble he'd been toying with during their conversation. With his frustration building, he swung his toes at it. The small rock skittered across the ground before toppling over the cliff.

He peered over the edge. The pebble smacked off the rocks below and bounced a few times before coming to a stop among the others.

The release did little to soothe his nerves. The conversation with Celine had not gone at all the way he'd hoped. She still preferred him to leave.

He did not want to abandon her. Another thought crept into his mind. Perhaps there was another reason she preferred him to go. Only yesterday he'd found out he was adopted. Their tenuous connection as cousins had been further shredded by the revelation. He'd been Josie's cousin before. Now he was nothing.

Perhaps Celine felt it was time to sever ties with her nonfamily member. He shook his head to clear the thought. He was being ridiculous. Celine only wanted to protect him.

Still, the recent development couldn't have come at a worse time. He'd have preferred to find his family, to sort things out for himself and with Celine before another crisis smacked them in the face.

So much for that, he thought, as he shoved his hands into his pockets and strode along the path. No matter how tenuous the connection, he would stay and help her, he vowed to himself.

The trees surrounded him as he continued along. In order to protect her, he needed to protect himself. He needed a way to ensure Celine didn't need to worry over him every moment.

If he could pull that off, at least to some extent, he could more easily make the case that remaining with her was the best plan.

The path continued past the edge of the woods surrounding him. He stopped at the tree line and stared up at the large white columns holding the roof at bay. If there was a way to ensure his safety from the likes of Dominique, Alexander could help him locate it.

He stepped out of the cover of the trees and into the sunshine. White clouds dotted the blue sky, giving no indication of the trouble that lay ahead. At least the weather was pleasant, he mused, as he strode toward the stately home.

He pounded the lion's head door knocker against the plate, shoving his hands in his pockets as he waited. No one answered.

Damien wrinkled his forehead at the door, trying the door knocker again. He stared up at the brick home as he waited, wondering if Alexander wasn't there. After a few moments, the door popped open.

Alexander sucked in a breath as he greeted him. "Damien, good morning."

"Good morning. Did I disturb you from something?"

"No, though I've only just returned home. Come in."

Damien crinkled his brow as he stepped into the home's expansive foyer.

"Oh, sorry, I didn't realize you were out."

Alexander waved his hand in the air as he shook his head. "I wasn't." Damien scrunched up his face in confusion. "I was at the main house. Celine insisted I stay there. She did not wish me to return home alone with Dominique on the loose."

"Ohhh," Damien murmured in understanding.

Alexander motioned for Damien to enter the sitting room. "I'm surprised you're out and about and she hasn't got you under lock and key until you can be spirited away."

"That's the thing," Damien said as he padded across the thick area rug in the sitting room. He plopped into an armchair. "I already told her I'm not leaving."

"An argument I doubt you'll win, Damien," Alexander said as he settled into a chair across from him.

"I'm going to try. But I'll need your help."

Alexander raised his eyebrows. "I am always interested in helping, though…"

"What is it?" Damien prompted.

"I cannot say I disagree with Celine." He offered Damien an apologetic glance.

Damien's shoulders slumped. "But surely–"

"She's not overreacting," Alexander interrupted. "Make no mistake about it. Dominique is an extremely dangerous entity. And I cannot say her demand that you leave is out of line."

"We've faced dangerous entities before."

"Not like this," Alexander said. "It should speak volumes

that she preferred even I not roam the estate alone after her appearance."

Damien let his arm flop against the chair as he sighed.

"I don't mean to sound so defeated," Alexander continued, "but this is a very serious situation. You witnessed her total lack of regard for human life last evening. She will not think twice about ending your or Michael's life if she deems it to her advantage."

"There has to be something we can do."

"Leave," Alexander said with a nod, "as Celine suggested."

Damien pounded his fists against the arm of the chair as he leapt from it and paced the floor. "I don't *want* to leave."

"I understand. And I realize how difficult this is for you, but it may come to that."

"I'd prefer to prevent that."

"Damien, there is no shame in retreating to preserve your life."

"There has to be something we can do. Some spell or talisman. Something that can provide some protection for us."

Alexander sucked in a long breath. "I'm afraid it may not be that easy."

"There has to be *something*," Damien insisted. "People aren't being killed right and left by people like Dominique."

"People don't typically come into contact with entities like Dominique."

"Can't we just spend the day looking through your library and trying to find something to help?"

"I'm not opposed to searching for something, but I am warning you that we may not find anything. You may need to face the unfortunate fact that the best way for you and Michael to remain safe is to leave."

"We'll cross that bridge if we come to it. But I'm not

willing to just throw in the towel. We can help here. We're part of this team now."

"Then let's get to it," Alexander said, rising from his chair.

Damien offered him a smile and a nod as he stalked to the wall filled with bookshelves and began to peruse the selection.

* * *

Celine climbed the steps leading to Marcus's seaside home. She paused for a moment outside the wooden front door. Her hand formed a fist, ready to knock, but she hesitated. After a moment, she banged against the door and waited for a response.

Dembe pulled the door open moments later.

"Good afternoon, Miss Celine," he said in his Nigerian accent.

"Hello, Dembe. Is he here?"

Dembe bowed his head and signaled for Celine to enter the foyer. Once inside, the quiet man motioned toward the sitting room.

"Thank you," Celine said with a fleeting smile.

She stepped into the boxy room, finding Marcus studying a book in the armchair nearest the fireplace. Celine cleared her throat to announce her presence as she shuffled into the room.

Marcus continued to peruse the book for a few more moments before he snapped it shut. He snapped his gaze to her.

"Celine! I would say this is a lovely surprise, but I am not at all shocked by your presence."

Celine cocked her head at him, a frown embedded in all her features. "No, I can imagine you are not shocked at all by any of the recent events."

With a groan, Marcus pushed himself to stand. "I assume you are referring to the recent arrival of your ne'er-do-well cousin."

"An arrival you were all too aware of."

Marcus crossed the room to the drink cart, pouring himself a brandy after offering one to Celine. She shook her head in response.

"I tried to warn you," Marcus said as he filled his glass.

Celine scoffed at the statement. "Really, Marcus? Pulling me aside in the In-between to offer your cryptic warning and then denying it later was a rather weak attempt."

Marcus shrugged as he sipped at the amber liquid. "But it was an attempt."

Celine narrowed her eyes at him. "You could have just said Dominique is coming."

"And would it have altered your decision to return here?"

"No."

Marcus raised his eyebrows as he waved his glass in the air. "Then it did not matter what I said."

"Only you could reason your way to that conclusion."

"Informing you of the events to come would have made no difference. You insisted on returning here even after you were told it was a mistake."

Celine shook her head but did not answer the statement. "Have you spoken with her?"

"Yes."

"Why did I think the answer would be anything different?" Celine mumbled as she plopped onto the couch across the room.

"I did not ask her to come. In fact, I prefer she did not. So, before you lump us together into one unholy alliance, know that I dislike her as much as you do."

"Have you convinced her to leave yet?"

"Unfortunately, I doubt I will be able to do that. She is out for blood."

"She's already spilled some."

"Oh?"

"A local. She killed him last night."

"On purpose or by mistake?"

Celine shrugged. "I'm not sure. She revived him as a zombie."

Marcus took another sip of the brandy. "Classic Dominique. Are you certain you do not want a drink?"

Celine waved her hand in the air, signaling a no. "What did she say to you?"

"The usual."

Celine narrowed her eyes and shook her head. "No, you said she is out for blood. Whose?"

"Anyone's. Everyone's. This is Dominique we're discussing. The woman lives for vengeance. It courses through her veins and keeps her stony heart beating."

Celine's lips curled at the corner and her eyebrows raised. "I never realized how much you dislike her."

"I detest the woman. Had you paid a bit of attention in our previous encounters you would have known this."

"No, you never voiced this strong of an opinion against her before. I can only imagine your more recent hatred has been stoked by your own encounter with her."

Marcus flicked his gaze to her. "I suppose I should be pleased by her arrival."

"Pleased?"

"Your acrimony can be directed toward her rather than me. At least I never threatened your precious Damien."

The amusement left Celine's face in an instant. She hardened her gaze at Marcus. "What did she say about Damien? Tell me!"

"Calm yourself, Celine. She made no direct threat. But

know she did notice them. She has already mentioned both Damien and Michael."

Celine leapt to her feet, her hands balled into fists. "Tell me what she said."

"Nothing specific. But judging by the temper she displayed last evening during our brief encounter, I would suggest removing your human compatriots until the situation can be sorted."

Celine sank back to the couch, parsing through the statement. "I would very much prefer to do that."

The corners of Marcus's lips twitched at her words. "Meeting with resistance, are you? I am not surprised. Your dim-witted friends are exceptionally difficult to work with. They seem to lack the ability to follow orders." Marcus took another sip of his brandy. "In fact, it seems they do the exact opposite of what is requested."

Celine stared at him, confusion on her features.

"I told them specifically not to engage with Tobias Greene. Not twelve hours later, the imbeciles admitted to having had a conversation with the man."

"I suppose that was my fault," Celine said with a sigh, recalling making the introduction when Michael and Damien visited 1842.

"They informed me it was. I suppose you shall have to employ those legendary skills of persuasion again to ensure they depart unharmed until the danger has passed."

"And when will that be?"

"How should I know?" Marcus questioned with a shrug.

"Do you really expect me to believe you have no idea of her plans?"

"I do because it is the truth. Dominique does not tend to share with me her dastardly agenda. Though you can be sure she is not here for the sea air."

Celine squeezed her eyes shut and heaved a sigh. "Her timing is terrible."

"I wasn't aware there was a good time for trouble like Dominique to surface."

"There isn't. But right now is a tricky time to force Damien, in particular, to leave."

"The boy tends to be rather sensitive, doesn't he? What is he fretting over this time?"

Celine slumped back against the couch and rubbed her palm across her forehead. She flailed her arms in the air. "I suppose you'll find out eventually." She puckered her lips before she spit the words out. "Damien was adopted."

Marcus raised his eyebrows in response and sipped his brandy.

"That's why Monica appeared in town last week."

"And the news has rattled dear Damien?"

"Of course, it has. It would rattle anyone."

"I am not judging. And did your dear mother inform him who his real family is?"

Celine shook her head and tented her fingers. "No, she didn't even tell Damien herself. She told me. I told him."

"And you did not ask?"

"She didn't know. At least that's what she said."

"Hmm," he murmured. He sipped at his brandy again as he focused on nothing in particular, a pensive expression crossing his features.

Celine narrowed her eyes at him. "What?"

He shrugged and shot a glance over his shoulder at her. "Nothing."

She cocked her head, her eyes still slits. "Do you know something, Marcus?"

"I didn't say that."

She stood and approached him, studying his face. Her

shoulders pressed away from her ears and her eyes widened. "No," she whispered.

He offered her a sideways glance.

"Oh, no. No, no, no."

His face scrunched with confusion, and he set the brandy glass down. "What?"

She squeezed her eyes shut and shook her head, her voice breathy. "Oh, please, no."

Marcus gave her an unimpressed frown. "Are you planning to tell me what you're babbling about?"

Celine grimaced and swallowed hard, biting her lower lip. She slowly raised her eyes to meet Marcus's gaze, her voice just above a whisper. "Please tell me you are not his father."

Marcus's face twisted into a mask of surprise. He blinked several times. "Did the poison on that rose leave a lasting effect on your brain?"

Celine studied him, seeking an answer, verbal or otherwise.

He scoffed. "Oh, you cannot be serious."

She shrugged, breaking eye contact with him and licking her lips before detailing her case. "You're both highly intelligent–"

"And that is where the similarities end," he interrupted. "If you can even make the case that we are similar on that front. Celine, you cannot possibly believe I fathered that ungainly boy."

Celine raised her eyebrows at him, her jaw unhinging to argue. He answered before she could speak. "To be clear, no, I am not Damien's father." He rolled his eyes at her.

Celine breathed out the breath she'd been holding. "Thank goodness. That's a relief."

Marcus's face scrunched into a frown. "He could do far worse. Though I still fail to see how you even considered it."

"It's not that far-fetched."

He took another sip of brandy before refilling his glass. "I spent centuries chasing you, Celine. Not other women."

Celine offered him a shrug and a penitent glance. "It was plausible."

"I am not his father. Plausible is a stretch. You'll need to search elsewhere."

"I certainly am relieved as I'm sure Damien will be. If you were his father, he'd likely suffer an identity crisis the likes of which the world has never seen before. At least we'll avoid that."

"But you will not avoid the need to find his parents during a time when he should be far away from Bucksville."

Celine flicked her gaze up to him. "Is that another of your vague warnings?"

"No, just a statement of obvious fact. Dominique is here for a reason. And her reasons are never benign."

Celine sighed. "I'm sick of her already."

"As am I."

"You mentioned that already. What happened between you two to ignite such animosity?"

"I told you before I have always disliked her."

"Not this much. In fact, you two had an alliance. A tenuous one but still... an alliance."

"You exaggerate."

"What did she say to you?"

"Let it go, Celine."

Celine ground her teeth as she considered her next statement. "If you dislike her so much, surely you'd warn me of what she's up to."

He arched an eyebrow. "I have no idea."

Celine cocked her head. "She didn't tell you anything?"

"No."

"Then what did you speak about?"

Marcus shot her a perturbed glance. "Celine, you really

are quite annoying with this. I have told you several times I have no idea what her plans are, she did not share them with me."

"So, she just stopped by to say hello and let you know she's in town?"

"If you must know, she stopped by to express her extreme displeasure over the situation with my soul marker."

Celine lowered her gaze to the floor, the weight of the black stone representing Marcus's soul weighing heavily in her pocket.

"I don't suppose you'd be willing to give it back. Perhaps then I can convince her to leave."

She snapped her eyes up to his face. "Not a chance, Marcus."

"Then I suppose you should prepare for an extended stay by your infamous cousin."

Celine backed up a step and spun to leave. She twisted back. "She's not going to win. I won't let her."

"You may not have a choice," Marcus warned her as she stalked from the room. "Be careful, Celine. She's dangerous."

Celine thundered down the stairs and into the bright sunshine. The conversation had not gone as expected. She learned nothing new except that Dominique's plans seemed to trouble even Marcus. Though there was no love lost between the two of them, their plans usually aligned. What was she after this time that he disagreed with?

Perhaps because they were at odds over the loss of his soul shard. Celine slipped the smooth black stone from her pocket and studied it. The only leverage she had against him. She couldn't give it up. She closed her fist around it, squeezing it tightly.

No matter what their argument was, she needed to convince Damien to leave town until this situation resolved.

CHAPTER 8

Celeste spun to face Teddy as the door closed and Celine's footsteps sounded on the steps leading off the porch. Her eyes widened as she fought to control her breathing.

Teddy poured a scotch from the decanter across the room. Celeste did not miss the slight shake of his hand when he lifted the glass to his mouth.

"What are we going to do?" she demanded after a moment.

"What can we do?" he responded after another sip of scotch.

"Leave," Celeste suggested. "Pack our bags and go." She stalked to the window, wringing her hands.

"Do you expect that will work?"

Celeste paced the length of the room. "She hasn't come to visit us. Hasn't sought us out. We could quietly depart with no one being any the wiser."

"Except your sister."

"Celine would never say anything."

"Perhaps not, but she certainly would think you a coward."

"At least we would be alive."

Teddy paused for a moment, staring into the distance. "What do you suppose she wants?"

Celeste flung her arms out. "How should I know?" She resumed her pacing and wringing of her hands.

"Perhaps she'll leave us alone."

"And perhaps she just hasn't gotten to us yet." Celeste raced across the room and squeezed her husband's arm. "Oh, Teddy, we need to leave."

"Calm yourself, Celeste. We cannot simply run away. It does us no good."

"I'd argue it does us a world of good. Out of sight, out of mind. Which is preferable when dealing with Dominique."

"Do you imagine she'd be angry with us? I can't see why."

"We've assisted Celine. She won't like that. She must be here because Marcus has failed again to convert her to our side."

"And you believe she'll be upset with us by extension?"

"I know it," Celeste answered. "

"Perhaps not. She hasn't sought us out."

"She will. Teddy, please. Let's leave."

"I'm shocked you'd want to leave Celine at a time like this."

"You don't know Dominique the way I do."

"I beg to differ, Celeste. Over the centuries, we've had many dealings with Dominique."

"And we've always been on her side."

Teddy puckered his lips and narrowed his eyes. "And you no longer are?"

"She will believe we no longer are given the events of the past several months."

"And are you willing to turn on your sister to save your-self? It may come to that."

"That's why I'd prefer to leave. I'd rather my sister think me a coward than be faced with a decision that may cost me her affection for the next two centuries as the last one did."

Teddy sipped at his scotch. Celeste's eyebrows arched toward her hairline and she fluttered her eyelashes. "What are you thinking, Teddy?" Silence met her inquiry. "You're thinking of betraying Celine!"

Teddy tilted his head. "Perhaps not so much betraying as convincing Dominique that we do not stand in her way."

"Dominique is not so easy to please! Merely promising not to stand in her way will likely not be enough. She will demand loyalty. And proof of it."

"As Marcus has done for centuries. And we have managed to–"

"To create centuries of animosity from my sister. I've only just managed to repair my relationship with her."

"But you've always strongly believed she belonged with Marcus. You agreed her marriage to Gray was a mistake. Has that changed?"

Celeste spun away from him, lowering her eyes as she considered his question. After a moment, she answered, "My thoughts on the matter are of no consequence. Celine is a grown woman and we should not have meddled in her affairs."

"So you have changed your mind."

Celeste twisted to face him. "When the chips were down, my sister gave up everything to save me. The least I can do is allow her the life she chose."

Teddy sighed. "All right, Celeste. We'll go. If that's the way you feel, you are correct. We should not risk Dominique's wrath."

Celeste firmed her jaw and nodded. "I shall pack a few things. We'll leave as soon as I am ready."

Teddy nodded and Celeste flew from the room. Her feet pounded up the stairs as her mind scrambled to sort through the things she'd need. With labored breath, she pushed into the bedroom she shared with Teddy and raced to the bed. She fell to her knees and dug two overnight bags from underneath.

With the zippers tugged open, she tossed the bags onto the silver duvet and darted to the wooden dresser across the room. She flung the drawer open and rifled through the clothing before selecting a few items.

She hastily folded them and dumped them into the larger of the two overnight bags. A lock of hair shifted from her chignon, falling across her cheek. She shoved it behind her ear as she hurried to the closet. She flung the door open and perused the clothing. Teddy's suits hung neatly across the bar.

She ripped shirts, jackets, and pants from hangers, rolling them into a ball and shoving them into the black bag. Her breathing turned ragged as she dashed across the room to the second closet. Hangers swung wildly as she yanked dresses, blouses, and pants from them. After tossing them into her bag, she stormed into the bathroom, bag in hand.

With one motion, she swiped the items from the countertop into her bag and zipped it shut. Her fingers struggled to wrap around several more items of Teddy's and carry them into the bedroom. She dumped them into his bag and tugged the zipper closed.

She shouldered her bag and took one final glance around the room. With a hard swallow, she lifted Teddy's bag off the bed and hurried from the room. Teddy met her as she clamored down the stairs. He lifted his bag from her grasp, shoving passports and money into the side pocket.

"Let's go," Celeste said, breathless from her race down the stairs.

Teddy nodded at her as he slung the bag's strap over his shoulder. Celeste reached for the doorknob and swung the front door open. An icy blast of air blew into the foyer.

Celeste leapt back a step, stumbling into Teddy. Her eyes widened as she stared out the open front door.

* * *

Damien slammed the book shut and tossed it on the desk. It skittered across the marred wooden surface, coming to a rest as it smacked into the other books strewn across the area. He slouched in his chair with a sigh.

Alexander glanced up at him, his eyebrows raised.

"Dead end," Damien reported.

Alexander lifted his shoulders. "I warned you we may not find much."

"Much?" Damien inquired, his voice incredulous. "We've found next to nothing!"

Alexander stared at him, an apologetic expression on his face.

"Outside of a vague reference to a talisman made of—what was it? The tears of a unicorn?"

Alexander chuckled at his statement. "I do not believe it was that storied."

"It may as well have been." Damien sat up and shuffled a few open books around before tapping on one. "Here it is, 'containing water sourced from the underground river in Hielosol,' whatever that means."

"Rare, I agree, though not impossible. But perhaps unlikely given the current circumstances."

"What is Hielosol?"

"It means Land of the Icy Sun, loosely translated."

"Sounds like a pleasant place."

"It's a treacherous world, encased mostly in ice. Even the sun, which shines quite brightly there, is frigid."

"And we need to find a flowing underground river in a world of ice." Damien flung his hand in the air. "Is that even possible?"

"Assumedly the river is deep enough underground that the sun can't freeze it."

"That doesn't–" Damien shook his head. "Never mind." He leapt from his seat and paced the floor. "Why should anything make sense at this point?"

"Damien–"

"Don't say it," he answered as he spun and crossed the room. "Don't even say it."

"We need to face–"

Damien hurried across the room to the desk and pawed through the books. "We'll keep looking. There has to be something else."

"This is extremely difficult."

"There has to be *something*! People live their lives all the time with this danger around and are perfectly safe. Has this never happened in the history of the world? Haven't people like you been around since the dawn of time? No one ever had to protect a loved one from a bad witch before?"

"Yes, of course. But you must remember the situation is not common. And solutions are few and far between, particularly given the range of powers you may be facing."

"There was a reference somewhere to another talisman type of thing."

"We could attempt to get Celine's soul shard back. It may offer some protection to you. But it would only cover you, not Michael."

"Okay, that's a start. Maybe we can get another piece of her soul for Michael."

"That would take some work and it would weaken Celine."

Damien snapped his gaze from the books to Alexander, a concerned expression on his face. "Did the first one?"

"Slightly, yes. Though it was only a sliver."

"So, we'll just take a sliver again."

"It's not that simple."

Damien snapped the book shut and shoved it away. "Nothing ever is."

"Damien, we'll figure something out."

"Yes, and that something will be run with my tail between my legs and hide until this blows over."

"That's not exactly how I would phrase it but remain safe and hidden until the situation is handled is the general idea, yes."

"The problem with that is, it's not a guarantee either. Things could go horribly wrong either where I am or here. Splitting up is a terrible idea."

"We can continue to search. And, in the meantime, we can devise a plan to retrieve the one soul shard we do have."

Damien plopped into his chair. "From Marcus Northcott. Wonderful."

"I doubt he'll give it to us. But with a bit of maneuvering, we may be able to steal it back."

Damien sighed and pursed his lips. He shook his head as he stared at nothing. "To be safe, we've got to attempt to steal from the Duke. I can see why Celine wants me to leave."

The comment earned another chuckle from Alexander. "Why don't we take a break? We'll both give some thought to retrieving Celine's soul shard. And we can continue to search for other solutions. Shall we meet back here for a game of chess and a strategy session later?"

Damien blew out a long breath and nodded. "Sure.

Though we can keep going now." He pointed toward the stacks of books still on the shelves.

Alexander shook his head and snapped his book closed, rising from his chair. "No, you need a break. Take a walk. We'll reconvene later."

Damien rose and put his hands on his hips. "Okay. I'll see you later." He stalked to the door, twisting before he exited in the foyer. He rapped his knuckles against the decorative trim. "Hey, thanks. I appreciate you helping me."

"Of course, Damien. We're a team."

Damien smiled before he spun and stalked across the foyer, pulling the door open and stepping into the bright sunshine. He shielded his eyes against it as he stalked toward the woods.

He entered under the canopy of the trees, wandering along the path aimlessly. He wiggled his shoulders to try to release the tension in them. His neck ached from hours of pouring over the books.

He could accept the pain if they'd been closer to a solution, but they weren't. In fact, they were further away, if that was possible. They'd found so little that it seemed an impossible task. He'd have nothing to aid in his impending argument with Celine. She'd demand he and Michael leave, and he'd have nothing to defend his position with, outside of simply wanting to stay.

He emerged from the dense trees. The ocean spread before him, gently rolling. Its calm waters glittered in the sun. He approached the cliff ahead and stared out over the water.

His eyes fell to the rocks below. A smile turned up the corners of his lips. Below him on the rocky beach, stood Celine. Her blonde curls rustled in the light breeze from the sea.

He shuffled along the path, picking his way down to the

beach. As he navigated the shifting rocks, he called out to her, "Hey, great minds think alike, huh?"

She snapped her head in his direction, a soft smile forming on her full lips. She shoved a lock of hair behind her ear. "Hey, D."

He grinned at her as he joined her to stare out across the sparkling water. After a moment, his eyes slid sideways, and he snuck a glance at her.

She flicked her gaze to him and offered him a weak smile. "I didn't find anything good on my travels."

"I didn't say anything."

"I know. Because you didn't want to ask in case that was my answer." She turned to face him fully and flung her arms out. "I'm sorry, D."

He lowered his gaze to the rocks below, preparing for the argument.

She spun back to face the ocean. "I did find out one thing that's good."

He snapped his gaze up to her. His heart leapt with the hope that they'd found a solution. "What?"

She gave him a sideways glance and winced. "I ruled out one person as being one of your parents."

Damien wrinkled his nose. "Who?"

"Marcus."

His eyes widened and he tilted his head as he stared at her. "Are you serious?"

"Yes. I considered it good news. I thought you'd be happy to know Marcus is not your father."

"I'm actually shocked you thought he might be. And that you asked him! Celine!"

Celine shrugged at him. "Sorry, it just–during our conversation, it came up and he acted a bit coy. I thought, perhaps, it was because he was your father."

Damien made a face as though he'd just eaten something

disgusting. "Oh, please. How could you possibly make that leap?"

"That's the same thing he said. It's not that much of a stretch."

Damien's eyes shot side-to-side. "Are we talking about the same Marcus? Tall fellow, dark hair, dark eyes, dark soul."

Celine shot him a glance, her lips puckered. "Yes, we're talking about the same Marcus." She shook her head. "It's not that big of a stretch. You both reacted the same way to this. Both of you were incredulous."

"No kidding! You literally just told me you suspected Marcus Northcott was my father." Damien shoved his hands into his jean pockets and shivered. "Gives me the creeps just thinking you actually considered that."

"You're both highly intelligent–" Celine began.

Damien flicked his hands at her. "And that is where the similarities end."

Celine's eyebrows shot up and she side-eyed him. "Not really. But in any case, he's not your father."

Damien remained silent for a moment. He squeezed his eyes closed and dropped his shoulders with a groan. "Ugh, now this is all I can think about."

"But it's not true, so you can put it out of your mind."

"Really? It's not true? Because he said so? That guy lies like a rug. How do we know he's not just lying about it."

"As odd as this may be to say, Marcus probably wouldn't lie about this. If he was your father or even suspected he was your father, he would have, at the very least, not denied it."

"You put way more faith in him than I do."

"We can do a simple DNA test to be sure if you'd like."

"Yeah, because I'd love to ask him for a cheek swab to prove he's not my dad."

"Trevor was your dad, D. We just need to find your biological father."

"Whatever, I don't want to deal with him to find out."

"I'll deal with him," Celine offered.

Damien stared out over the gently rolling water. "Maybe I don't want to know where I came from."

Celine snorted a laugh at him. She reached over and squeezed his arm. "Yes, you do. We'll find your parents and whoever they are, we'll face it together."

"Until you make me leave."

Celine pulled her hand back and shoved it into her hoodie pocket. "D–"

He spun to face her. "Alexander and I have been looking for another solution. We haven't found one yet but–"

"And you're not going to." Celine shook her head. "Alexander should know this."

"At least he's willing to try!"

"Well, I'm not willing to risk your life. And quite frankly, I'm surprised Alexander is!"

Damien circled around her, running his fingers through his hair. "He's not. Don't blame him. I think he's humoring me. He told me straight out that leaving may be the only solution."

"Good!" Celine exclaimed.

"*But*," he stressed, "he agreed to help me search for another solution."

"There isn't anything safer than you and Michael leaving town until we can get this situation under control."

"We're going to be sure of that. Because, honestly, splitting up is the worst solution ever."

"It's not. Damien, Dominique is dangerous."

He flung his arms out. "So was every other enemy we've faced! We never ran away before."

"This is different. The others–they were focused on me."

"And Dominique isn't? She flat out told you it was about you last night. You join her or she'll kill us all."

"Exactly!"

"And how is that any different from the others?" He counted them on his fingers. "Marcus wanted you, Tobias wanted you, Dominique wants you."

Celine sighed and flung her arms out. "It's just different, okay?"

"How?" Damien placed his hands on his hips. "Tell me how."

"Dominique has no conscience. She will kill you, Michael, Gray, anyone, if she thinks it's to her advantage."

"So would the others."

Celine shook her head. "No. They may have killed you if you got in their way. She will kill you just to make a point."

Damien squashed his lips together in frustration. "Celine–"

"No, D. No! I will *not* take a chance with your life!"

He bent down and grabbed a stone, flicking it into the sea. "It's not your decision to make."

"It is. This is on me. Dominique is here for me. I don't want your death to be on my hands."

"It won't be. That's what I'm trying to tell you!"

Celine spun away from him, her jaw tensing as she stared out over the ocean. She blew out a long breath through her nostrils as she pursed her lips.

Damien bit his lower lip, shaking his head. They were getting nowhere, going round and round with the same argument over and over. Damien dragged his feet along the rocks. They clamored around, clacking into each other. He leaned over and snatched another one from the beach.

Something stung his finger. He dropped the stone shaking his hand as he gasped.

Celine snapped her head in his direction. "What is it?

What happened?"

Damien continued to flick his fingers in the air. "Ow! I don't know!" He blew out a breath. "Whew, that stings!"

Celine grabbed him and dragged him to the ocean, dunking his fingers in. The cold water rushed around their legs, soaking their shoes and pants. "Better?"

He nodded as he caught his breath. Celine pulled his hand out of the water and studied the fingers. Splotchy red spots covered the tip.

Damien peered at his finger. "What is it? A bite? Some beach bug or something?"

"No. It almost looks like a burn, but what burned you?"

Celine rose from her squat and strode a few steps up the length of the beach to where they had just stood. She scanned the beach in search of the source.

Damien joined her, scouring alongside her. Celine stooped down, narrowing her eyes at the mix of whitish-gray and pink spotted rocks. Damien squatted down next to her.

She reached out toward a speckled rock. She swiped a gooey green substance from it, raising her hand to her face to study it, rubbing it between her thumb and forefinger.

"What is that?" Damien inquired. He glanced down at the rock, reaching for it.

"No, don't!" Celine shouted.

He froze mid-reach, his eyes sliding sideways toward her.

"That's what burned you." Celine rose and headed for the water, swishing her hand in the salty sea to clean it.

"What is it? Some kind of nuclear waste? How did it get here?" Damien questioned.

Celine rejoined him, drying her hand on her pant leg. She shook her head as she studied the rock she'd swiped. A swath of green still covered it.

"No," she said. "It's blood."

Damien screwed up his face. "Huh?"

Celine narrowed her eyes and stared up the beach. She picked her way across the rocks, pausing and stooping over to stare at another spot. Damien followed her.

"It's blood," she repeated.

"Umm," Damien murmured as he scratched his head. "Like human? Ohhh, zombie?"

Celine continued to hop across the stones, following a trail of green splatter. "No, not human. Not even zombified human."

"How do you know it's blood?"

Celine stared down at a large pool of the green goo. "I've seen it before. It's poisonous to humans, but not immortals. But what's it doing here?"

Her brow furrowed as she studied it before her eyes rose to the cave entrance at the edge of the beach.

"I'm confused," Damien said.

Celine stalked toward the cave entrance. She pulled her cell phone from her pocket and toggled on her flashlight as she ducked inside.

She stopped after taking one step in, throwing her arm out sideways to bar Damien from entering.

He stared at her. "What?"

"Careful," she said, her voice breathy as she focused the flashlight on the cave's floor. He wrinkled his forehead as she edged toward the side of the cave, stepping around something.

Damien glanced down at the cave's floor, lit partially by the sunlight filtering through the entrance and Celine's flashlight. He gasped, stumbling back a few steps and nearly sprawling across the rocks outside.

"Holy crap!"

Damien's jaw hung open as he stared at the object in front of him. His lower lip bobbed as he tried to formulate words. None came.

CHAPTER 9

On the ground in front of Damien lay a massive, scaled creature the likes of which he'd never seen before. Not even in the illustrations.

"Stay back, don't touch it," she warned.

Celine's light revealed pieces of the hulking beast, curled into a fetal position on its side. The light whipped away as Celine pressed her cell phone to her ear.

Light filtered in from the cave's mouth, highlighting features of the mammoth being. Damien leaned closer, studying the thing with wide eyes.

Thick dark red scales covered it from head to toe. Two large wings were folded against its back. A long, thick tail ending in a barbed tip extended from underneath the wings. It measured at least five feet behind the creature with a base as round as a small tree trunk.

Two bulky legs jointed like dog legs extended from its core. They ended in three-toed webbed feet with long claws poking from the end of each of toe.

Damien stepped toward the head of the beast, noting its

human-like face. A large green tongue lolled from the side of its partially open mouth. Two pointy fangs extended from the top jaw. Thick, gooey green globs oozed from a large gash under its chin.

Large scaled, hooded eyelids covered partially closed yellow eyes. Two pointy horns poked from the top of its scaled, hairless head.

Celine spoke in the background. "It's me. Can you come down to Widow's Cove? There's something I think you'll want to see."

She pulled the phone from her ear and tapped at it before directing her flashlight toward the creature.

"What the hell is this thing?" Damien questioned, glancing up at her as he squatted next to the beast's head.

"It's a Dracopire," Celine answered. Her face pinched. "But what's it doing here?"

Damien rose to stand, his eyes still wide. "A what now?"

Celine flicked her gaze to him. "A Dracopire. Basically, a supercharged vampire. It gets its name from the dragon-like wings and scales and the fact that it survives on blood."

Damien lowered his gaze to the mammoth creature on the ground. He swallowed hard. "Like human blood?"

Celine shook her head, his statement eliciting a small giggle. "Not usually. They don't live in the Earthly realm in general. Outside of a small colony of them that live in the mountainous regions in Romania."

"They live on earth?" Damien exclaimed.

"Just a handful of them. In a really remote region."

Damien's gaze darted around the cave as he parsed through her statement. "Romania..." he repeated, his voice trailing off. "Like... Transylvania?"

Celine pointed a finger gun at him. "Bingo."

"You're kidding. Vampires in Transylvania." He scratched his head. "Is that where–"

"Dracula comes from. Yeah."

"This just gets weirder and weirder." He returned his gaze to the creature at his feet. "So, wait, Dracopire because of its dragon-like wings. Are there dragons?"

"No, D," Celine said, flicking him an amused gaze. "This isn't Lord of the Rings."

The rocks rattled outside the cave. Damien snapped his head toward the entrance, his heart pounding as he wondered if another one of the blood-sucking creatures approached.

"Celine?" Alexander's voice called from the beach.

"In here!" Celine shouted.

Darkness hovered at the entrance before Alexander ducked inside the cave. He smiled at Celine before his gaze flicked to Damien.

"Oh, hello, Damien. I didn't realize you were–" His words cut off as his eyes found the Dracopire at his feet. "Oh my!"

Celine grinned at him. "I told you you'd want to see it."

Alexander leaned over to study the body. "Is this–Is this what I think it is?"

Celine squatted behind the beast, shining her light onto its form. "Yep. A Dracopire."

Alexander blew out a sharp breath, his eyebrows raising. "My goodness." His eyes roamed up and down the body. "I've never seen one in person before."

"I've seen them alive and kicking," Celine admitted. "What I haven't seen is a dead Dracopire on the coast of Maine."

"Is Gray still in town?"

"Yeah. I texted him and told him to come here right away."

"He's bleeding here," Damien said, pointing to the neck wound.

Celine shifted her light and stance to study the wound.

Alexander shot out a hand to prevent Damien from

coming too close. "Careful, Damien. The blood is poisonous to humans."

"Yep." He shot a glance at Alexander. "Found that out the hard way."

"He picked up a stone covered in blood earlier and got burned," Celine explained. "Looks like his throat was slit. Likely out on the beach by the pattern of the splatter. He must have stumbled into here then died."

Damien pulled his cell phone from his pocket, tapping around on it before snapping a picture of the beast.

"Yes," Alexander concurred. "But why? How? How long has he been here? And why is he here?"

Celine stared down at it, deep in thought. "Since last night."

Alexander lifted the hand-like paw at the end of the creature's arm. "How do you know?"

"Last night, I was checking on Damien and I thought I saw the moon go dark. He must have been flying in."

Damien huffed out a breath. "They fly?"

Celine circled around him and knelt behind the body. "Yes, that's what the wings are for."

"They don't look big enough. I thought they were decorative."

Celine tugged at one, unfurling it from the creature's back. She rose to stand, stretching the wing as far above her head as she could. "They're larger than they look. Little guy like this probably has a wingspan of about twelve to fifteen feet."

"Little?" Damien inquired, his eyes widening as he stared down at the beastly creature. He estimated it had to stand at least seven feet high.

Celine nodded as she eased the wing back into place. "He's pretty small. I'd say he hasn't reached maturity yet.

They typically grow at least eight feet. Wingspans about twenty feet."

"What are they doing outside of Sangmond?" Alexander asked.

"Same question I had."

"Aren't they from Romania?" Damien inquired.

"No, just a small colony of them. But," Celine explained, "he is not from the Romanian colony." She pointed to a large black symbol on his upper bicep. "This marking indicates his clan. This is a Sangmond clan. Not a Romanian one."

"He's been pierced through the heart," Alexander said as he stared at a hole in the beast's chest.

Celine joined him, squatting down and tilting her head. "So, he has."

Damien opened his mouth to inquire further about this when the rocks clattered outside again.

"Hey, Damien!" Michael's voice called. "What did you want me to–"

Michael entered the cave, stopping dead as he saw everyone. His eyes fell to the large beast on the ground. He stood speechless for a moment.

"Anybody want to tell me what the hell that thing is?"

"A Dracopire!" Damien explained. "There was no way I could ever describe it accurately to you, so I thought you should see it for yourself."

"A what?"

"Dracopire," Celine repeated.

"Super-charged dragon vampires," Damien said.

"Why?" was all Michael could manage.

Damien added a question. "And what's Sangmond?"

Michael's gaze darted around the cave, and he crossed his arms over his chest. "Sangmond? Oh, please don't tell me there's some other weird creature lurking around here."

Celine shook her head. "Sangmond is a place."

"Another realm," Alexander explained. "Where most Dracopires live."

"It means Blood Moon," Celine explained.

Alexander shook his head as Michael leaned over the creature, a disgusted expression on his lips.

Damien threw his arm out to hold Michael back. "Don't touch it. Their blood is poisonous to us."

"Why is a Dracopire on Earth?" Alexander said.

"That's my question, too."

"And who killed him?" Damien asked.

"And why?" Michael chimed in.

"I can make an educated guess on who killed him," Celine said.

She glanced up, finding three sets of eyes on her. "Dominique."

"Maybe she's not so bad after all," Michael murmured.

"Celine!" Gray's voice called from outside.

"In here!" she answered.

He ducked into the cave, joining their group. "Why the group meeting in the—whoa!"

"That has been everyone's reaction so far, Gray," Alexander said.

"Is that a Dracopire?"

"Yep," Celine answered.

"What's it doing here? And how did it die?"

Celine shrugged. "No idea on the first question. As for the second—" she flicked her light toward the creature's sliced neck "—someone slit his throat then pierced its heart. And I can pretty much guess who."

Gray stared down at the body. "Why would Dominique kill a Dracopire? What was it doing here in the first place."

"Maybe it attacked her," Damien suggested.

Celine pursed her lips as she considered the situation. "I'm not sure, but I don't like this."

* * *

Celine stalked onto the beach, her arms crossed tightly over her chest. She stared out over the ocean as she tensed her jaw. The others followed behind her.

Gray put his hands on his hips as he stared at her. "I don't understand how a dead Dracopire definitely relates to Dominique."

She twisted to face him. "Oh, come on. Dominique shows up here and suddenly there's a Sangmond Dracopire dead on our beach. It's not a coincidence."

"Maybe not but why was it even here? It makes no sense."

Alexander tapped his lips with his finger. "I, too, am struggling to see the connection. I understand the timing is suspicious, but if he is related to Dominque's arrival, why would she kill him?"

Damien nodded as he stared into space, processing it. He jabbed a finger in Alexander's direction. "He makes a point. Why would Dominique bring him here and then kill him?"

"Which then suggests Dominique didn't and this is purcly a coincidence," Gray insisted.

Celine's lower lip jutted out and she shook her head. "That doesn't make sense."

"It does," Michael argued. "You don't want to see it because Dominique's arrival has made you paranoid."

Celine narrowed her eyes at him, her expression turning sour. "I'm not being paranoid. You don't know what Dominique is like."

"Okay, then explain why this guy is here!" Michael shot back.

Celine's jaw hung open as she attempted to formulate a response. After a moment, she sighed. "I can't. But this cannot be a coincidence."

Gray stalked toward her and put his hands on her shoulders. "Celine, you're upset about Dominique. And that's understandable. But we can't read into everything."

"I'm *not* reading into things. This is not normal. And abnormal things when Dominique is around tend to be because of Dominique. What else would a Dracopire be doing on a Maine beach?"

"But why would she kill him if she brought him here?" Alexander asked again.

"Maybe they got into an argument. She is not exactly the most self-controlled person. She could have killed him in a fit of rage."

Gray flung his hands out before he gripped her arms. "Well, then, it's over. He's dead and gone. And we don't have to worry."

Celine shut her eyes and shook her head, not agreeing with the response from her husband. After a moment, she flicked them open. "We can't leave the body here."

"Alexander and I will take care of it," Gray promised. He gave her a brief smile. "Take Michael and Damien home."

Celine considered it for a moment before she nodded. She grabbed his forearm and squeezed it. "Be careful, Gray. We don't know where Dominique may strike next."

He kissed the tip of her nose. "We will be."

She smiled at him before flicking her gaze to Alexander. "You'll come back to the main house after?"

"I will, Celine. Try not to worry. We'll be careful."

"Thanks."

She looped her arm through Damien's and tugged him down the beach with her. Michael followed behind them.

She gave one final glance back as Gray and Alexander disappeared into the cave.

Something about the situation still bothered her, but she could make no sense of it. Perhaps time would reveal the reasoning behind the Dracopire's arrival on Earth. She prayed the reason wouldn't be as dire as she imagined.

CHAPTER 10

$\mathcal{C}$eleste swallowed hard as she stumbled back several steps, bumping into Teddy behind her.

"Careful, Celeste, I–" he began. The sight at the open front door ceased any further words. He staggered back several steps, dropping his bag on the floor next to the foyer table.

Dominique sashayed through the door, a smirk on her face. She shoved her hands into her leather jacket and cocked her hip. Her eyes flicked down to the bag still clutched in Celeste's hand, then up to Celeste's face. She raised her eyebrows.

"Going somewhere, Celeste?"

"Dominique!" Celeste exclaimed in faux surprise. "I didn't realize you were in town. How lovely to see you again."

Dominique tilted her head and narrowed her eyes. "Didn't you?"

"No," Celeste fibbed, struggling to keep her voice measured. "Did you just get in?"

"Do you need somewhere to stay? We have the room!" Teddy added.

Dominique studied them both, her features twisting into an amused grin. "How you two ever made it through life when you are this bad at lying is beyond me?"

"Lying?" Celeste questioned.

The smirk on Dominique's face eroded into a scowl. She ripped the overnight bag from Celeste's hand.

"Yes, lying," she spat. She unzipped the bag and dumped the contents. "What were you planning to do with these?"

"I was–well–" Celeste stumbled.

"You were what?" Dominique glowered at her as she stalked toward her. Celeste inched backward. "Taking them to the local church to donate? Hmm?"

Celeste smacked into the table behind her. It screeched across the floor as she stumbled.

"No, I just–"

"Just what, Celeste?" Her eyes glowed red as she snapped her gaze to Teddy. "And what you about, Theodore?"

She reached her hand over the bag he'd discarded on the floor. It flew up into her grasp. She pulled the passports from the pocket and waved them at him.

"What's the matter, Teddy? Cat got your tongue?"

She lunged at him and grabbed hold of his tonguc as his lower lip bobbled, trying to formulate a response.

He moaned as she held it between her thumb and forefinger.

"Dominique, please. You've got this all wrong."

Dominique flung Teddy across the room. He smacked into a wall and slid to the floor below. She snapped her head toward Celeste.

"Have I, dear cousin?"

She held out her hand and drew Celeste into her outstretched fingers like metal to a magnet. "And what have I got wrong?"

Celeste dangled from her clutches as she lifted her from the floor. She pulled at her fingers as she choked.

"Please–let me–explain," Celeste choked out.

Dominique dropped her in a heap on the floor. "Yes. I think you'd better explain why you have been disloyal to the cause."

"We haven't been," Teddy assured her as he climbed to his feet.

"That's not how it looks from my end."

Teddy smoothed his blazer and cleared his throat. "Perhaps not. Though I can assure you–"

Dominique balled her hands into fists and stamped her foot. "I want more than assurances, Teddy. I want results."

"And you shall have them," Celeste promised as she rose to stand.

"Yes, I will," Dominique answered. "With or without your help."

"With it," Celeste said with a nod.

"Tell me why when Marcus Northcott had Celine contained you helped her escape."

"That's not exactly what happened," Teddy contended.

"Isn't it?" Dominique questioned, her head snapping toward him as her eyes returned to their blue color. "It is my understanding he had her imprisoned and she had agreed to marry him." She jabbed her finger at Celeste. "And you let her out."

Celeste wrung her hands. "Celine restored me from my vampiric state. I owed her."

"So, you did betray us?" Dominique said, her lips curling into a sneer.

"No," Celeste answered, backing away from Dominique. "Celine's acquiescence to Marcus's demands was a ploy. I realized that. I did all I could to appear on her side. We'll get more information from her this way."

"She's right, Dominique. You wish to break her, but Celine is not so easily broken. She spent three years with Marcus and did not break. We must take a different approach."

Dominique flexed her jaw and narrowed her eyes. "Don't mansplain to me, Teddy. I'm not your wife nor your ward."

Teddy held up his hands. "My apologies. I did not mean to offend you."

Dominique returned her attention to Celeste. "Tell me about these humans Celine is involved with."

"What?' Celeste croaked.

"The humans. The two men I saw at the Buckley house. Tall, gangly fellow with brown hair. Seems afraid of his own shadow. And the blonde. Handsome, arrogant, my type of guy."

"Michael and Damien," Teddy answered.

"Oh good, we've identified their names. How helpful. Tell me about Michael and Damien."

Celeste swallowed hard and cleared her throat. "They are from her days as Josie."

Dominique lifted her shoulders toward her ears. "That tells me nothing."

Celeste licked her lips and motioned toward the sitting room. "Perhaps you'd like to sit down–"

"I'd like to find out about Michael and Damien. Not sit down, not have tea. Tell me what I want to know."

Celeste nodded. "All right. When Celine disappeared, she was reborn as a human. She spent almost twenty-five years with a human family in upstate New York."

"Knowing Celine, she probably liked this existence."

"She fought quite hard to remain in it, yes," Teddy said, circling around Dominique to join Celeste.

Dominique rolled her eyes at the statement. "She's such a goody-goody."

"Damien was Josie's cousin," Celeste explained. "When she returned here, he followed her."

"And Michael? Is he a cousin, too?"

"No, he–"

"He what? Spit it out, Celeste."

"He was her ex-boyfriend. He followed her here assuming she was Josie and hoping to rekindle their romance."

Dominique burst into laughter, doubling over. "Oh-ho, that's rich. So, her ex-boyfriend is literally living under her husband's roof." She righted herself, still chuckling. "I can see why she keeps him around. She always did love a pretty face."

"There's more," Teddy said.

"Oh?" Dominique raised her eyebrows at him then flicked her gaze to Celeste, who resumed wringing her hands.

"Michael and Damien are–" Celeste heaved a few breaths. "They're the men who helped Celine on her sixteenth birthday."

Dominique's eyes shot skyward as understanding dawned on her. "I see."

Silence consumed the space as Dominique mulled over the latest information.

"Dominique, what is your plan?" Celeste said.

Dominique flicked her gaze to Celeste and narrowed her eyes. "It will be revealed as necessary. In the meantime, the powers that be demand a reaffirmation of your devotion, a show of loyalty."

"Of course," Teddy answered. "We can easily confirm our loyalty."

"I'm afraid it won't be as easy as saying it, Teddy."

"What then?"

"I have a task for Celeste to complete. Accomplish it and The Order will welcome you back into the fold. Fail to and, well–" Dominique shrugged her shoulders. "We'll cross that bridge if we come to it."

Celeste side-eyed Teddy before she returned her gaze to Dominique. "What is it?"

Dominique arched an eyebrow at her as the corners of her lips curled into a wicked smile.

* * *

Celine slogged through the door to the Buckley mansion with Michael and Damien in tow. She stalked into the sitting room and poured herself a drink, sipping at the brandy as her mind pondered the latest development.

Damien followed her inside, shoving a hand into his jeans pocket. "You okay?"

Celine took another sip of the brandy and nodded. She pressed her lips together. "Yeah."

"That doesn't sound convincing," Michael said as he poured a brandy.

Celine stalked to the fireplace and stared at the dancing flames.

"Celine, it'll be okay," Damien said.

Celine twisted to face him. "We can't be sure of that. Until we know more, you two should stay in the house. Don't go out without someone with you, okay?"

Damien shot a glance at Michael. "Okay," he agreed.

"Seriously?" Michael questioned.

"Yes, seriously, Michael."

Michael shrugged as he sipped at his drink. "It just seems like overkill."

"Dominique is dangerous. Not to mention if there are more Dracopires around."

"Are those things nocturnal like vampires?" Michael asked.

"No, not always. They tend to be more active at night, but Sangmond's sun cycle is quite different to ours."

"Really?" Damien inquired.

Celine nodded. "In Sangmond, the moon rises and sets like the sun. The sun has cycles like our moon."

"The sun and moon are reversed there?"

"Essentially yes. And the moon is a blood-red color. They spend most of their time awake when the moon is up. They sleep for the few hours when the sun is out. In our world, this would correspond to the hours of about eleven in the morning to four in the afternoon."

"So, in theory, we're safe if we go out between those hours."

Celine slammed her empty drink glass on the mantle. "No, Michael, you're not. Dominique prowls around at all hours of the day."

"Okay, okay. I just—we're not children. We'll be okay."

Celine squeezed her eyes shut. "I just want to be sure nothing happens to you. At least until we can find a safe place to hide you."

Michael firmed his stance. "I already told you I'm not running away."

"And I already told you both, that only applies if I am sure we can keep you safe."

Michael opened his mouth as Celine stalked across the room and stepped through the doors into the foyer.

"Where are you going?" Damien inquired.

She rubbed at her forehead. "There's something I need to check. I won't be long."

Damien leaned back and caught her free hand, tugging her back. "Hey, you okay?"

She sucked in a deep breath. "Yeah. I'm fine. Just worried. I'll be back soon. Don't leave the house, okay?"

"Sure," he agreed, letting her hand slide from his.

Her footsteps pounded across the stone floor in the foyer. Moments later the door banged shut.

Damien glanced after her before shoving his hands further into the pockets of his jeans. He flicked his gaze to Michael and made a face.

"She's on edge," Michael answered. "Let her go."

"Yeah, I get that, but the problem is I don't want her sending us packing."

Michael shrugged. "I'm not leaving."

Damien stalked to the drink cart and poured himself a brandy. "I get that. I don't want to leave either, but–"

"But what? She can't *make* us go. I mean, what's she going to do? Throw us out of the house? She won't even let us leave the house right now."

Damien stared into the amber liquid before taking a sip. "No, but she has a point."

Michael raised his eyebrows as he dropped into an armchair near the fireplace. "How so?"

"Maybe this is getting too dangerous. I don't want to be dead because I was too stubborn to listen to Celine."

Michael shot him a glance as he eased into the chair across from him. "We've been up against some tough enemies, Damien. We're not kids and we're certainly not new enough that we don't know how to navigate in this world."

"Dominique seems dangerous, though."

"She's a hothead. Yes, it makes her dangerous. It also makes her stupid."

Damien bit his lower lip as he tried to parse through the logic.

Michael leaned forward, placing his elbows on his thighs. "She'll pop off at the worst possible moment and leave herself open to an attack she never saw coming. Celine is all over this. She's never going to let her win."

Damien's leg bobbed up and down as he considered it.

"Come on, man, where's your faith in Celine?"

Damien licked his lips as he studied his drink. "I–"

"Do you think she can't beat Dominique? Didn't Gray say she was more powerful?"

"I don't think she'd let anything happen to us. But I don't want to see her hurt or worse in a desperate attempt to save us. Nor do I want to see us hurt or worse because we insisted on staying and Dominique gets one over on Celine while she's busy defending herself against someone else."

"So, you want to leave?"

"No!" Damien said, leaping from the chair and pacing the floor. "But I don't want to make this worse either. I've never seen her so rattled. Not even when she nearly died!"

"Did you come up with anything promising in your research?"

Damien kicked the tassels on the area rug. "Nope. Nothing. Not even anything good in Alexander's library outside of some odd reference to something nearly impossible to get."

"So, we're stuck. No lucky charms or special spells that'll keep us safe from whatever kind of powers Dominique has."

Damien sighed as he swirled the liquid in his glass. "Nope. Nothing that would–" His voice cut off as his brow furrowed.

"That would what?" Michael stared at him when he got no response. "Damien?" He rose to his feet. "You okay, buddy?"

Damien snapped his fingers and pointed to Michael. "Stop us from dying, that's it!"

"Dying? I'd prefer not to, though I suppose I could come back as a vampire-like Celeste if worse comes to worst."

Damien shook his head and set his glass down on the table, his pace quickening as he paraded around the room.

"No, the point is *not* to die, right?"

"Yeah."

"And what's a good way not to die?"

"Uh, stay away from Dominique?"

"But what if that's impossible?"

The crease between Michael's eyebrows deepened as he considered the question. "I am really not following you, man."

Damien paused in his pacing, holding his hands in front of him as he explained. "Why is Celine more worried about us than she is about Gray and Alexander? She's not asking them to leave town. Just us."

"Because we're human. We're in way more danger than Gray or Alexander. They're immortals."

Damien's eyes lit up. "Right! They're immortals. They're not impervious to danger or death but they have some level of protection from it, right?"

"Right. So what?"

Damien lifted his eyebrows, the corner of his mouth turning up as he answered. "So, we become immortals, too!"

CHAPTER 11

Celine stalked down the path away from the house. Worry consumed her with every step. The discovery of the Dracopire struck fear in her heart. What was it doing here? Its arrival coincided with Dominique's and could not be coincidental.

She needed answers. She wasn't sure if she would get them, though she'd try. She disappeared into the canopy of trees. In the cool darkness under their leaves, she scoured the surroundings for signs of more of the creatures. They would be asleep now. But had there been others here? Did something happen on Sangmond to send them to the Earthly realm?

She saw nothing, even after scanning the sky for their flight. She continued to the edge of the woods, pushing out into the open field beyond.

The seaside home of Marcus Northcott rose in front of her. With a deep inhale, she stalked forward toward it. Her fingers wrapped around the wooden railing as she climbed the stairs, wondering if she would find her cousin inside.

With her fist raised, she hesitated a moment before she banged against the door. Dembe opened it moments later.

"Good afternoon, Miss Celine," he said with a head bow.

"Hello, Dembe. Is he here?"

The quiet man nodded and motioned for Celine to enter the foyer. She stalked into the space, her heels clicking against the wooden floorboards.

"He is in the sitting room, Miss Celine," Dembe said.

"Is my cousin here?"

"No. Miss Dominique left yesterday evening and has not returned as of yet."

"Thank you, Dembe."

The dark-skinned man nodded and offered her a bow before disappearing down the hall. Celine sucked in a deep breath as she rounded the open entrance into the sitting room.

"Ah, Celine, I thought I heard you speaking with Dembe," Marcus said as he closed his book. "What brings you by? I don't suppose you'd like to return my soul marker so your dear cousin is appeased?"

Celine shook her head. "More's the pity," he said as he dumped the book on the table next to him and rose from his chair. He crossed the room to the drink cart, pouring himself a brandy. He waved the decanter in the air at her in a silent offer.

She waved a hand to decline. "I need some information."

"Oh? I'm not sure I'm in a very sharing mood given your obstinance over my soul marker."

"This concerns you, too."

"I fail to see how whatever you're after should be of any concern to me."

"I found a dead Dracopire on the beach."

Marcus froze as he raised his brandy glass to his lips. He shifted his eyes sideways toward her.

"Yes, you heard me correctly. A Dracopire. Its throat slit and its heart stabbed."

He set the brandy glass down and twisted to face her. "And why are you telling me this?"

"Do you know why a Dracopire would be here?"

"I did not invite him if that's what you're implying."

"It's not. I'm simply looking for an explanation."

"I have none."

Celine narrowed her eyes at him. "I don't believe that."

Marcus snatched the brandy from the table and stalked across the room. "I don't much care, Celine."

Celine followed him with her gaze. "Oh, someone is testy since Dominique's arrival."

"Your cousin does not bring out the best in anyone."

"Is she connected to the Dracopire's appearance?"

He glanced at her over his shoulder. "How should I know?"

"You know her. You've spoken with her. Did she say anything?"

"So have you. Did she confess her plans to you?"

"Don't be ridiculous," Celine huffed.

He twisted to face her. "Why would you think it any less ridiculous that she shares the plans with me?"

Celine held back an eye roll. "You're on the same side."

"Hardly."

"Really? You are not both beholden to the same shadowy overlord?"

"That does not mean we agree on everything nor that she shares her plans with me."

Celine flung her arms out and stalked toward him. "Come on, Marcus. Do you really expect me to believe you know nothing?"

Marcus studied the liquor remaining in his glass before

he flicked his gaze up to her blue eyes. His lips twisted into a sneer, and he tensed his jaw.

"Dominique has a… tenuous alliance with the Fugarde clan."

Celine's jaw dropped open and she shook her head as she tried to understand the statement. "What? How?"

Marcus stalked across the room and refilled his glass. "She cultivated the relationship over decades."

Celine joined him and helped herself to a glass of brandy, sipping at it before she responded. "What does that mean?"

"It means if you found one here, there will soon be bigger problems than the simple arrival of Dominique."

Celine flicked her gaze to Marcus's dark eyes. "How? The adjudicators will never allow the Dracopires to form another colony on Earth."

"I do not believe they wish to form a colony."

"Then what?"

"Dominique did not secure their allegiance to rehome them. She obtained it to ensure a powerful ally when she required one."

"Again, there is no way the adjudicators will allow her to bring them to Earth."

Marcus sighed. "I am not sure she much cares what the adjudicators will or will not allow."

"So, what are you saying?"

"Prepare yourself, Celine. There is trouble coming."

* * *

Dominique stepped into the cool ocean breeze. Her dark hair blew across her face as she stomped down the stairs to the gravel path below. Her blue eyes flicked up to the sky. Dark clouds raced up the coast, creeping further inland as they approached.

Lightning danced across the sky and thunder rumbled in the distance. A storm was coming. In many forms.

Dominique recalled the expression on Celeste's face when she'd imparted her task. A show of unequivocal loyalty. Her lips twisted into a sinful grin at her cousin's reaction.

She sauntered down the path as large rain drops began to pelt her, falling intermittently as the clouds threatened to break loose.

In her pocket, her cell phone chimed. She pulled it from the confines of the dark fabric and flicked on the display. A text message awaited her: *Is it done?*

She paused in her walk as her thumbs flew across the keyboard. *It is. Celeste will complete the task. And then we'll continue our plan.*

As she reached the tree line, a new message arrived. *Have you seen her?*

She rolled her eyes as her nostrils flared with aggravation. *Yes.*

She followed up with a second message. *I have a new way in.*

A new text message on the screen: *Just get it done.*

Her jaw flexed and her eyes narrowed as she read the text. Her nose wrinkled as her lips twisted into a scowl. She slid the phone into her pocket and continued along the path, tossing her hair over her shoulder.

She had things to accomplish, whether or not they were appreciated. The cool air gusted past her again and the rough ocean waters pounded the nearby shore. Why did Celine enjoy this horrid place? Why would anyone?

She preferred the French coast, the Caribbean, or anywhere with the glitz, glamour, and warmth so few humans could afford. She closed her eyes as she stalked along the wooded path. On top of the horrible climate, Celine clung to these pitiful underlings like they mattered.

Weak, sniveling, and useless. Three words to describe the Buckleys. And, it appeared, the two newcomers who were only human. That would make destroying them almost too easy.

Celine would bend to her or watch as her family was picked off one by one. The idea warmed her soul.

She pressed ahead toward another seaside home. The lights of Marcus Northcott's home blazed against the black clouds rolling behind it. She thundered up the steps to the porch and flung the door open, stepping inside as the heavy clouds let loose.

Rain pounded down on the porch's roof and lightning tore through the sky. Despite it being the middle of the afternoon, the black clouds blotted out the sun, making it appear to be night.

Dominique brushed a thick, dark curl away from her face as she stalked through the foyer and into the sitting room. She ground to a halt as she stepped through the doorway, jerking her head back as her eyes widened.

She blinked rapidly as she stared at the scene inside. With puckered lips, she cocked her head. "Well, well, well, what do we have here?"

Dominique sashayed into the room to the drink cart and poured herself a bourbon. She scanned the others over the rim of her glass as she sipped her drink.

"Celine Devereaux sharing a drink with Marcus Northcott. Are we finally coming to our senses, Celine?"

Celine slammed her glass onto the drink cart with a heavy sigh. "It's Celine Buckley."

Dominique bit her lower lip and raised her eyebrows. "Oh, come on, the suspense is killing me! Am I going to have the opportunity to kill your entire family or not?"

Celine sniffed as she glowered at her cousin. "I'm not even going to dignify that with a response."

She spun on her heel and took a step toward the foyer.

"Oh, good. I'm glad. I was *really* looking forward to killing a few people. It's just–who to start with?"

Dominique stared into space, tapping her lips with her finger.

Celine clenched her hands into fists as she squeezed her eyes shut. She spun to face them. "Leave them alone, Dominique."

Dominique continued as though Celine had not spoken. "Alexander?" She pressed her lips together as she narrowed her eyes in a show of fake consideration. "Hmmm. No, not hard-hitting enough. What about one of the humans?"

"Don't touch them, Dominique."

She flicked her gaze to Celine. "Now, *that* would be a tragedy. Defenseless human souls under your care, snuffed out like they never mattered." Dominique narrowed her eyes as she scanned the room. "Which one is Michael, again? Is he the hot one or the dorky one?"

Celine's nostrils flared and she balled her fists tighter. With a stomp on the floor, she shouted, "I said leave them alone, Dominique."

"Is this really necessary?" Marcus inquired as he set his steely gaze on Dominique.

She flung her arms out. "Why are you glaring at me? If I started randomly slaying people, everyone would be criticizing me for not giving her fair warning. As far as I can see, I'm doing her a favor."

"If you lay even one finger on them, Dominique–"

"You'll what?" Dominique spat, flicking her gaze to Celine.

Celine squashed her lips together in a thin line.

"Look, it's really this simple. If you want your precious little family to live, give them up! Otherwise, prepare yourself because I'm going to start the massacre soon."

"Spare me your threats. If you want to come for someone, you come for me."

"Oh, I'd love to," Dominique said as she flung her glass across the room. It slammed into the wall near the fireplace and shattered into pieces. Glass skittered across the floor as Dominique lunged through the air at Celine with a shriek.

Celine braced herself, widening her stance and summoning a fireball. She whipped it at Dominique. The impact stunted her flight. She dropped to the floor on one hand and one knee, raising her eyes to glower at Celine.

Celine scowled at her. "Don't be an idiot, Dominique." She spun on her heel and took a step toward the foyer.

Dominique rose to stand, flinging her hair away from her face with a twist of her neck. "I spoke out of turn before." She tugged her jacket down as she caught her breath. "I'll kill Damien first."

Celine froze, her muscles stiffening. Her fingers curled into tight fists again and she trembled with anger. She spun and flung herself across the room, flying through the air with an ear-splitting shriek until she collided with an unsuspecting Dominique.

The two women toppled together in a tangle of limbs as Dominique sought to defend herself against Celine's attack. She shoved her arms forward, blowing Celine back with a blast of lightning-filled energy.

Celine floated toward the ceiling before she began to fall, landing on her feet like a cat and balancing herself with her left fingertips. She snapped her head up and growled at Dominique, who climbed to her feet across the room.

In rapid succession, Celine fired two sharp bursts of white-hot fireballs across the space. One narrowly missed her opponent, slamming into the wall with crackling energy. The other smacked into the defense field Dominique created before it could strike her.

Celine growled with frustration when she failed to hit Dominique and leapt to stand. Her dark-haired twin threw out her hand, sending a lightning ball her way. She dodged it easily.

The two women danced around each other like wolves circling trapped prey. Electricity crackled between Celine's fingers. Flames danced around Dominique's.

With a shrill cry, Celine lunged at her, wrapping her electricity-laden fingers around her cousin's throat. Dominique latched on Celine's shoulders with her flaming fingertips.

The two fell to the floor, rolling across the hardwood slats in a tangled ball. They smacked into a wall, bringing their movement to a halt. Dominique landed on top of Celine. She straddled her, pressing down against her as she crushed her windpipe.

With gritted teeth, Celine grasped her attacker's arms. Unable to move them, she resorted to a different tactic, conjuring a blast from both hands in a concerted effort. The impact blew Dominique upward.

Her hair dangled as she flew backward toward the ceiling. She smacked into it with a sickening thump. Her arms flailed as she began her descent, falling toward the floor at a quick pace.

Celine's eyes widened and she rolled across the floor, leaping to her feet as her cousin thudded against the hardwood.

With a groan and strained breaths, Dominique pushed herself upright. Purple-red blood trickled from the corner of her mouth. She swiped at it with the back of her hand, grimacing at the purplish streak left behind. She sucked in air and narrowed her eyes at Celine as she took a stumbling step forward.

Her chest heaved with effort. "Is that all you've got?"

"Not even close," Celine spat back, throwing her arms out to the side as she summoned an attack.

A large fireball sailed between the two women, exploding against the floorboards and driving them both back and away from each other.

"Enough," Marcus barked from across the room.

Dominique sneered at him. "I don't think it is."

"Me either," Celine retorted. She lunged toward Dominique when another fireball landed between them, driving her back.

"I said enough!" Marcus said. "I will not continue to police you like two school children."

"Feel free to leave anytime, Marcus," Dominique said. "We're adults. We promise not to play nice."

"You cannot destroy each other outright. You are locked in an unending battle."

"I'm willing to find out if that's true the hard way," Dominique answered.

"Me too," Celine added.

Marcus grabbed Celine's arm and dragged her toward the doorway. "Go home, Celine."

"Go say goodbye to Damien," Dominique shouted behind her.

She twisted toward the woman, rage apparent on her face. Marcus grabbed hold of both her arms, holding her back. "Stop."

"Threaten him one more time, Dominique, and I swear I'll find a way to kill you once and for all."

Dominique arched a dark eyebrow and pulled her lips back in a half-smile. She snorted a laugh. "So, Saint Celine does have a dark side. Welcome to the party."

Marcus wrangled Celine from the room, through the foyer, and out the front door onto the porch. Rain still fell in a deluge. Thunder rumbled overhead.

"You should have let me kill her," Celine shouted as she paced the porch's floorboards to release her energy.

"You cannot kill her outright and you know it."

Celine stamped her foot on the porch's floorboards. "I can damn well try."

"You're speaking out of turn, Celine." He eyed her forehead, reaching out to touch a piece of singed skin. "She's left a mark."

Celine winced and shoved his hand away. She jabbed her finger toward the sitting room window. "If she so much as lays a finger on Damien, I will find a way to end her."

"She's testing for a weakness. And you've just shown her your largest."

"Damien isn't a weakness. He's a person–"

"Who Dominique will target to get to you."

"Oh, like you wouldn't. That's a move straight out of your playbook."

"I saved Damien's life more than once."

Celine gritted her teeth as she stared at the falling rain. "Keep her away from Damien," she growled before she stepped into the rain.

"Celine, wait–" he called after her.

She ignored him, continuing through the downpour toward the trees.

* * *

Dominique sipped at a fresh glass of bourbon as Dembe swept away the glass she'd broken earlier. The front door slammed shut and a gust of damp air swept past her.

She turned and leaned her hip against the drink cart as Marcus reentered the room. "She gone?"

"Yes," Marcus answered, stalking across the room to pour himself a brandy.

Dominique sipped her bourbon as she approached the fireplace.

"You should have let me try to kill her."

"You cannot kill her, and you know it," Marcus said. "The powers that be simply will not allow it."

He smirked at her as she ground her teeth and wrinkled her nose at the words. She curled her fingers tightly around the glass in her hand, squeezing it until it shattered under her grip.

Through a clenched jaw, she said, "I am sick of the worship of Celine."

"Too bad," Marcus said as he stalked toward her. "I doubt it will end anytime soon."

She glared at him. "You've gone soft, Marcus. You kowtow to her. It's no wonder she's eluded you for centuries."

"She's eluded *us* for centuries because she is extremely powerful and loyal to the family she's chosen. One of us needs to stay on her somewhat good side."

Dominique features pinched. "Why? Why is everyone so concerned about pleasing Celine?"

Marcus shrugged. "You are antagonizing her. Which is one way to achieve the goal. However, if I remain sympathetic, it lends us a peek into her strategy."

Dominique snorted a laugh as she gave him an incredulous glance. "Do you really believe Celine is going to share her strategy with you?"

"Perhaps not wholly, however, she did seek me out to discuss the latest events, didn't she?"

"My arrival?"

"The arrival and subsequent death of a Dracopire. Which I can only assume is related to your arrival."

Dominique side-eyed him as she sipped her bourbon. "And she sought your counsel?"

"Yes. Which allows us to learn what she knows and what she thinks. And from there we can infer her strategy. Understand where her focus lies. And modify our plans accordingly."

Dominique narrowed her eyes as she stared at the flames leaping in the fireplace. "I suppose it could be somewhat useful. Though my plans are quite simple." She turned to face him, her features stony. "Kill the Buckleys and anyone associated with them."

"She will remain loyal to them."

"We'll see how long that lasts when I pick them off one-by-one."

"She will seek a way to destroy you if you do that."

"Let her try."

"You aren't all-powerful, Dominique."

"I have a few tricks up my sleeve. I don't intend to lose. I will break her." She stalked toward the door.

"I'm warning you, Dominique. You are picking a fight you may not win. Particularly if you continue to threaten Damien."

She stopped, a grimace forming on her lips. She spun to face him, her eyes narrowed and cold. "I am going to destroy Celine Devereaux. And I'm going to start by killing Damien."

CHAPTER 12

Celeste paced the floor of their square sitting room, wringing her hands as she stalked to and fro.

"Sit down, Celeste, there is nothing you can do at the moment," Teddy said from his armchair. He clutched a glass of brandy in his hand, balancing it on the arm.

Celeste flung her arms out to the sides, then let them fall to slap her sides as she huffed out a breath. "How can I relax?"

"We'll figure out a way to get around this. Perhaps a consult with Marcus is in order. We've always been loyal to the cause. He knows this."

"I betrayed him once. He may not be as helpful as you are assuming."

Teddy puckered his lips as he considered it. "It cannot hurt."

Celeste grimaced as she collapsed into a chair, letting her chin rest in her palm. "Pinning our hopes on Marcus may not be wise."

"We've always depended on him in the past and it has always worked in our favor."

Celeste's knee bobbed up and down as she bit her lower lip.

"We have no other alternatives, Celeste."

"Perhaps we should go to Celine. Explain–"

Teddy leapt from his chair and stalked to the window, glaring into the rainy darkness. "Explain what? There is nothing to explain."

"We could–"

"Celeste! There is nothing to explain to her. If you do that, you have clearly chosen your side and the punishment will be swift and severe. You yourself have already experienced the effects of failing our masters. You've only just recovered your true self after having your membership revoked, as it were. Is it an experience you wish to repeat?"

"No, but–"

"Then there is no choice. We owe our lives and our souls to the cause. We owe them to Marcus, to Bazios. And by extension, to Dominique and the nameless master she serves."

Celeste lowered her eyes to her lap.

"We made our choice long ago, Celeste. We cannot change sides now."

Celeste stared at the floorboards, her eyes dull and glassy and her features blank. "Perhaps we chose incorrectly all those centuries ago."

"You did not think so then." Teddy paused and twisted to face her. "And you do not think so now. Until a few months ago, you continued to encourage your sister to reject her marriage and join Marcus."

"That's not true," Celeste shot back, fire in her eyes as she snapped her head to glare at him. "Since her return from her human life, I have never encouraged that." She leapt from her chair, her hands balled into fists. "And lest you forget, it was

Marcus Northcott who robbed me of my so-called member-ship. And it was Celine who saved me."

"In a calculated move to ensure Celine's return to immor-tality. You were merely a pawn in the game, Celeste. He did not intend for you to pay the price for long. He knew how Celine would react."

Teddy stalked across the room and put his hands on Celeste's shoulders. "No, the cause has always been loyal to us. Marcus included. Dominique's request is… difficult, I understand. But we do owe her."

Tears brimmed in Celeste's eyes and spilled onto her cheeks. She buried her face in her hands. "I cannot do it."

Teddy pulled her toward him in a tight embrace. She snapped her head up to study his dark brown eyes. "You do it. Do it for me."

His eyebrow arched up and his breathing hitched. He released his grip on Celeste and stalked across the room, his hands clutched behind his back. He swallowed hard as he composed his response. "I suppose I could. Though I am uncertain if my completion of the task will restore faith in our loyalty to the cause."

"What difference would it make as long as the deed is done?"

Teddy shrugged, the corners of his mouth turning down as he shook his head. "I am not certain, though perhaps we should run it past Dominique, just in case."

"You don't want to do it," Celeste accused.

Teddy twisted to face her. "That's not true. I simply do not wish to incur the wrath of our allies for bungling a task."

"It is not bungled if it is completed."

"But must it be completed by you? Is this a test of your loyalty?"

Celeste crossed her arms over her chest and stalked to the

window, a brooding expression on her features. "Perhaps our best option is for you to complete the task and simply remain quiet about it. We shall allow Dominique to simply believe I did it."

"I suppose that is an option. My only concern would be if it should ever come out."

"How would it?"

Teddy shrugged. "I'm not suggesting it would, but just mentioning the possibility." He stalked toward her and tipped her chin up. "I think the best thing to do right now is not panic. We'll figure this out. But let's not rush into any decisions just yet."

Celeste gave a slight nod and a fleeting smile. Despite her acquiescence, her mind continued to churn. With no clear solution in sight, she would spend a sleepless night searching for a way out of her current predicament. Though she did not see a clear path. Only a path to her own destruction. No matter what she decided.

* * *

Celine slogged through the front door and into the large foyer. She crossed to the massive, centrally-located stone fireplace, leaving a trail of water as she went.

Rain dripped from her soaked hair and drenched clothing. She stared into the dancing flames as the warmth relieved her rain-soaked chill.

Gray peered around the corner from the sitting room. He stepped into the foyer. "There you are. Where have you been? Damien said you stormed off."

"That's an exaggeration. I went to check on something."

Gray's eyes roamed up and down the length of her. "What?" He shook his head and waved his hand in front of him. "On second thought, that can wait. Change out of those wet clothes first."

Celine sighed. "Is Alexander here?"

"Yes, in the sitting room. Why?"

"Good. This is something you both should hear." She stalked toward the sitting room entrance.

"Don't you want to change first?"

"No," she said simply as she ducked inside.

Damien and Alexander played chess near the fireplace.

Michael reviewed paperwork at the desk across the room. He glanced up as Celine entered the room. "Whoa. You okay?"

"I'm fine," she said as she peeled off her wet hoodie.

Damien leapt from his chair, grabbing a throw blanket from the back of the chair and wrapping it around her shoulders. "What happened?"

"I got caught in the rain."

Gray poured her a brandy and handed it off as she huddled on the couch, pulling the blanket tighter. "Why did you go out? You knew the storm was coming."

"I told you I had to check on something."

"You should have waited wherever you were until the rain let up," Michael said.

Celine set her jaw, her blue eyes turning icy. "That wasn't an option."

Damien eased onto the couch next to her. "What happened? Where did you go?"

"To see Marcus."

Gray closed his eyes and huffed.

"Why, Celine?" Alexander inquired, switching chairs to one closer to her.

"I wanted to know if he knew anything about the appearance of the Dracopire."

Michael settled into a nearby chair. "And?"

"According to him, Dominique has a rather dubious alliance with them."

"Well, that doesn't make sense," Gray answered as he paced the floor. "Why kill one then?"

"I don't know, but this points to it not being a coincidence."

"Perhaps it's nothing to worry about. If she's killed him, the alliance may be ended," Gray suggested.

Celine shook her head. "I'd love to believe it will be that easy, but with Dominique nothing is."

Alexander studied her face. "Celine, are you hurt?"

Celine swiped at the blackened skin on her forehead. "No, I'm fine. It'll be gone by morning."

Gray rushed across the room, studying the mark. "What did he do to you?"

"Marcus didn't do this." She glanced up at the concerned faces around the room before she returned her gaze to the area rug's intricate pattern. "I had the misfortune of running into Dominique while at Marcus's."

Gray threw his arms in the air. "Celine, you have *got* to stop going to him. I can't believe he let her do that to you."

Celine sighed and shrugged. "You can't blame this on Marcus. It was my fault."

"I cannot see that being true," Gray said.

Celine tugged the blanket tighter. "It is. I was leaving and she made a remark that made me see red. I attacked her and it led to a full-blown fight." She raised her eyes to Gray. "Which Marcus stopped, I might add."

Gray pressed his lips together and shook his head. "At least he is good for something."

"I don't agree. He should have let us continue. Maybe I could have ended her."

"I doubt it. Did she sustain any damage in the fight?" Alexander inquired.

"She was bleeding and a bit disoriented after I threw her against the ceiling."

A laugh escaped Alexander's lips at the statement.

"Good for you, Celine," Michael said.

"Thanks. But that isn't the point. The point here is that the Dracopires *are* connected to Dominique. And the situation is now far more dangerous. Particularly given our encounter."

"What did she say to set you off?" Michael asked.

"She threatened everyone."

Alexander pinched his eyebrows together. "That's not new."

"She said she'd start with Damien."

Alexander winced.

"Boy, she really knows how to twist the knife, doesn't she," Gray said, his arms crossed tightly over his chest.

Alexander twisted to face his cousin. "She always did. My question is how she came upon the knowledge that that particular threat would upset Celine."

"Northcott, where else?" Gray retorted. "He's probably feeding her every bit of information he has. Including anything you two let slip on your little escapade into the past with him." Gray poked a finger at Michael and Damien.

Celine leapt from the couch, shedding her blanket. She paced the room, her wet hair springing back into soft curls as it dried.

"It doesn't matter where she got the information. She has it. And now we have to do something about it. We can't let her come after them. They're too exposed as humans."

Gray shrugged. "I don't disagree."

Alexander flicked his gaze to Damien. "I have to agree with Celine at this point. I'm sorry, Damien. But if she's threatened you directly, you really should go for your own safety."

Damien shot a glance at Michael. "But–"

"No buts, D. You've got to go. I'm not taking a chance with your lives. She named both of you specifically." She jabbed a finger toward her burned skin. "You can see what she can do. And I'm an immortal. Now, imagine how easy it will be for her to hurt you. Or worse."

Damien held his hands out in front of him. "Just a second, just a second, just a second. There may be a better solution."

Celine flung her arms out to the sides. "What?"

Damien glanced around the room. "Okay, just hear me out."

Alexander motioned for him to continue. "I would love to, Damien. We didn't find much earlier. Did I miss something?"

Damien shot a glance at Michael. "You okay with this?"

Michael shrugged, his hands on his hips. "Go for it, man."

"Michael and I had a conversation earlier about this and, while we both have a few reservations, it's not enough to hold us back, especially right now given the circumstances."

"Spit it out, Damien," Gray said, his arms crossed tightly over his chest.

Damien's posture stiffened and he swallowed hard. "Wouldn't it be better if Michael and I were… like you."

Celine's eyebrows shot up. Alexander's jaw dropped and he shot a glance at Celine.

"You don't know what you're saying," Gray shot back.

"I do. Sort of," Damien said.

Celine's forehead wrinkled and her shoulders slumped. "You don't, D."

"It would solve so many problems!"

Celine flicked her gaze to Michael. "You're okay with this?"

Michael shrugged. "Admittedly, I have some reservations, but not enough to hold me back."

Damien squeezed his eyes shut at Michael's admission.

"There you have it," Gray shouted, motioning toward Michael. "He's not on board."

"I'm on board enough," Michael said, shooting a glare at Gray.

"Michael's right," Celine said. "You should have reservations."

"I don't. Not if it solves our problems. Because us running away doesn't."

Celine approached him, offering a tight-lipped smile as she grabbed his hands. "You're not running away, D. You're just staying safe."

"But isn't this a way to do that?"

"There are things that can go awry," Alexander stated.

Damien's forehead crinkled as the disagreement over his suggestion continued. "You all did it!"

"Mine was accidental. You know that. And it's not something I'd want for anyone else. Especially if they weren't one hundred percent sure." She shot a glance at Michael.

Damien grabbed her hands. "I'm sure."

"Alexander is right. Things can go wrong," Celine said.

"How? What?" Damien questioned.

"Suffice it say," Gray barked, "things can go wrong. Trust that we're doing this for your own good."

Alexander shrugged. "On top of that, none of us are able to perform the ceremony."

Damien's eyes fell to the floor. Celine squeezed his hands.

"I just don't understand why you can't do it?"

"Yeah," Michael chimed in. "Isn't there like a guidebook or something."

Gray snapped his head toward Michael. "That's a wonderful idea. Yes. Perhaps one or both of you would like to take the chance of transforming into something… different. Maybe a vampire like Celeste. Perhaps a werewolf."

Damien snapped his head up to stare at Gray. "There are werewolves?"

Celine slid her head sideways, getting into his line of vision. "D, none of us are adept enough to do this. Not even me. And I don't want to try it on either of you in case something goes wrong. Look at what happened when I bought Celeste back, and she was already immortal."

"I trust you, Celine."

"I don't trust me, D. I'm sorry. This isn't a solution."

Damien puffed out a long breath and tossed his arms out to the side. "Okay, so let's find someone qualified."

"Easier said than done," Alexander informed him.

"Particularly under the circumstances," Celine said. "By the time we did this, you could be…Dominique's timetable may be faster than we're prepared for. We don't have time to waste."

"But–"

"But nothing," Gray interrupted, "you heard Celine. Now, go pack your bags."

Damien blinked as a frown formed on his lips. "Fine," he murmured with a sniff. He stormed from the room into the foyer, disappearing toward the stairs.

"D–" Celine called after him.

"Let him go," Gray said, "we've got bigger problems to deal with."

Celine pressed her lips together and shot a glance at Michael. He held his hands up after setting down his glass. "I'll go after him."

"And pack your bag, too!" Gray shouted as Michael stalked across the room.

"Yeah, yeah, yeah," Michael murmured as he crossed the foyer.

Gray stalked toward the fireplace, staring at the flames as Celine sank onto the couch. Alexander squeezed her shoulder.

"You did the best you could, Celine. This is the best way to keep him safe."

Celine pressed her palms against her forehead and sighed. "I should go after him."

Gray twisted to face her. "Let him go. He'll get over it."

"He's just so upset. And right after the adoption bombshell."

"He'll be fine," Gray insisted.

"It isn't the best timing, but Dominique has given us little choice, I'm afraid," Alexander admitted. "And if she has threatened them directly…"

"It's best that they go," Gray finished for his cousin.

"Gray's correct."

"So, let him go blow off steam and pack his bags."

Celine pursed her lips as she stared at the coffee table. Alexander gave her shoulders a rub. "Give yourself a break, Celine. Dominique will require a tremendous amount of your focus. This is the best thing that can happen."

Celine nodded. "I'm going to head upstairs and get into some dry clothes."

Gray grabbed her hand before she left the room. "Hey, this is going to be okay."

She offered him a fleeting smile and squeezed his hand, giving him a silent nod. She pulled her hand away and sauntered across the foyer.

Tears formed in her eyes as she mounted the stairs. Damien's upset face before he stalked from the room danced in her mind. She blinked the salty liquid away. She had no solutions. There were no other options.

Damien's idea wasn't terrible and it solved a few issues,

but they had no means to achieve the goal. Particularly in the short time they had.

A potential solution crossed her mind as she reached the doors to her suite. Her fingertips lingered on the brass door-knob a moment before she shook her head, dismissing the idea. That plan was simply too risky.

CHAPTER 13

$\mathcal{D}$amien thundered up the stairs and threaded through the halls to his door. His fingers hesitated as they wrapped around the doorknob. He thudded his head against the carved wood. Perhaps he should return downstairs and continue the argument. Had he thrown in the towel too early?

He shook his head. It was no use. They weren't listening. They'd made up their minds.

He threw it open and stalked inside, slamming the door shut behind him. Darkness crept over the horizon as the sun set on the opposite side of the house. He stalked to the window and pushed it open.

The cool ocean breeze gusted into the room. He gulped it in, hoping it soothed his frayed nerves. He'd never known Celine to give up like that. To give up on him.

Perhaps she was that worried about Dominique. Or perhaps given the recent news of his adoption she preferred to get rid of him.

A shadow crossed the waning light outside. Damien snapped his gaze toward it, trying to discern what it was.

A knock sounded at the door. He stared at it, his heart lifting. Perhaps it was Celine. Maybe they'd had a change of heart. He hurried across the room and pulled the door open.

Michael stood with his hand on the door jamb. "Hey, man, you okay?"

Damien sighed and motioned for him to enter. "Not really."

"Celine's pretty upset, too."

Damien returned to the window, staring out it as he chewed his lower lip.

"I thought you'd want to know that."

Damien remained silent, staring out over the rolling ocean as the sun continued to descend and darkness crept over the surroundings.

"Look, I don't think this is easy for her, either. And it wasn't a terrible idea, man. But if we can't pull it off… I don't see what we can do."

"I went to Shadow World. We've been to Alterra with a *way* creepier version of her. You've been bitten by a vampire. We've defeated a soul eater. This doesn't feel impossible. And how could she think I'd make this decision lightly?"

"I don't think she does."

"That's what she said!" Damien shouted as he spun to face Michael. He squeezed his eyes closed. "Sorry. I'm just…upset."

"I get it. It's fine to vent."

Damien paced the floor. "I refuse to accept that there's no solution here."

"Outside of some research, I'm not sure there's much we can do. I mean, Gray's adamant that we go. Celine is too worried about Dominique. And I can't blame her. That burn on her forehead looks pretty nasty. Even Alexander isn't on our side for this."

"I'm really surprised about that. He's usually so open-minded."

Michael cocked his head. "Either he doesn't want to upset Celine or he really thinks we can't pull this off."

"I wish I could ask more questions, but I feel like all of them are going to play it close to the vest since they've told us we can't do it."

"Alexander is usually pretty honest, right? Maybe he's not lying."

Damien spun to stalk in the opposite direction. "You're right. Maybe it is impossible."

"So, what do you want to do?"

Damien twisted the other way, shuffling toward the window. He rubbed his chin with his fingers as he completed his circuit. "Then again, maybe it isn't impossible."

"Wait, I thought we just established it was based on Celine's answer and Alexander's agreement. Gray's useless. The guy hates us no matter what, so we don't count him. But based on the other two, this is impossible to pull off. We don't know anyone who can perform this ceremony that'll change us, right?"

Damien ceased his pacing and stared at Michael. "Except we do."

Michael's eyes narrowed. "Celine? I mean, I trust her, but she didn't seem to think she could."

Damien shook his head. "No, not Celine."

Michael shrugged. "Who then?"

Damien stared at him. "Who turned Celine?"

Michael's brows knit for a moment before realization dawned on him. His expression turned to one of concern. He cocked his head. "Damien, that's–"

"Probably a terrible idea. I know, I know," Damien said, returning to his pacing. "But it *is* an idea."

"Come on, man. Going to Marcus Northcott?"

"He's helped in the past."

"But we'd owe him. And doing it behind Celine's back. I don't know, man. This is risky."

Damien bit his thumbnail as he pondered it while wandering around the room.

"Are we seriously considering this?" Michael asked after a moment.

Damien collapsed into an armchair in a heap with a sigh. "I don't know." He shook his head. "Maybe it's a horrible idea."

Michael narrowed his eyes as he sank into the chair next to Damien. "We've worked with some terrible ideas before, though."

"And come out on top."

"Damn right, we did. We've worked with worse odds."

"And won."

Michael nodded as he drummed his fingers on the chair's arm. "So, are we actually considering going to Marcus Northcott?"

Damien leapt from his seat, pacing again. "I don't know. This is one of those things I'd love to run past Celine or Alexander, but–"

"But we can't. No way. They'll *never* go for this."

Damien shook his head. "You're right. So, we're on our own for this decision."

"We've been on our own before," Michael said.

"What's your gut say?"

Michael chewed the inside of his cheek as he considered it. "It's a solution to our problem. It may also be the stupidest decision we've ever made in our lives. Trusting the Duke is a huge risk."

"He's come through before."

"He has."

Damien pointed a finger at him. "In spades."

"True. But not in circumstances like this. Remember, he's supposedly on Dominique's side."

"And I don't want to owe her my soul."

Michael winced and shook his head. "Me either. Nor him."

"Maybe we can make a deal where we don't."

"Can we trust that deal, though?"

"Only one way to find out." Damien stalked across the room toward the door.

"Whoa, whoa, wait a minute. Where are you going?"

Damien pulled the door open. "To find out from the source what we can expect if we make a deal with the devil."

Michael leapt from his seat. "Whoa, wait. There's no way I'm letting you go alone."

"I'm not going to do the deed right now. But you should wait here."

"You're not sidelining me! You just complained about them doing that."

"I'm not sidelining you, Michael. But you should wait here… in case I don't come back."

Michael shook his head. "This is a terrible idea, man. You shouldn't go alone."

"I'll be fine. But just in case, get Celinc if I'm not back in an hour."

* * *

Dominique stared out over the evening sky. The waves crashed on the rocks in front of her, the ocean remained stormy even though the violent weather had passed for the moment. She drummed her fingers against her forearm as the stars began to twinkle in the darkening sky.

She wiggled her shoulders and rolled her neck in a few directions. Her muscles still stung from her altercation with her cousin. The impact she sustained when she hit the ceiling had been enough to draw blood as she bit into her lip.

A frown formed on her lips and her nose wrinkled with acrimony. Pure jealousy fueled some of her animosity. Celine had grown stronger over the centuries. Or perhaps her anger over the threat to Damien burrowed that deeply into her soul.

Dominique's frown twisted into a cruel smile. She hoped Damien meant that much to Celine. It would make it all the more delicious when she destroyed him.

A rustling sounded to her left and she twisted to find an eight-and-a-half-foot Dracopire stalking toward her.

"It's about time, Cassian. I've been waiting here for an hour."

"I came as soon as I received your message," the beast answered in his deep voice. "I have only just returned to the realm."

"Not my problem. Did you do as I requested?"

He nodded his scaly head. "Yes. The army is being prepared."

"Excellent."

"You should know, there was some... outrage over Crispin's death."

"Crispin betrayed me. He paid the price with his life. As will anyone else in your clan who betrays me."

Cassian stared at her with his yellow eyes. "Some of them may challenge you."

"Let them. I have no issue destroying Dracopires who do not understand their place in this arrangement."

He nodded, his tail swishing behind him. "I will keep you informed of the progress as we move forward." He spun, unfurling his wings to take flight.

"Just a moment," Dominique said.

The hulking creature twisted back, his wings folding close to his body.

"I have another task for you."

"What is it?"

Dominique slid her cell phone from her pocket and toggled it on, tapping around on the screen before she pivoted it to face Cassian.

"Find him and kill him."

Cassian nodded his head in silent agreement before his wings swept outward and he leapt toward the sky.

Dominique's hair whipped around as his wings created a wind tunnel as he sought to gain height. She stared after him as he disappeared into the night sky. Her eyes fell back to the phone still clutched in her hand. The gleaming screen displayed the face of her latest victim. Dominique toggled on her pencil and drew a large red "X" over the smiling face of Damien Sherwood.

* * *

Celine peeled off her wet pants and draped them over the towel rack before she pulled on a dry set of clothes. Her mind refused to settle as she tugged her shirt over her head and slipped a cardigan on over it. She wrapped the bulky sweater around her midriff and crossed her arms over it.

She glanced in the mirror, catching sight of the blackened burn on her forehead. She tapped it with her finger, wincing as it stung. At least it had already begun to recede.

She shook her head as she stalked into the bedroom. Her mind dwelled on Damien's face as every one of them shot down his idea. It wasn't terrible. But it wasn't feasible either.

The best thing for him was to go as far away from Dominique as possible. He didn't understand that. Not after everything they'd been through together.

Some of their experiences gave them a false sense of security. She imagined the turmoil they'd lived through made them believe they could navigate this new world easily. They were wrong. Dominique presented a new challenge. One they were not prepared for.

Celine sank onto the bed, the image of Damien's heartbroken face still emblazoned in her brain. Her leg bobbed up and down as she tried to move her mind to another topic. She couldn't.

With a sigh, she dragged herself off the bed, through her sitting room, and into the hall. She stared at Damien's door. She ran her fingers through her hair as she pushed herself to walk toward his room.

She hovered outside it, hesitating to make contact with the door to knock. She shook her head. She'd just let herself in. Privacy be damned.

"Hey, D–" she said as she pushed the door open. She stopped short when she found her cousin missing from the room.

Michael leapt from one of the armchairs across the space.

"Oh, hey, Celine. Didn't expect you."

She tugged her sweater around her as she scanned the room again. "Where's Damien?"

"Damien? He's, uh, not here at the moment."

Celine's face pinched as she stared at Michael's fumbling response. "Where is he?"

"Umm, just not here." Michael offered her a grin as he rubbed the back of his neck. "He just, you know, needed a minute."

Celine licked her lips and narrowed her eyes at him.

"He was pretty upset."

She nodded as she crossed the room and stared out the open window. "So am I. I'd really rather not leave things like we did."

Celine stared out at the darkening sky. The moon rose overhead, bathing the landscape in ethereal white light.

"Yeah, well, we need to all agree on a solution. Right now, everyone's upset, so I think we've just not found the right solution yet."

Celine's mind raced as Michael droned on behind her. Where was Damien? Retrieving a snack, perhaps. But then why not say that?

A shadow flitted across the moon's light. Celine cocked her head as she stared out, searching for the source. Her lips parted as her heart began to beat faster.

She twisted to face Michael. "Where is Damien?"

"I told you, he's–"

"Where, Michael? Did he leave the house?"

"I mean–"

Celine's voice raised an octave. "This is important. Did he leave the house?"

Michael swallowed hard. "Yeah, he did."

Celine glanced out over the landscape again as another shadow swooped past. "Oh, no," she groaned as her knees threatened to buckle.

She spun and raced past Michael into the hallway. Michael followed her as she sprinted down the hall, winding her way to the main staircase.

"What is it?" he shouted after her as they ran.

She flew down the stairs, careening around the corner at the landing and spilling onto the foyer floor below.

"Celine, what's wrong?" Michael shouted as he struggled to keep up with her, still rushing down the massive staircase.

She stopped in the middle of the foyer, pushing her hair back from her face as she scanned the room. She stormed toward the fireplace and grabbed a poker. With the end raised, she studied the tip before she nodded and headed for the door.

Gray and Alexander appeared at the doorway to the sitting room.

Gray's chin jutted backward as he spotted Celine's panic. "Celine, what's going on?"

"Damien left the house," she said, breathless as she flung the door open, "and there's a Dracopire out there."

"Oh no," Alexander murmured. "Wait, we'll help find him."

"I'll go, too," Michael offered.

"No, you wait here," Celine argued.

"I can help," Michael said.

"It may be best to keep him close," Gray suggested. "Leaving him here alone leaves him open to an attack by Dominique in the event that this is a ruse to draw you from the house."

"Fine. He'll go with me. You two go toward the cliffs. He likes to go there and to the beach below. We'll take the path closer to the house."

Alexander and Gray nodded. The group tore out of the house in search of Damien. Celine and Michael veered left as Alexander and Gray continued forward toward the cliff's edge.

"Stay close to me," Celine warned, grabbing his hand and tugging him toward her. "Do you have any idea where he may be?"

Michael winced, his eyes darting from side to side. He shook his head. "No, he just said he needed some air. Maybe this way."

Michael pointed toward the path they used to go to Marcus Northcott's. Celine veered onto it, craning her neck to scan the sky.

Michael followed her gaze. "Is there really a Dracopire out here?"

"Yes," she answered as she continued to scour overhead.

"And it would attack him?"

Celine thundered down the path. Michael puffed as he struggled to keep up with her. "Dominique directly threatened him. So, at the very worst, Dominique has asked it to attack him. At the least, it may just be hungry and looking for a snack. Either way, it's dangerous."

Michael pressed his palm to his forehead as they blazed down the trail.

A loud squawk sounded overhead, followed by a roar.

Michael froze and whispered, "What was that?"

Celine broke into a run. "Dracopire hunting cry. He or she has found something to attack." Celine sprinted ahead, calling for Damien. Michael raced behind her.

A black shadow blotted out most of the moon's light, plunging them into darkness. The shrieking cry pierced the air again, followed by another grumbling roar.

"DAMIEN!" Celine screamed as she tracked the movement overhead.

The sound of flapping wings beat against their ears. Celine and Michael skidded around a corner in the path. Celine's eyes widened as she spotted a figure ahead on the path.

"Damien!" she called.

The figure stopped and turned to face her. Her shoulders slumped with relief as she recognized him.

"Celine!" he called as he hurried toward her. The cry reverberated above them again.

"Damien! Don't move."

He froze, his eyes raising toward the canopy of trees above them. Without warning, the leaves and limbs parted. A dragon-like beast tore through the opening. Broken sticks and wayward leaves rained down on them as the Dracopire dove toward Damien.

CHAPTER 14

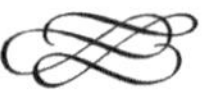

$\mathcal{D}$amien danced backward. The beast narrowly missed his target as he pulled upward, wings beating hard to regain altitude.

Celine closed the gap between them. She spun, keeping Damien behind her, as she searched the skies above them. The Dracopire shot through the trees, disappearing from sight.

"Whoa!" Damien exclaimed.

Michael jogged toward them.

"Michael, get back under the cover of the trees," Celine shouted, waving him to the side.

He nodded and hurried off the path, slipping into a thicket of trees. Celine crouched in a ready position, returning her gaze upward.

"Do you think it'll–"

Damien's question was cutoff when the Dracopire shot through the canopy of trees again, barreling toward them.

They dove apart in separate directions. Damien tossed himself to his left, landing hard on the ground and sliding to a stop. Celine shot forward and to her right. She somersaulted, landing on her feet and twisting to glance over her shoulder.

The Dracopire pulled up before it smacked into the ground. His wings created a wind tunnel, shaking the branches around them as he rose higher in the air.

He hovered above them, circling and scanning the ground below. His yellow eyes fixed on Damien, narrowing as his scaly lips pulled back in a threatening hiss, exposing long yellowed fangs.

"No!" Celine screamed as his body whipped around, tail flailing behind him.

The creature plunged toward Damien. Damien's feet scrambled to find purchase as he desperately tried to escape.

He twisted onto his belly, pushing himself upward as he tried to run for cover. The Dracopire swooped toward him, his massive hand-like paw swiping toward Damien's flailing legs.

Damien stumbled, grasping at the ground to pull himself along. He howled as the paw clamped around his ankle. The Dracopire's wings thrashed as he attempted to shoot skyward with his prey dangling.

The additional weight made his ascent slower. Celine whipped a fireball at him as he struggled to climb. The energy-filled ball failed to penetrate his scaled body, lightning crackling across his leathery skin.

The impact stung him, but not enough to wound him. He dropped Damien in a heap. With the air forced from his lungs after the impact, Damien struggled to recover.

The Dracopire spun to face Celine, his tail swishing violently. He growled at her, his teeth bared as he balled his paws into fists.

"Leave him alone!" Celine shouted, firing another ball at him. He glided sideways, dodging it. After a hiss at her, he spun in search of his prey. Damien crawled toward the cover of the trees.

The Dracopire landed, pounding across the dirt toward Damien with its three-toed feet. Celine shrieked as she raced toward him, brandishing the poker. She swung and struck the creature in the back with the electrically charged accessory.

The creature whipped its tail, knocking into Celine's legs. The force sent her spiraling through the air. She smacked into a tree, sliding down to the ground.

The Dracopire continued its lumbering walk toward Damien. Damien labored to move forward. The large creature reached him in three strides. Razor-sharp claws sliced at the air, catching hold of Damien's pant leg and shredding it.

Celine readied a fireball, slinging it toward the creature. It sailed across the distance between them, but before it could reach its target, the Dracopire swiped at Damien again. His lancinating claws tore into the flesh of Damien's leg.

Damien caterwauled in pain as blood spewed from the large slice. Celine leapt to her feet as her fireball smacked into the Dracopire's back.

With a growl, the creature twisted to face Celine.

"Leave," he snarled.

Celine narrowed her eyes and lunged forward into a menacing pose. "I don't think so," she said through gritted teeth.

The creature narrowed his yellow eyes at her and spun to face her fully. He lifted his head in the air and let out a deafening roar, flinging his arms out to the side. He stalked toward Celine who fired another shot at him. It glanced off his thick chest and he continued forward as though he wasn't hit.

Behind him, Michael skirted through the trees toward

Damien, who writhed in pain. The large creature continued toward Celine, oblivious to his presence.

The two circled each other. He dwarfed Celine, standing nearly one and a half times her height. She slipped under his arm as he swiped at her and cracked him with the poker.

He whipped around to face her again. She leapt over his tail as it sailed past her. He flung an arm out, knocking her backward like a rag doll.

The creature stalked toward his intended victim again. With a shrill scream, Celine leapt to her feet and flung herself between them.

"You can't have him," Celine said.

"We'll see," he taunted.

Celine wrinkled her nose as she sneered at him. She propelled herself through the air toward him, barreling into his chest. Her force knocked him back a few steps. He flailed his wings to keep himself upright as she latched on to him, striking with the poker again.

He grabbed the poker, stopping her from swinging. They struggled over it for a few moments before he wrenched it from her grasp and tossed it aside. It landed with a bounce near the base of a tree.

He grabbed her neck in his thick paw, lifting her from the ground. She kicked her feet wildly as she clutched at the scaly appendage. She gasped for air as he crushed her windpipe. After a second, she gave up trying to pry his paw away from her neck and instead flung an electricity-laden fireball into his face.

The fireball penetrated the more sensitive and less leathery skin of the beast's face. He roared with pain, dropping Celine to the ground. She coughed and choked as she rose to her hands and knees. Seconds later, she sailed through the air as the Dracopire kicked her in the gut.

She banged into another tree. It took a second to recover,

but she arched her back and leapt to her feet. Pine needles and branches stuck in her hair as she rose.

The Dracopire stalked toward Michael and Damien. Michael desperately tried to tug Damien back, but he was no match for the Dracopire's speed.

Celine raced toward the creature. She flung herself upward and wrapped her arms around its neck. He thrashed in an attempt to throw her, but she held tight to him. His wings beat against her as he sought to rid himself of her small body.

As a wing struck her side she grabbed it, leaping from his back and to the ground. With the wing clutched in her hands, she yanked it downward.

He roared in pain as she dug her fingers into the wing's sensitive skin. He whipped the wing away from her. His tail crashed down toward her, and she dove away as it banged against the ground.

She rolled toward the discarded poker. Her fingertips grazed the item before she was whipped backward. The Dracopire lifted her by her ankles and flung her across the trail. She tumbled through the air until she struck a pine tree.

As she recovered, he closed the gap between them, yanking her upward in his massive paw. With a throaty growl, he bit into her arm.

She shrieked as his teeth plunged into her skin. Warm blood ran down her arm, dripping to the ground below. He tossed her to the side, and she crumpled against the trunk of a tree.

Celine squeezed her eyes closed as pain throbbed through her arm. Her sight blurred for a moment as she craned her neck toward Damien and Michael. Her vision swam but she spotted the creature stalking toward Damien.

Celine dragged herself to her feet and stumbled toward the poker. With ragged breath, she wrapped her fingers around it and clenched her jaw. She craned her neck to stare at the creature.

With a deep inhale, she stormed toward him, breaking into a run as her bite wounds closed. She screamed as she sprinted toward him. He reached Michael and Damien, his arms reaching toward Damien's legs.

Celine raised the poker over her head and plunged it through the creature's back. Shock shone on Michael's and Damien's face as the poker passed through his thick body and jutted from his chest. A splattering of green blood shot toward them, burning any skin it touched.

The Dracopire howled and stumbled forward. Celine yanked the poker from his back as he collapsed to his knees. She circled around him, her face a mask of disdain.

"I told you you couldn't have him," she hissed before she drove the poker into his heart.

The creature gagged and seized twice before collapsing to the ground. A pool of green blood oozed around him.

"Is it dead?" Michael's frenzied voice asked from behind her.

"Yeah," she said with a nod as she hurried to Damien's side.

Damien writhed in pain, clenching his jaw as he reached for his injured leg. A groan emanated from his taut lips.

Celine knelt at his side. "Hold him still so I can look at this."

With trembling hands, he reached for Damien's shoulders and braced him against the ground. Damien wailed in pain as Celine teased the torn fabric away from his wound.

"Easy, D. I've just got to take a look."

Damien's cheeks bubbled as he puffed through the pain. He winced, another wail emanating from his clenched teeth.

"Take it easy, buddy," Michael soothed, his voice still shaky.

Celine eased the blood-stained fabric away. A foot-long gash ran the length of his shin. Blood oozed from the deep wound. His skin around it bubbled with burns from the poison secreted from the Dracopire's claws. The blood from the wound appeared to boil inside as it reacted with the poison.

Celine's heart dropped at the sight. They'd be lucky to save his life, let alone his leg. Her lower lip trembled as she assessed it.

"How bad is it?" Michael inquired as Damien continued to writhe. Sweat beaded on his brow as he squeezed his eyes shut.

"It's not good. He's poisoned. I'll try to remove the poison here before we move him."

Celine stared down at the torn flesh. "D, this is going to hurt, but I have to do it." She grabbed a branch from nearby. "Put this in his mouth."

Michael nodded. "Open up, buddy, tree bark sandwich coming in."

With his teeth clenched around the bark, Celine pressed her lips against the wide wound and sucked as much of the bloody mucus as she could. The metallic tinge of blood filled her mouth along with the bitter flavor of the poison.

Damien screeched in pain as she worked her way down the wound.

"That's all I can do here. We need to get him help right away."

"I'll carry him," Michael said. He slid one arm under Damien's shoulders and the other under his knees. The slightest pressure to lift him elicited a yelp from Damien.

Michael winced and glanced at Celine.

"Celine!" Gray shouted. She spun to face him. His wide eyes scanned the surroundings, his jaw hanging open in shock. "What the hell happened?"

Celine answered in a shaky voice. "The Dracopire attacked us. I killed him. But Damien's hurt. It's bad."

Gray pushed past her to stare down at Damien. "How bad? Will he survive?"

"I don't know," she answered. "We need to get him to the house."

Gray nodded. "I've got him." He scooped Damien into his arms. Damien's head lolled as the pain caused him to lose consciousness.

"Where's Alexander?" Celine questioned.

"At the beach."

"Take Damien straight to the house and have Millie assess him. I'll get Alex. I'll take Michael with me."

"Okay," Gray said with a nod.

"Gray, hurry. Every second counts."

He nodded as he set off in a run toward the main house.

"Come on," Celine said, grabbing Michael's hand. "Stick close to me. There may be more of them."

Michael swallowed hard, worry etched into his normally playful features. They threaded through the woods in the most direct line toward the cliffs.

"Is he going to be okay?" Michael asked after a few moments.

"I hope so."

"That doesn't sound good."

Celine ceased her frenzied walk for a moment and rubbed her forehead with her blood-stained fingers. A sob escaped her as she answered. "It's not. We'll be lucky to save his life. And I'm not sure we'll be able to save his leg."

The crease between Michael's brows deepened as the realization of the situation set in.

Celine wiped at her nose as she sniffled. She straightened her shoulders. "Come on. The faster we get back, the faster we'll have answers."

Michael nodded and followed her toward the cliffs. A shout sounded ahead of them. Celine quickened her pace, dodging around the thick tree trunks and into the moonlight beyond.

Her eyes widened as she took in the scene on the cliff's edge. Alexander hovered in the air over the rocky beach below. Dominique's hand held him in place, though she had no contact with him. He clutched at an unseen force around his neck.

His eyes flitted to Celine as she emerged. Dominique twisted to face them. "Oh, hey, Celine. Nice of you to join us. Alex and I were just having a little conversation."

Celine's features turned stony. "Put him down."

"Aw, why? We're having fun!"

Celine balled her hands into fists. "Fun's over. Your Dracopire is dead."

Alexander wobbled over the precarious drop as Dominique's shoulders slumped. "Ugh," she groaned. "Seriously?" She shook her head in a mock display of disgust. "Well, this night is not going my way at all, is it?"

"Put him down, Dominique."

Dominique narrowed her eyes at Celine. "You'd like that, wouldn't you?" She flicked her gaze to Alexander and shrugged. "Ah, you're right. I mean it's not going to kill him if I drop him. Only temporarily maim him a little. That's no fun."

She waved her hand across the sky, flinging Alexander away from her toward the trees. He somersaulted through the air before he landed hard on the ground, rolling toward the tree line.

Dominique turned her attention to Michael, who emerged from the woods behind Celine. She cocked her head as her lips turned up on the corners.

"You, however, will be more fun to play with." She

extended her arm toward him, reaching with extended fingers. "Come here, hot stuff."

Her hand drew him toward her like metal to a magnet. Michael's feet slid along the ground as Dominique pulled him with an unseen force.

"No!" Celine shouted. She extended her hand in a similar manner, stopping Michael's forward progress.

He hovered in the air as the two women fought against each other.

Dominique raised her other hand, bracing herself as she expended more energy to win the battle. Celine did the same. Sweat beaded on her brow as she fought to tug Michael back toward her.

Dominique barred her teeth as she sought to gain an edge over Celine. Michael began to inch toward the cliff.

"Give it up, Celine. Killing Cassian must have sapped your energy."

"Never," Celine said. She trembled with effort as she concentrated on stopping Michael from moving toward her cousin.

Alexander climbed to his feet and hurried to join Celine. He stretched out his hands toward Michael.

Michael's forward progress ceased, and he began to slide backward. After a few moments, Dominique tossed her hands in the air. Her grip on Michael released, sending him tumbling backward into Celine and Alexander. Celine climbed to her feet as Alexander pulled Michael to stand.

"Oh, just take him." She rolled her eyes. "You don't play fair. That was two against one."

"Spare me, Dominique. You never play fair. Just taking a page from your book. Now, leave my family alone."

Celine grabbed Michael's arm and tugged him toward the house.

"Oh, I don't think so, Celine. This is just the beginning."

She raised her voice as Celine, Michael, and Alexander continued to widen the gap between them. "You're going to suffer, Celine!"

When the cliffs were no longer visible, Celine grabbed Alexander's hand and squeezed. "Thanks for the assist."

"No problem."

"Yeah, man, thanks," Michael added.

"Thank you for getting her to drop me," Alexander said. "And did you really kill a Dracopire?"

"Yes," Celine answered. "But not before it wounded Damien."

"Oh, no. Is he all right?"

"I don't know," Celine admitted. "It was pretty bad. I tried to get most of the poison out of the wound. I hope Millie can clean it properly, but it didn't look good."

Alexander ceased walking for a moment. "Are you saying–"

"Let's just get to the house," Celine urged.

Alexander nodded and they resumed their frantic pace toward the glowing lights on the hill.

Celine raced across the lawn toward the sprawling mansion as they emerged from the trees. She slammed through the front door and skidded to a halt in the foyer, scanning the space for a clue to Damien's location.

A blood-curdling scream came from the direction of the west wing. Celine raced across the entryway and into the hall leading to Millie's lab as Michael and Alexander entered the house.

She pounded down the thickly carpeted hall toward the bright light shining at the end. She burst into the room and scanned the scene inside.

Gray struggled to hold a thrashing Damien on the table as Millie attempted to cleanse the wound.

"You must hold still, Damien," she shouted over the whir

of the centrifuge spinning. She doused his leg with a clear solution, eliciting another pain-filled shriek from him.

Celine hurried toward the exam table. Damien whimpered as Millie ceased her work on his leg for the moment.

"I'll need to close the wound," she said, "however, for now, I'm going to cover it. I'll need to put him under to close it. There's no way he'll tolerate the pain."

Celine wrapped her hand around Damien's as Gray moved away. Damien trembled as sweat beaded on his forehead. His breathing was ragged, and he gasped and gurgled as he fought through the pain.

Celine stroked his forehead. "Easy, Damien. Try to relax."

His head bobbed up and down as he continued to writhe.

"Have you given him anything for pain?" Celine questioned as Millie prepared a slide from the centrifuge.

Michael and Alexander hurried through the door as she answered. "Yes, several doses of morphine. It seems to have had little effect."

"Can we try something else?"

"There isn't much else more potent than what I gave him," Millie said as she leaned over her microscope.

Damien groaned, his face twisting into a mask of pain.

"The poison is in his bloodstream," Millie said. "I will begin a course of antibiotics to try to stop its progression. And we'll have to be careful with that wound. If it becomes infected, I'll have to amputate the leg."

Millie rose and crossed to the patient.

"You'll do everything you can to save it, though, right?" Celine asked.

"Of course, though saving Damien himself is the more vital task," Mille admitted.

Celine stared at her dark eyes behind her reading glasses. She cocked her head, her brow furrowing.

Millie pushed her glasses up on her head. "The wound is... bad and the poison's progression is–"

Her words were cut off as Damien's body jolted. Celine leapt, staring down at him. He moaned with pain, his teeth clenched.

"What's happening?" she asked, her eyes wide.

Millie consulted the monitor connected to Damien through a variety of leads. "His blood pressure's dropping."

"What does that mean?" Celine inquired.

Millie raced across the room without answering.

Damien groaned again. "It hurts," he murmured.

Celine returned her attention to Damien. She stroked his hair. "I know it does. But you've got to fight, D. Okay? We're all here with you and we're going to help you, but I need you to fight."

His face contorted again, his lips pressing into a thin line. Tears spilled sideways from his eyes, running into his hair. "There's so much pain."

"I know. Just hang on, Damien."

"BP's still dropping," Millie said as she pulled two paddles from a crash cart.

Celine's eyes went wide at the sight. She glanced down at Damien again. "Damien," she said, clutching his hand to her chest.

His eyes closed and he did not respond. His hand went limp in hers. "Damien!" she called again as a tremble shook her voice.

Her face turned into a mask of shock and tears spilled onto her cheeks. Her voice rose an octave as she raised a shaking hand to her lips. "Damien!" she screamed.

The monitor emitted a long, loud, flat beep. Celine glanced in horror at the blue screen as flat lines filled it.

illie ripped off her glasses and flung them on a nearby counter. "He's flatlined. Gray, pull her back."

Gray wrapped his hands around Celine's shoulders and tugged her backward. She clung to him as her knees wobbled.

Millie pressed the metal paddles to Damien's chest. "Clear."

Damien's chest leapt in the air as the defibrillator jolted him. The flat lines continued to parade across the screen.

Millie adjusted the machine and pressed the paddles against his chest again. "Clear." Another jolt. Another failure.

Millie fiddled with the machine again before pressing the paddles against his skin for the third time. Celine squeezed her eyes shut as tears dripped from her jawline. She clung to Gray's sleeve as he held her up.

Michael's red-rimmed eyes betrayed his upset as he clutched the counter, his eyes focused on Damien's limp form and his jaw tight.

Damien's chest jumped in the air, his back arching as

Millie activated the machine. He fell back to the table. A single beep sounded, followed by another, then another.

"We have a heartbeat," Millie announced as she tossed the paddles away.

The occupants of the room breathed a collective sigh. Millie loaded a syringe with medication. "We're not out of the woods yet. That poison isn't giving up."

"Can you stop it?" Gray questioned. "Reverse it?"

"I'm not sure. He's alive. For now. I do not expect it to last."

Michael's jaw hung agape. He flicked away a tear that dropped onto his cheek. "Are you saying... are you saying that he's dying?"

"I'm afraid the news is fairly dire. I had hoped to start an antibiotic regimen to counteract the poison, however, given the latest event, I fear we may be too late."

Celine's lower lip trembled as she stared at Damien's body. Her body shook as her eyes stared blankly ahead. She spoke, her voice just above a whisper. "What are you saying?"

Millie lowered her eyes. "I'm saying he's alive right now. But you may want to use this time to... say your goodbyes."

Celine blinked slowly. Michael raked his fingers through his hair as he bit his lower lip. Alexander's shoulders slumped.

"Celine, let's sit down," Gray said.

"No. No, no, no, no, no," Celine murmured.

"Celine," Gray tried again, "you should–"

"No!" Celine barked at him. She wiped away the tears dripping from her chin and sniffled. She stalked toward the door and spun back before she left. She jabbed a finger at Millie. "Keep him alive until I get back. Whatever it takes."

"Celine!" Gray called after her.

"I'll go," Alexander said. "Stay with Damien."

Celine rushed down the hall. Alexander jogged to catch up to her. "Celine–"

"Don't," she answered, waving a finger in the air.

He pursed his lips as they continued toward the foyer. "I realize this is a shock. None of us wanted this outcome, but–"

"He's not dying, Alex. Not today."

"I'm not certain we can stop it."

"I can. Stay here and make sure he stays alive."

His features pinched as he considered the statement. She barreled across the foyer and into the night air. She sprinted through the woods along the path until another home came into her view. She paused to suck in a breath before she continued forward.

She raced up the steps and shot through the front door. It banged off the wall as she flung it open and crossed the foyer. She hastened into the sitting room, coming to a halt, her breathing hard.

Marcus Northcott stood across the room at the drink cart, a glass of brandy in his hand. His expression conveyed concern. "Celine, what's wrong?"

She gasped for breath. "I need you."

He nodded and set down his glass. "Lead the way."

* * *

Celine pushed into the foyer, crossing it at lightning speed. She led Marcus down the long hall to Millie's lab. They burst through the door. Monitors continued to beep, with Damien's vital signs scrolling across them.

Marcus followed Celine to the exam table. Damien lay motionless covered in blankets, his skin gray and his lips white. Michael sat next to him, his palms pressed together in front of his face.

Marcus circled around the table as Michael moved back.

"What is his status, doctor?"

"Stable for the moment."

"And the wound is on his leg?"

"Yes," Celine answered. She pulled back a temporary cover Millie had placed on it.

"The wound is extremely large. Did you remove the poison?"

"As best I could at the site. Millie cleaned it here."

He cocked his head as he studied it. "How long ago did he sustain the injury?"

"An hour. Ninety minutes at most."

"Poison progression into his system?"

"Yes," Millie answered. "It entered his bloodstream and progressed." She paused a moment. "His heart stopped earlier. We had to use life-saving measures to revive him."

"And since?"

"Relatively stable since, but he has not regained consciousness. His pressure is a bit low and we're trying to keep him warm. I have given him several pain relievers and an antibiotic injection."

"Not a terrible set of first steps, but it will do little good."

"I've seen you save people who are worse, Marcus. I was."

"You were a special case, Celine."

Celine pressed her lips together to stop them from trembling. She cocked her head. "He can't die, Marcus."

Marcus eyed her across the table. "There are several things I will need."

"Tell us what."

* * *

Dominique stormed around the trunk of a large tree. Low branches scratched at her face and pulled at her hair. She fumed with each step, trying to follow the direction she'd seen Celine come from. The path through the woods appeared ahead.

She strode to it and scanned left and right. Her shoulder slumped and she bit the inside of her lip as she let her eyes slide closed. After a moment, she blew out a breath and stalked toward the beastly body splayed on the ground.

Her nose wrinkled as she stared down at the fireplace poker sticking from his chest. Green blood pooled around him, and his tongue lolled from his slightly parted lips.

She puffed out her cheeks and blew out a long breath. The overconfident idiot had likely failed in its directive. She assumed Damien still lived.

She yanked the poker from the body and studied the end with a frown before tossing it on the ground. She shook her head before she snapped a picture of the dead Dracopire and shoved her phone into her pocket. With a groan, she slogged down the path, leaving the creature behind.

She continued beyond the woods, stepping into the moonlight. Her mood soured with every step as the image of the dead Dracopire danced in her head. The situation would need to be handled. But she'd handle another situation first.

The seaside house loomed in front of her and she marched toward it, thundering up the steps and roaring through the front door. She stomped through the foyer and into the sitting room, heading straight to the drink cart.

Without a word to the room's other two occupants, she poured a bourbon and downed it before pouring another. After a sip, she spun to stare at the two startled faces.

Teddy and Celeste studied her with confused expressions. She narrowed her eyes at them and licked her lips, a sneer forming as she bit into her lower lip.

"Dominique? Is something amiss?" Teddy inquired.

"Oh, yes, something is amiss."

"What is it?" Teddy motioned toward the couch in front of him. "Please, sit down."

Dominique stalked across the floorboards. "No, I don't want to sit down. I want action. I want results."

"And you shall have them," Teddy assured her. "But–"

"No!" she shouted at him, hurling her glass across the room and into a wall. It slammed into the wood paneling, shattering and scattering bits of glass across the floor. "I'm done with excuses. And I'm sick of failure."

Celeste swallowed hard. "Perhaps you can tell us what's upset you."

"Celine killed a Dracopire tonight. *My* Dracopire." She shook her head as she gritted her teeth. "Now I'm going to have to explain this. I'll be leaving for Sangmond tonight. I'll be back by tomorrow night. I expect to have results on my request by then."

"On that note," Teddy began, holding a single finger in the air.

Dominique snapped her gaze to him as he continued.

"Would it be acceptable if the plan was slightly modified?"

Dominique folded her arms over her chest.

"I can explain," Teddy quickly added.

Dominique waved a hand in front of her, signaling him to proceed.

"Would it be satisfactory if, say, I were to complete it?"

Dominique scoffed at the request. She focused her eyes on Celeste. "Don't have the stomach for it, Celeste?"

"It's not that," Teddy said.

Dominique lowered her chin and narrowed her eyes. "Then there shouldn't be a problem. I told *her* to do it."

"But the result would be the same. Surely, it is the result that matters, not the method of achieving it."

Dominique sauntered to him, placing herself inches from his face. "If I wanted you to do it, I would have told you to do it." She jabbed a finger toward Celeste. "I told *her* to do it for a reason."

"Surely Celeste's loyalty isn't in question."

"Let's make that obvious, shall we?"

"It already should be! I can assure you she's been very active in helping Marcus–"

"I don't want to hear your assurances. I've already told you that. I want action. I want Celeste to do what I told her. And I don't want to hear any more about it."

Celeste's jaw dropped as her features pinched. "But–"

Dominique's eyes glowed red as she shot a perturbed glance her way. "No excuses, Celeste. Get it done. And get it done by tomorrow. Or I'll take my frustration out on you."

Dominique marched from the room and into the moonlight beyond the house. With a deep squat, she launched herself skyward, disappearing through the clouds and into another realm.

* * *

Celeste stared out the window as her cousin disappeared into the sky above. She wrung her hands as she stalked away, pacing the area rug near the fireplace.

Teddy puckered his lips as he poured two brandies. He sipped at one before wandering toward Celeste with both glasses.

"I'm sorry, Celeste. I tried." He held the glass out to her.

"Did you have to bring it up?"

"I thought we had agreed that you preferred not to do it."

Celeste yanked the glass from his grip. "And I thought you agreed to complete it for me and say nothing."

"I was worried someone may find out and it may put you in a worse position."

"Worse than the position I am in right now?" Her hand trembled as she lifted the glass to her lips.

"I agree it is not an enviable position, however, what must be done must be done."

Celeste closed her eyes at the statement.

Teddy spun toward the secretariat in the room, waving a finger in the air. "And it must be done soon. You heard Dominique. She wants it completed by the time she returns from Sangmond."

"Let us hope she does not return."

Teddy pulled the top drawer open. "I doubt that will happen."

"How did Celine kill a Dracopire? Why?"

"I don't know, but I doubt that will prevent Dominique's return. She'll likely paint it as Celine's fault despite her inviting the creature into this realm."

Celeste took another sip of brandy. "She will use the incident to fuel their rage against Celine and the Buckleys, yes."

"And we should not interfere. And give her no reason to set her sights on us."

"Teddy, she's my sister."

"And she will be perfectly fine, Celeste. You know very well Dominique will not harm her. She doesn't have the latitude to do so."

"Will she be? This may kill her."

"I doubt it." Teddy set his glass on the table and strode to Celeste, wrapping his hands around her face. "We are so close to victory, Celeste. Let's not fall short now. The centuries may have blurred your initial convictions, but don't lose sight of the endgame. We are nearly there."

Celeste licked her lips as she stared into her brandy. Teddy returned to the open drawer of the secretariat. He lifted a knife from the drawer, holding it flat in both hands.

"Now, let's get this finished so Dominique has no reason to question your loyalty."

Celeste eyed the sheathed ceremonial dagger, dipped in a poison capable of killing an immortal. She set down her glass and strode toward it, lifting the ornate handle from Teddy's hands. She glanced up at him and he firmed his lower lip, giving her a nod.

"We'll celebrate when you return with the task complete."

She arched an eyebrow as her fingers wrapped firmly around the hilt. "I'm not certain I'll feel like celebrating."

He offered her a fleeting smile. "Remember the endgame, Celeste. We shall be victorious and then you shall reap the benefits of this difficult situation."

Without a word, Celeste slipped the dagger into her cardigan pocket and stalked from the room.

CHAPTER 16

eline sniffled as she wrapped her fingers around Damien's limp hand. Her swollen eyes glanced up at the monitors. A steady beeping announced his life on a second-by-second basis.

She lowered her gaze to his pale form. His eyes remained closed, and a tube extended from his mouth. A machine breathed for him.

She glanced down at the large bandage pushing at the blankets covering him. They'd cleaned the wound again and Millie had bandaged it. Blood oozed from the white covering by the time they'd draped the first blanket over him.

With Marcus's assistance, Millie had prepared an anti-venom and administered one round. Whether or not he received it in time to counteract the poison only time would tell. For now, Celine kept vigil at his bedside, counting his breaths and his heartbeats.

If he lived past the first twenty-four hours, he should survive. Marcus's voice rang in her head as he offered his prognosis. She questioned it, uncomfortable with the "if" in the statement. Marcus's response had been characteristic of his overconfident personality. He offered her his usual half-smile, half-smirk and informed her that she should not doubt him.

She took solace in that confidence now, willing herself to believe he'd live. Twenty-four hours, she repeated in her mind. It had already been two hours. Twenty-two to go.

Millie warned if he did not wake up in that time frame, his prognosis would be grim. Even if he survived, he may never awaken.

Tears formed in her eyes, and she bent her head toward Damien's hand, resting her forehead against his cool skin. "Damien," she sobbed. "Please come back."

A hand squeezed her shoulder. "Hey," Michael said as she glanced up.

Celine wiped the tears from her cheeks with the back of her hand. "Hey," she sniffled, grasping his hand and squeezing.

"Any change?"

She returned her tearful gaze to Damien and shook her head. "No," she choked through a stuffy nose.

"It's only been two hours," Michael said.

"Yeah."

"He'll pull through."

Celine nodded, fighting back the tears that threatened to spill over again.

"He's a fighter."

Celine's lower lip quivered, despite the strong clench of her jaw. "How did I let this happen?" she sobbed.

Michael squatted next to her, rubbing her shoulder. "This isn't your fault."

"I was supposed to keep him safe. To keep both of you safe."

"You did. You have. He was just in the wrong place at the wrong time."

Celine swallowed, trying to clear the lump in her throat. Her voice broke as she spoke. "I told him not to go out. Why did he go?"

"Look, if you're going to blame yourself, I'm just as much at fault. I let him walk out the door. Didn't say anything. Didn't tell anyone. I thought it would be okay."

"You don't know the dangers of this world like I do."

"You told me. I ignored it."

Celine shuddered as she sucked in a breath. She stared straight ahead at nothing.

"He's going to be okay, Celine. Marcus Northcott doesn't like to fail."

Celine mustered a half-hearted smile at the joke. "He doesn't."

Michael nodded and stared at Damien.

"Why don't you take a break and let me sit with him for a while."

"I'm okay," she insisted. "It's only been two hours. I'd like to stay until he at least shows some sign of improvement. Maybe a little color in his face."

"I'll let you know if anything changes. Plus, it'll give him time to improve. When you get back, he may turn a corner."

"I want to be here if something happens."

"Celine–" Michael began when a quiet knock sounded.

"Celine," Gray said, sticking his head through the door. "Your sister's here. I wasn't sure what to tell her."

"Oh, I'd better go talk to her." She rose from the chair and faced Michael. "You'll be here?"

Michael gave her a tight-lipped smile. "I'll stay with him."

Celine blew out a long breath and smoothed a lock of hair behind her ear as she wobbled to the door on unsteady legs. Gray wrapped his arm around her as Millie flitted into the room.

Celine twisted to eye her as she stared at the monitors and then scribbled a few notes on her clipboard.

"Millie?" Celine asked just above a whisper.

"Vitals are stable. With any luck, we'll see some improvement soon."

Celine nodded, giving her a weak smile as Gray rubbed her shoulder. "Maybe when you get back."

She allowed him to lead her from the room and through the halls to the sitting room. Celeste stood as she entered, her eyes wide.

"Celine?" she inquired as she studied her disheveled sister.

Celine stepped toward her, her eyes focused on the ornate area rug. She opened her mouth to speak, but no words emerged. Instead, she collapsed forward against Celeste. Celeste caught her, wrapping her arms around her sister as her shoulders shook with sobs.

Celeste shot a confused glance at Gray and then Alexander as she eased Celine onto the couch. Celine wiped at her eyes as Celeste rubbed her back.

"Celine, what is it?"

Celine choked through her brief statement as she hung her head in her hands. "It's Damien."

"Damien? Has something happened to him?"

Celine nodded as she fluttered her eyelashes, raising her eyes to the ceiling in an attempt to force her tears to recede. "He was attacked by a Dracopire."

Celeste's eyes widened. "Is he–"

"He's still alive," Gray said as he poured a brandy and handed it to Celine.

"Though he had a difficult time of it," Alexander added.

Celeste glanced between them, her shoulders slumping. "Well, that's good news."

"He's alive," Celine explained. "For now. We almost lost him. His heart stopped and Millie–"

Celine's voice quavered and cut off before describing the life-saving measures they'd employed to keep Damien from becoming a member of the deceased.

Gray hovered over her, rubbing her upper back. Celine lifted a trembling hand to wipe away her tears.

"Oh, you poor darling," Celeste said as she stroked her hair.

Celine sniffled again. Her features hardened from upset to angry. She balled her hand into a fist and leapt from her seat.

She paced the floor in front of the couch. "This is Dominique's fault."

Celeste fluttered her eyelashes. "Perhaps you should sit down, Celine. Let's not worry about that now. You should focus on Damien and taking care of yourself."

"Celeste is right, darling," Gray said.

Celine bit her lower lip, her features icy. She flicked her eyes sideways toward Celeste.

"Have you seen her yet?"

Celeste swallowed hard. "Yes," she admitted, keeping her eyes focused on her lap. "She stopped by after you warned me about her arrival."

"And?" Celine prompted.

"She was her usual unpleasant self."

"Did she say anything to you? Anything about her plans?"

"No. She seems to be playing things quite close to the vest."

Celine plopped onto the couch next to Celeste and covered her face with her hands for a moment before she smoothed her hair back with a sigh.

"Celine!" Celeste cried. "What is this?" She rubbed her thumb against the black mark on the edge of Celine's hairline.

Celine winced and pulled away, shoving at her sister's hand. "It's nothing. It'll be gone by morning."

Celeste wrinkled her nose in confusion. "Did you get that from the Dracopire?"

"No," Celine admitted, leaning forward to rest her elbows on her thighs, "from Dominique."

"What?" Celeste gasped.

"We had a little… skirmish earlier."

Celeste's jaw hung open and her eyes widened.

Celine shot her sister a sideways look. "Don't worry, I gave as good as I got."

"You cannot go around picking fights with her. You know how volatile she is," Celeste chided.

Celine rose to her feet, pacing again. "Don't lecture me, Celeste. She threatened Damien."

"And you could not tolerate it and attacked her," Celeste surmised.

"I should have killed her."

"You may have ended up in the same way had your fight continued that long."

Celine's features hardened again, and she narrowed her eyes. "She sent that Dracopire after Damien."

"And now that you've killed it, she's gone to Sangmond to smooth over ruffled feathers." Celeste flicked her big blue eyes to her sister, looking up through her eyelashes. "You can be sure she's blaming you."

"Let her," Celine said. "I'm going back to check on Damien." Celine stalked to the door. She twisted back as she grabbed the door jamb. "Oh, Celeste?"

"Yes?"

"If you see Dominique again, tell her if she lays another

finger on my family, I'll kill her." Celine rapped the wooden frame with her fingers and disappeared into the foyer.

Celeste stared after her as her sister disappeared. She focused her attention on her lap again, smoothing the fabric of her dress, and adjusting the hemline.

Gray swallowed the last of his drink, setting his glass on the mantel. "I think I'll go with Celine to check on Damien in case the news is grim. If you'll excuse me." He glanced at Celeste. "I assume you can show yourself out."

"Of course," she said with a demure smile. "Oh, please keep me informed of his condition."

Gray nodded before disappearing from the room.

Alexander eyed her from across the room, his lips puckering. Celeste offered him a polite smile, her full lips curving upward and her eyelashes fluttering. The fire crackled in the fireplace, providing the only sound in the room.

After a moment she stood and stalked to the drink cart, pouring herself a scotch. She sipped it, glancing over the rim to find Alexander's eyes still on her.

"You're staring," she said.

"I'm thinking," he answered.

"About?"

"You."

Celeste fluttered her eyelashes again. "My, that sounds tawdry. You do realize I am a married woman."

He stalked toward her, pouring himself another drink. "I have no interest in you as a life partner, Celeste."

"How direct. The least you could do is feign interest. It's no wonder you're still single."

"I also have no interest in your opinion on my social life."

"Then what is your interest, Alexander?"

"Your relationship with Dominique."

Celeste twisted away from him, stalking toward the roaring fire. "What about it?"

"Exactly how close are you?"

"We are cousins. Like you and Gray."

Alexander raised his eyebrows as he stared into his brandy, considering the information. "As cousins, Gray and I are quite close."

Celeste twisted to glance at him. "I don't think I care for what you are implying."

"I am implying nothing. Perhaps your guilty conscience is stretching my words."

Celeste studied the liquid in her glass. "I have nothing to be guilty over."

The corner of Alexander's mouth inched upward as he studied her. "We'll see. I'm going to check on Damien. Excuse me."

He set his glass down and strode from the room.

Celeste sucked in deep breaths, her chest heaving with effort as she allowed the upset of the conversation to wash over her. She stalked to the fireplace, collapsing against the mantle, her forehead resting on the back of her hand.

Her other hand trembled as it traveled to the bulge in her sweater pocket.

A voice startled her. "You okay, Celeste?"

She leapt, her eyes wide and her mouth hanging open as she glanced to the door.

"Michael!" She stared at the tall blonde's boyishly handsome features, twisted into a mask of concern and confusion.

"I'd offer you a drink, but it looks like you have one," he said as he strode across the room and poured himself one.

"Yes," she answered, her heart still pounding hard against her ribs.

He spun to face her and sipped at his brandy. "Everything all right?"

She blew out a shaky breath as she stared at the floor. Her forehead crinkled and she pressed her mouth into a thin line.

Her left hand slid into her cardigan pocket, her fingers wrapping around the hilt of the dagger hidden there.

She tightened her grip on the weapon before her eyes slowly slid up to Michael's.

CHAPTER 17

*D*ominique landed on the reddish-brown dirt making up the ground in Sangmond. The blood-red moon glowed high overhead, bathing the surrounding landscape in reddish hues. The blue tree leaves glowed with a purplish tint under its light as they rustled in the gentle, warm breeze.

Dominique rose to stand, shaking her head to toss her hair over her shoulders. She stared up at the craggy mountains rising beyond the tree line.

Lights glowed from inside several of the round domiciles. Her eyes rose to the top of the mountain where Sanguine Palace stood. Its turrets and towers poked high into the sky. A reddish mist floated at its base, giving it a celestial appearance.

Despite the muggy warmth clinging to the air, Dominique tugged her leather jacket tighter around her and set off for the palace. She trudged up the difficult terrain, past the houses.

The shrieks of Dracopires filled the air from the forest she'd just left. Some of them swooped through the air, landing and disappearing into the living spaces after a successful hunt. Some carried their prey with them, likely bringing dinner for their family.

A gray, hairless creature flew toward her. With beady, black eyes, it studied her before hissing, barring its triangular, razor-sharp white teeth. The creature stopped short as a chain leash jerked to its limit. Dominique barred her teeth at the Gobgoyle, the Dracopire's equivalent of a pet dog.

She pushed against her thighs with her hands as she continued the long, steep trek. She skipped across several crumbling stones providing a shortcut to the winding path up before she leapt across a large gap and back onto the dusty trail.

As she reached the mist, the dirt turned to cobblestones. Her high-heeled boots clicked off them as she trudged upward to the massive iron gates closing off the palace from the dwellings below.

Dominique reached the doors, over four times her height. She stared up at the knocker. With a deep squat, she leapt up, flying ten feet in the air to grasp the giant iron ring. With her feet braced against the doors, she tugged on the knocker and let it drop as she slid down the door to the ground below.

She landed as a smaller door opened to the side of the massive entrance. A Dracopire stepped from within and stared down at her.

"What do you want?" he asked in a deep voice.

"Dominique Devereaux to see Queen Anika."

The Dracopire narrowed his yellow eyes at her. "Are you expected?"

"No. But I come bearing grim news." Dominique pulled the claw from her pocket and held it out, balanced between her two palms.

"Where did you get that?"

"From Earth. Where my cousin, Celine Devereaux, has killed two of your kind."

The creature motioned for Dominique to enter before returning to the small room next to the entrance. The metal doors banged as a chain clanked, tugging them open.

Dominique passed between them and continued toward the palace rising in front of her. The Dracopire that greeted her joined her on the path. They approached the large drawbridge leading into the castle.

Her companion spoke to the guard at the door in their native language of Drakish. Dominique caught a few words between them before the guard nodded and lowered the drawbridge, allowing them into the entrance.

Within moments, her heels echoed off the walls as she stepped onto the palace entry hall's red and gold marble floor. Mined from the nearby caves, the hue glowed, lighting the room.

"This way," her companion said.

Dominique nodded and followed him, increasing her pace to keep up with his massive stride. At only half his size, she hustled to stay in step with him.

He led her toward a large room. An empty throne sat on a raised platform across from the entrance. Two Gobgoyles lounged near it, curled on the floor. One snored quietly. Both leapt onto all fours as Dominique entered the room. They both bared their teeth, hissing and snarling at her.

A large Dracopire, a red velvet cape draped over her shoulders, obscuring armor underneath, stalked into the room. She clapped her paws and barked in her native language at the two creatures near the throne.

"Grimon! Muzut!" The two animals snapped their heads toward her upon hearing their names. "Nish!"

The creatures ceased their hissing and eased down to a

deep squat, their knobby knees coming to a rest near their large ears and their wings furling against their back.

The hulking Dracopire turned her attention to Dominique. She strode across the room, towering above her at a whopping ten feet tall.

"You have some news?"

Dominique nodded, refusing to bow her head to recognize the royalty. Instead, she simply removed the claw and held it out toward the creature.

Anika's yellow eyes clouded, turning green, then blue, a sign of distress in their race. "Cassian?" her deep voice whispered.

Dominique nodded. Anika chuffed, smoke puffing from her nostrils as she closed her paws around her son's finger. She twisted away, stalking a few steps from Dominique.

"How?"

"My cousin, Celine Devereaux, killed him."

The Dracopire remained silent.

"I am here to offer my condolences." Dominique paused for a moment. "And remind you of your obligation to provide the army."

Anika whipped around to face Dominique. "Why should I send my army after this?" She waved the claw in the air.

"To avenge your son's death. And Crispin's."

"You killed Crispin."

"No," Dominique said. "Celine killed Crispin. And Cassian. And she will destroy more if we allow her."

"Why should I help you? It has only led to my nephew's death and my son's death."

Dominique sauntered across the room, her heels echoing off the marble floor as she slowly strode around. "To avenge them."

"And how many more will die?"

"To expand your community. You are overcrowded here. You need space."

"The adjudicators will not allow that."

Dominique paused to glance out the peaked window at the blood-red moon hanging in the sky. "Leave the adjudicators to me."

"It is not worth the fight."

Dominique spun to face her, her eyes burning red. "Might I remind you, Anika, that you owe me?"

"An agreement can be revoked under these circumstances." Anika waved the claw again.

Dominique narrowed her eyes. "The agreement cannot be revoked under mine."

The Queen strode to her throne, climbing the stairs to it and collapsing in it. Her paw reached for the Gobgoyle on her left. She stroked its hairless head. Its eyes slid to slits, a mewling sound escaping its lips.

"I must think," she said.

Dominique tilted her head. "Unacceptable."

"You lay this at my feet even as you deliver news of my son's death?"

Dominique stared at the Queen as she stalked toward her, climbing up the large stairs. She leaned toward the Dracopire, clutching each arm of the throne.

"I'll lay even worse at them if you betray me."

Anika's blue-green eyes narrowed and slid sideways to stare at Dominique. Dominique did not back down. She did not flinch.

"You shall have your army. In one week."

Dominique's lips curled into a vicious smile. "I knew we could come to an agreement."

* * *

Celeste's fingers grasped the ceremonial knife's hilt as she flicked her gaze away from Michael's boyishly handsome features. Her lower lip quivered, and her eyes filled with tears.

"Celeste?" Michael questioned again. "Are you all right?"

Her shoulders slumped forward, and she released her grip on the knife, burying her face in her hands.

Michael set his glass on a nearby table and hurried across the room to her. "Hey, hey, what's going on?"

Celeste sobbed as she flung her arms around Michael. "Oh, Michael, I'm in terrible trouble." Tears slid down her cheeks, dripping onto his dress shirt.

Michael wrapped his arms around her as she wept and offered a few quiet consolations. After a few moments, he led her to the couch and eased her onto it.

She wiped at her cheeks with the backs of her hands, sniffling. Michael crossed the room and swung the doors closed. On his way back, he retrieved her glass and refilled her drink, offering it to her before perching on the couch next to her.

She accepted the proffered glass, sipping it before she continued wiping at her cheeks.

"Feel better?"

Celeste sucked in a shaky breath. "No," she admitted, another sob escaping.

"What's wrong?"

Celeste firmed her jaw, though it continued to tremble. "You wouldn't understand. No one will."

"That's not true."

"It is," Celeste insisted, gulping down another swallow of brandy.

"Okay, maybe I'm not the best person to discuss this with. What about Celine?"

"Celine is under enough pressure. And I doubt she'd understand."

"What about Teddy?"

Celeste's face pinched at the mention of his name. "He is of no help in the matter."

Michael raised his eyebrows. "All right, well, that leaves me. Unless you'd prefer to confide in Gray or Alexander."

"Ha!" Celeste barked.

"Like I said," he said with a coy grin, "that leaves me."

Celeste leapt from the couch, pacing the floor. "You wouldn't understand either. No matter what I do, I am a dead woman."

Michael rose and followed her pacing, stepping in front of her as she turned. He placed his hands on her shoulders and stared down at her. "I'll understand."

"You will despise me."

Michael shook his head. "I won't."

Celeste licked her lips as she studied his face. She flicked her gaze downward. "I can't."

"Well, you obviously can't face it alone either. Or we wouldn't be in this position. So, you may as well confide in me and let me help you."

"There is no help for me. I have reached the end of my usefulness. No matter which choice I make, I shall be cast out."

Michael narrowed his eyes at the statement as Celeste wrestled herself from his grasp and stalked to the fireplace.

"I'm assuming this has to do with Dominique."

"You assume correctly."

"Has she threatened you? Because if she has, Celine will–"

"No," Celeste interrupted. "It's not that."

"Then what?" Michael inquired, his hands finding their way to his hips.

Celeste swallowed hard and spun to face him. Her

sparkling blue eyes studied the man in front of her. Could she trust him? Either way, she was a dead woman, most likely. What could it hurt?

"She has demanded a pledge of loyalty."

"From you?"

"Yes," Celeste answered, her voice breathy with nerves.

"And did you give it?"

"The pledge–" Celeste lowered her eyes to the floor. "It came with a demand. A task I must complete to prove myself."

"Which is?"

Celeste paused for a moment, swallowing hard before she answered. "I'm supposed to kill Gray."

Michael's eyes widened and he collapsed onto the couch behind him, blowing out a long breath.

"See, I told you you wouldn't understand. I should have known better." Celeste shook her head and hurried toward the closed doors.

"Whoa, whoa, wait just a minute," Michael said, bouncing up from his seated position and flinging an arm out to stop her. "I didn't say that."

"Your reaction was quite enough. I suppose you'll tattle to Celine and then she can toss me into a ceiling like she did with Dominique."

"I'm not going to tell anyone. I'm assuming you're not going to do it?"

Celeste licked her lips again and flicked her gaze to Michael's blue eyes. Her lower lip trembled as she considered her answer.

Michael cocked his head. "Oh, Celeste, come on. Are you seriously considering killing Gray?"

Her chest collapsed as she blew out a breath.

Michael's eyes widened. "You're considering it?"

Celeste wrung her hands. "I didn't say that."

"You didn't say you weren't either. You can't do this. Celine will flip her lid. Especially on top of the whole Damien incident."

"I'm surprised you haven't thrown me out yet."

"Well, I'd rather you didn't. Gray and I don't exactly see eye to eye, but Celine loves him. This would kill her. You can't be considering it."

"I don't see what choice I have. Dominique will most certainly end my life if I do not succeed."

"And Celine will end it if you do."

"Exactly."

"Well, you've got to pick a side, Celeste. You can't toggle back and forth."

Celeste stalked to the window staring out into the night sky. "Do you think Celine would kill me for it?"

"Ah, yeah." Michael bobbed his head up and down. "She was pretty ticked at the Dracopire that attacked Damien and she made fairly short work of him."

Celeste wrung her hands again.

"Celeste, you can't actually be considering this."

She spun to face him, throwing her arms out at her sides. "Michael, I have no choice. You don't understand. Dominique demanded this of me. I've already tried to get out of it."

"Well, try harder. Look, Celine's not going to stand by and let you kill–"

"Shhh, please," Celeste said, holding her hands in front of her to signal his silence.

Michael lowered his voice. "She's not going to let you kill Gray and do nothing. And, let's be honest, Celeste, do you even want to?"

Celeste squeezed her lips into a thin line. A tear rolled down her cheek again. "I've just restored my relationship with her." Her face twisted as more tears fell.

Michael's head lolled to the side as he sighed. He shuffled to Celeste and pulled her into an embrace, holding her until she no longer sobbed.

As she regained her composure, he pulled back. "Oh, Michael, what am I going to do?"

"Well, like you said, you just got your relationship back with Celine. So, unless you're willing to wreck it again, I wouldn't kill her husband."

Celeste squeezed her red eyes shut. "Then I must say my goodbyes."

Michael shook his head. "You need to tell Celine what Dominique asked you to do. She can help."

"I can't. Not with the worry over Damien."

"She'll help, Celeste. Regardless of Damien's issue, we stick together."

Celeste's chest heaved up and down as she considered his words. A knock sounded at the door.

Gray appeared. Celeste spun away from him. He glanced between Michael and Celeste. "Am I interrupting something?"

"No," Michael said. "Just chatting."

"Damien's awake."

"I'll be right down."

Gray nodded, shooting another glance at Celeste's back before he disappeared from the doorway.

"Celeste–" Michael began.

"Go to your friend, Michael. I have to go."

Michael opened his mouth to reply but Celeste dashed from the room. The front door slammed moments later. He sighed as his shoulders slumped at the final reaction. He had no idea what she'd do, but he certainly hoped it wasn't to kill Gray.

CHAPTER 18

Celine clutched Damien's hand as he remained unresponsive. The machine continued to push air into his lungs as he struggled to turn the corner. He remained deathly pale, his hands still cold.

Millie had added another warm blanket on her last check. His vitals remained steady with no decline, but still no improvement.

Gray rubbed her shoulders. "Maybe you should get some rest. I'll stay with him."

Celine shook her head. "I want to be here when he wakes up."

"I'll get you the moment he even flutters an eyelash."

She firmed her lower lip in a half-smile and squeezed Gray's hand, glancing up at him. "I'm staying. I want to be here in case he needs me."

Gray raised his eyebrows as he reached for another chair to drag toward the exam table. "Okay. I'll stay with you."

"You don't have to. But thank you."

He wrapped his arm around her shoulders and pulled her close to him, kissing the top of her head. She relaxed against him as she focused her eyes on the rise and fall of Damien's chest under the heavy load of blankets.

She closed her eyes for a moment, allowing the constant beep of the machines to inform her of Damien's status. Her head began to loll as tiredness overcame her. She jolted awake as the cry of a Dracopire echoed in her head.

"Hey, it's okay," Gray soothed, stroking her hair. "I think you dozed off."

"Yeah," she said with a sniff. "I did. I thought I heard another Dracopire. Everyone's in the house, right?"

"Yes, as far as I know."

Celine rose from the chair and stalked to the window, ducking her head to glance outside. The clear night showed no signs of the flying creatures. The moon stood clearly against the black sky, unobscured and glowing brightly.

"Do you want me to check?" Gray inquired.

"Please," Celine said with a nod. "Just make sure Michael is here and Alexander, too."

"Don't want me to check on Northcott, too?"

Celine chuckled at his grumbled statement. "No, Marcus can take care of himself. Though I suppose we should keep him alive in the event that we need him."

"You have more concern about his well-being than I do," Gray said with a cheeky smile. "I'll be right back."

"I'll be here," Celine promised as she eased into the chair next to Damien's bed and reached for his hand again.

She leaned forward wrapping her other hand around his and stroking the back of his hand with her thumb.

"If you can hear me, D, it's time to wake up now. You don't want to ding Marcus's ego, do you?"

She studied his features, hoping the words may have done some good. He remained comatose. She puckered her lips and sighed, checking the time.

It had only been six hours since Millie administered the

serum. Perhaps he needed more time. Eighteen more hours until he'd be in the clear. And for him to wake up.

Celine puffed her cheeks out as worry consumed her. She stared down at his hand in hers. An acute change in the steady beeping caused her to snap her head up. She stared at the monitor, her eyes widening. The beeps, formerly slow and steady, increased in speed. Spikes filled the screen.

"Oh, no," she murmured as she vaulted from the chair and raced into the hall. Millie already hurried toward her.

"What's happening?"

"I don't know. He was fine a second ago then the monitors started going wild."

The doctor swept past Celine into the room and studied them as she swung her stethoscope from around her neck.

She held a finger to his pulse before she seated the earbuds in her ears and pressed it against his chest.

"Is he okay?" Celine inquired.

"His heart rate is spiking. That could be for any number of reasons."

"Such as?"

"Such as he is in pain, his heart is failing," Millie answered as she pried his eye open and flicked the light into it, "or he is waking up."

Celine wrapped her arms around her torso. She stared down at her cousin. "Which is it?"

Millie straightened as she checked the monitors again. "His pupils are responsive, so I am hoping–"

Damien groaned, his eyelids squeezing shut.

"Damien!" Celine exclaimed. She grasped his hand and rubbed his arm. "Damien, are you waking up?"

His eyes fluttered open. He stared at the ceiling for a few moments before his eyes slid sideways. A tear slipped from the corner of his eye, falling to his hairline.

"D? You're okay. Squeeze my hand if you can hear me, okay?"

Damien spun his hand around to hold hers and squeezed. The corners of Celine's mouth turned up and tears formed in her eyes. She patted his hand.

He grunted, his other hand pawing at the tube.

"Easy, Damien," Mille said. "We'll get the tube out."

Millie buzzed around the room, preparing things. "Celine, if you'd step out–"

"I'll stay if you don't mind."

"All right. Damien, I'm going to remove the tube now. I want you to take a deep breath and then cough. All right?"

Damien nodded and his chest rose with his deep inhale. He forced the air out in a cough as Millie eased the tube from his throat. He gasped in a breath and coughed again.

"Easy, Damien," Millie said, holding his shoulders. "You'll probably have a sore throat. That is perfectly normal. Take a few moments to relax and then let me know how you're feeling overall."

Millie drew a sample of blood from his arm. Celine wiped the tear streak from his face and smoothed his hair back as she smiled down at him. "Hey, buddy, it's good to see those blue eyes again."

His forehead crinkled as he fidgeted.

Gray stuck his head in the door, a grin forming on his face. "Hey, you're awake!"

Damien and Celine both nodded. "That's great. We were all worried about you. Celine especially."

"Can you let Michael know?" Celine inquired.

"I'll tell him."

"Thanks."

Damien fidgeted again.

"Easy, don't try to move too much until Millie checks you."

"What happened?" he asked in a hoarse voice.

Celine's features pinched as the incident flooded back into her mind. "There was a Dracopire. It attacked you."

Tears formed in Celine's eyes, and she swallowed hard as a lump formed in her throat again.

"Hey," Damien's throaty voice breathed, "I'm okay."

Celine offered a weak, wobbling smile. "Yeah."

Millie jotted notes on her clipboard. "You are correct, Damien. You are going to be okay. It appears you've turned the corner. We were afraid you may not awaken but the anti-venom appears to have done its job."

Celine snapped her gaze to Millie. "The poison's gone?"

"It is receding. And with his awakening, I'd say the prognosis is good."

Celine's shoulders slumped. "Thank God."

Millie tossed the blankets back and began to cut open the bandage around his leg. "I'm going to look at your wound, Damien. Can you tell me if you are experiencing any pain?"

Damien glanced down, unable to see anything over the mound of blankets. He attempted to sit up.

"No, stay down, D," Celine said, pressing a hand against his shoulder.

"Ow!" Damien shouted with a wince as Millie peeled back the bandage. He shot upright, staring down at his wound. His jaw dropped open and he fluttered his eyelashes.

"Easy, Damien," Millie said again.

"It's okay, D. We're going to fix it," Celine assured him.

His forehead wrinkled further as he stared at his ravaged skin.

"Are you experiencing pain in the leg?" Millie asked again.

Damien's lip bobbed up and down before he resorted to nodding in silent response.

"I'll give you something for the pain before we proceed

any further." She left the table, crossing the room to fill a syringe.

"It's okay, D. Just relax."

He gulped in air. "Am I going to lose my leg?"

"I hope not," Millie said, tapping the syringe to bring the air to the top.

"You hope?" Damien questioned.

"We must watch it carefully for infection. If we can prevent that, we will be in the clear. Though I don't think you'll be running any marathons anytime soon."

Damien swallowed hard, wincing slightly as Millie poked him with the needle and injected the pain reliever.

"This should ease the pain. If you still feel discomfort, let me know."

Damien nodded as Millie circled the table to assess the wound again. He flicked his gaze to Celine.

"I'm sorry, Celine."

Celine finger-combed a lock of hair from his face. "For what?"

"I shouldn't have gone out."

"Damien, let's not worry about that now."

"But–"

"Hey, buddy!" Michael called from across the room. A broad grin spread across his face as he crossed to the exam table. Gray followed him inside.

A smile formed on Damien's lips as he glanced at his friend. He reached out to grab Michael's hand.

"We were worried, man. You took quite a beating from that thing."

"So, I see," Damien croaked.

"But you turned the corner. I knew you would."

Damien smiled weakly as Gray circled to put his hands on Celine's shoulders. "Told you he'd be okay."

Damien's eyelids fluttered and he swallowed hard again.

Celine shook his hand. "You okay, D?"

He offered her a tight-lipped smile and nodded.

"Are you in pain?" she asked.

He shook his head. "No, not really."

Millie glanced up over the glasses sitting low on her nose. "Damien, if you are feeling any discomfort, you must let me know. Do not try to be brave. If we do not get ahead of the pain, we'll struggle to contain it later. And you need to rest comfortably."

He glanced down his nose at her. "No, I'm okay. I just…" His jaw contorted into a wide yawn. "I'm suddenly really tired."

Millie offered a tight-lipped smile and nodded. "That's a normal side effect of the painkiller. I'm not surprised. Close your eyes and rest."

"But I just woke up," he joked in his raspy voice.

"Rest, buddy, you deserve it," Michael encouraged him.

Damien's eyelids slid closed before fluttering open again. Celine squeezed his hand. "It's okay, D. Get some rest."

"I'm afraid to close my eyes," he admitted.

"I'll stay here with you. I promise," she said.

"And me," Michael answered.

"Thanks, guys," Damien said, grasping both of their hands. He winced again as he blinked a few times.

"You sure you're not in pain?" Celine asked.

He nodded. "I'm sure," he said, his words slurring a bit and his eyes heavy.

"Okay, close your eyes."

He inhaled a shaky breath as his eyes slid shut. The heart monitor registered a slowing rhythm as he drifted off to sleep.

"This is normal, right?" Celine inquired of Millie.

"Perfectly. The dosage was quite high. He'll likely sleep for hours."

"His slurred speech?" she added.

"Yes. All side effects of the heavy pain medication."

Celine nodded and returned her attention to Damien's sleeping form. She rubbed a thumb against his forehead.

"Whew, I'm glad he woke up," Michael said. "And sooner rather than later."

"Me, too," Celine answered. "Someone should probably tell Marcus."

Millie answered, her eyes never leaving the wound. "I can retrieve him when I've finished. I'd like him to look at the blood samples."

"I'll go," Celine said. "As long as someone will stay with him in case he wakes up again."

"I'll stay," Michael offered.

Gray echoed Michael's offer. Celine spun to grasp his hand and pecked him on the cheek. "I won't be long."

"I hope not. Don't make me come looking for you. I'd rather avoid Northcott entirely. It makes me uncomfortable that he's even in this house."

"I know and I'm sorry, but–"

"It's fine, Celine. I understand why he's here."

Celine gave his hand another squeeze before she dropped it and crossed the room, heading down the hall. Alexander approached from the foyer.

"How is he?"

"Asleep again. Millie gave him another massive dose of painkillers so she could redress the wound. I'm sorry you missed him for the few minutes he was awake."

Alexander offered her a slight smile. "It's fine. I'm glad you and Michael were able to speak with him. I'll catch him on the next round."

"You're just as important to him as Michael and me. He'll want to see you as soon as he can keep his eyes open longer than five minutes."

"Are you heading off to get some rest?"

"No, to update Marcus. Gray didn't have the stomach for it."

"Oh, I can handle it if you'd like," Alexander offered. "I also detest the man, but I can tolerate him for your sake."

Celine smiled at him. "Thanks, Alex, but I can do it."

He nodded at her as she stepped away. "Oh, Celine," he said, ceasing her motion.

"Yeah?"

"Have you discussed Dominique at any length with Celeste?"

"No, why?"

Alexander waved a hand in the air. "No reason. I was merely curious about her reaction to the arrival of your dear cousin."

Celine nodded at him before continuing down the hall. She crossed the foyer, ducking into the back hall and continuing to the library. She pushed the double doors open and found Marcus perusing one of the bookshelves across the room.

He glanced at her before returning his gaze to the shelf. "The selection here is rather pitiful, I'm afraid."

Celine held back an eye roll. "Sorry the books are not as intriguing as you'd like."

"Most of these appear to be rather a bore. Though I did manage to find this to pass the time. Rather a decent read."

Celine eyed the book's cover. A pirate ship floated in dark waters. The red letters *Rise of a Pirate* were emblazoned across the top.

"I'm so glad. Damien is awake."

Marcus arched an eyebrow. "Oh? And how is he?"

"Millie's taking a closer look at him now. She's given him a heavy dose of pain medication, so he's resting. She's assessing the wound again."

Marcus stared at her as she puckered her lips, her eyes downcast to the floor below. She flicked her gaze up to his face as she sucked in a deep breath. "Marcus–"

"Yes?"

"Thank you."

"You are welcome, my dear. Is there anything else you'd like to say?"

Celine furrowed her brow. "You saved Damien's life and I'm grateful for that."

"And?"

Her eyes darted from side to side. "Uh–"

"And I'm sorry I doubted you, Marcus."

Celine pressed her lips together and shook her head at him. With a sigh, she said, "I didn't doubt you. I was just concerned. Damien means a great deal to me. I couldn't bear it if he died."

"But he will. One day. He is, after all, only human."

Celine's eyes fell to her feet again. "I know."

Silence spanned the next few seconds before Marcus spoke again.

"Well, I suppose I should look in on the patient in case any adjustments must be made on my end."

He stepped past her, and she spun to follow his movement. "Marcus, wait."

He ceased his motion and twisted to face her.

"There's something we need to discuss," she said.

CHAPTER 19

Celeste hurried away from the large house, her breathing ragged. She paused as the trees surrounded her, leaning against the base of one of the large, leafy ones. She clutched her stomach as she let her eyes slide to the ground.

Her forehead creased as she fretted. Why had she told Michael about Dominique's demand? He'd surely tell the others. And that would finish her. If Dominique didn't beat them to it. She'd failed in her task.

She wiped a wayward tear from her cheek and forced herself to continue along the path. She wandered through the pathways, avoiding any houses, including her own.

She reached the cliffs and stared out over the rolling ocean. She inhaled the salty air, wondering if it would be the last time she'd smell the sea or watch the waves.

Tears formed in her eyes. She had less than twenty-four hours to complete the demand. If she didn't, Dominique would take her revenge. If she did, Celine would.

With a sigh, she blinked her tears away and continued

along the path toward her seaside cottage. She lumbered up the steps and slogged through the door.

Teddy appeared in the doorway leading to the sitting room with a champagne flute in each hand.

"I heard you coming up the steps," he said with a grin. "And I wanted to welcome you home. Is it done? Are we clear?"

Celeste glanced at him, her features pinched.

He read the signs immediately. "What's wrong? Did something happen? Were you unable to complete the task?"

She shuffled toward him, grabbing a flute and downing the champagne in one shot. She crossed the room to the bucket and poured herself another glass.

"Celeste?" Teddy questioned.

"I didn't do it," she choked out after another sip.

He set his glass down, a slack expression on his face. "Why not?"

"I couldn't."

"You couldn't? Or you wouldn't?"

Celeste shrugged as she took another sip. She pulled the dagger from within her sweater pocket and tossed it onto the coffee table.

"Couldn't. Wouldn't. Both? Does it matter?"

"I think it matters very much, yes. If you were simply unable to do it because you had no access to Gray that may buy us some time. However, if you chose not to do it... well, that is another matter entirely."

Celeste stared into the bubbly liquid in her glass. "I did not have a moment alone with Gray. And even if I had, I'm not sure I would have done it."

"Why, Celeste?"

"Damien is gravely ill. He was attacked by a Dracopire earlier. Celine is a wreck."

"And you took pity on your sister and could not add to her misery," Teddy surmised aloud.

Celeste stared into the glass again. "Something like that."

"Will the boy live?"

"He woke up before I left. I suppose that's good news."

"Excellent. Then the situation is not as grim as you assumed. Perhaps you can still manage to complete the task before Dominique's return tomorrow."

Celeste chewed her lower lip without responding.

Teddy approached her and gripped her shoulders. "Why don't you get some sleep. I'm sure this ordeal is taxing on you. With a good night's rest, you'll feel better in the morning. And you'll see the point I'm making. I realize this is not ideal, but it will bring about the plans we've aimed for since we met and married."

Celeste lifted her eyes to him, studying his face. "Was this truly our aim?"

He drew his chin back as he stared at her. "Celeste, what are you saying? You know the goal has been a union between your sister and Marcus. That can only be achieved with Gray's death."

Celeste glanced away from him.

"You do realize that, don't you, Celeste?"

With a sigh, she nodded. "Yes. I suppose I do."

"There's a good girl. Now, let's get some rest and face the problems fresh tomorrow. It will all be over soon."

Celeste took a final sip of her champagne and set the glass on the table before leaving the room. She climbed to the second floor and readied for bed, slipping between the sheets next to an already sleeping Teddy.

Celeste stared at him for a few moments before she rolled to her other side, staring out the window at the moon-bathed landscape.

She rolled onto her back and stared at the ceiling. Teddy's

words rang in her mind. "It will bring about the plans we've aimed for since we met and married."

Celeste recalled those moments. She had attended a ball in Paris with her Aunt Genevieve. She'd spent the season in Europe. Her aunt insisted, telling her father she would make a far better match there than in Martinique.

She recalled the glitz and glamour of those grand affairs. The fashions, the hairstyles, the grand ballrooms decorated to the hilt. Sparkling chandeliers, champagne flowing freely. And the attention of as many men as she could muster.

"You are pretty, my dear," Aunt Genevieve had said. "You should easily capture the attention of any man you choose."

That night in Paris, she had dressed in a rose-colored ballgown. She had worn a silk ribbon in her hair. One Theodore vanWoodsen had asked her for a dance early in the evening. She had obliged him. Her first dance partner had extolled Teddy's virtues as an esteemed lawyer and financial expert. "Destined to be someone who knows everyone," he had said.

The idea appealed to her. Teddy could provide a solid position for her in society. She discussed the matter later with her aunt.

"You do not wish for a title, dear?" her aunt questioned.

Celeste considered it. "I wish for a comfortable life where I shall want for nothing."

"Ah, you prefer money to stature, then?"

"I prefer money and influence, yes. I understand Mr. vanWoodsen has both in ample amounts."

"He does. As well as connections with some of the most influential people in Europe. He can provide well for you."

The corners of Celeste's mouth had twisted upward. "Then I think I shall choose him."

The memory faded from her mind. Teddy had courted her for months before offering marriage. He'd tempted her with grand plans for an influential place at a certain Duke's side when he ruled the world. Celeste had offered her own sister to solidify the plan, not realizing her sister would choose love over any of the things Celeste prized.

Centuries later, Celeste wondered if her sister had made the better choice. Perhaps she had. But perhaps Celeste had made a decent enough choice. She loved Teddy. At least she thought she did.

Her eyes slid sideways to his sleeping form. She considered waking him. Perhaps she could explain her feelings to him, justify her reservations. Celeste imagined the conversation unfolding. Teddy insisted she follow Dominique's plan. Would he change if she poured her heart out to him? Doubtful, she concluded.

With a pout, she threw back the covers and climbed from her bed, pulling on her silk robe. She tied it around her as she padded across the room to stare out the window. Her mind churned with questions for which she had no answers.

Her face fell, her chin dipping to her chest. Loneliness overcame her. She felt lost and alone. She had no one to turn to. No one to help. She had no one.

An image formed in her mind, and she crinkled her forehead as she considered it. Perhaps she wasn't alone. Perhaps someone could help her.

She twisted and eyed Teddy, still sleeping soundly. She approached the bed, gazing down at him. After a moment, she swiped her cell phone from the table and padded from the room and down the stairs. She opened her message app as she eased onto the couch. Her fingers flew across the virtual keyboard. Her thumb hovered over the send icon.

She sucked in a deep breath and squeezed her eyes closed as her thumb tapped the arrow and the message went on its way.

She toggled off the phone's display and sank her forehead

into her palm. The chime of her phone startled her. She pursed her lips as she stared at the blank screen, afraid to read the response.

With trembling hands, Celeste toggled on the display. It opened to the message screen she'd just used. A response awaited her: *I'm up and yes, I'm still willing to help*

Tears sprang to her eyes and she blew out a long breath, sucking in another shaky breath. Michael had answered and his offer still stood. She was not alone. She had help. Would it be enough to save her life?

* * *

Damien panted as he ceased running for a moment to catch his breath. His leg ached and his chest hurt from the hard pace he'd set. He gasped for air, doubled over with his hands resting on his thighs.

A loud screech sounded overhead followed by a roar. Damien's heart thudded against his ribs, and his stomach turned over. He scanned the sky. A shadow passed overhead.

With a last gasp, he sprinted down the path. A large hulking beast landed in front of him. He skidded to a halt. The Dracopire threw back its head and screeched again before it stormed toward Damien.

He opened his mouth in a wide scream.

* * *

Damien's eyes fluttered open. He glanced around his room. Next to him, a monitor kept track of his heartbeat. It beeped steadily, a spike appearing every second or so. Michael dozed in a chair next to his bed, his legs kicked up on the mattress.

He recalled being moved last night after sleeping off a

massive dose of painkillers. He'd asked about his leg and Millie had been vague at best. At this moment, his leg ached.

Damien winced as he fidgeted in his bed. The movement shook the mattress, disturbing Michael's sleep.

He startled awake, rubbing at his face and blinking his eyes. He focused on Damien. "Hey, man, how long have you been awake?"

"Just a few minutes," Damien answered.

Michael pulled his legs off the bed. "You in pain?"

"A little."

"I'll call Millie. She said not to let the pain get ahead of you."

"Can you grab me some water, too? These pain meds are giving me cotton mouth, ugh." Damien turned his lips down as he flicked his tongue inside his mouth.

Michael hastened from the room to retrieve the doctor for another round of pain meds and a cup of water.

He settled back in the chair after Millie departed following a brief exam.

"Is Celine resting?" Damien inquired.

"Yeah, finally got her to take a break. She'll be upset she wasn't here when you woke up."

"She's been here every other time. She needs a break, too."

"Yeah, and the truth is, I wanted a minute alone with you." Michael leaned forward with his elbows on his thighs.

Damien sipped at his water. "Sounds ominous."

"Not really," Michael admitted. "The thing is I didn't tell Celine why you were outside. I said you went for a walk, and we didn't realize how dangerous it was. I wanted you to know that in case you thought I ratted you out and spilled the beans to Celine."

"So, she has no idea I was going to see Northcott?"

"None. And maybe we should keep it that way."

Damien nodded.

"Especially since I think you're right."

Damien snapped his eyes to Michael.

"We can't keep doing this, man. You almost died. And then Dominique almost threw me off a cliff."

Damien's eyes widened and his muscles stiffened. "What? When? Are you serious?"

Michael pursed his lips and nodded. "Yeah. Right after the whole Dracopire thing. Gray brought you here, Celine took me to get Alexander. When we got to the cliffs, Queen D had Alex hovering over the rocks below. She tossed him down and tried for me."

"How'd you get away?"

"Celine and Dominique had a forcefield battle. I trust Celine, but I've never been so scared in my life, especially when I started to slide toward Dominique."

Damien cocked his head.

"Apparently the Dracopire fight took a little out of Celine. With Alexander's help, they managed to overpower Dominique. Thankfully."

Damien cast his eyes downward and shook his head. "Surely now Celine will agree with us."

"But she can't do anything about it even if she does. And she's never going to go for Northcott doing the deed."

"You're sure you're cool with it?" Damien inquired.

Michael pursed his lips before he began nodding his head. "Yes."

"Not that we'll really get the chance to talk to him now. I'm not exactly going to be walking around anywhere and you probably shouldn't be sneaking out either before you end up a Dracopire snack."

Michael scoffed. "Talking to Northcott may be easier than you think."

"Did you get his number?"

Michael smirked. "You have no idea what's gone on here the last twenty-four hours."

Damien crinkled his brow. "Huh?"

Michael grinned and shook his head. "You were pretty bad off, man."

"Yeah, I know. My leg's pretty bad. I don't think Millie's certain it can be saved."

"No," Michael said with a shake of his head. "I mean, you were *bad* off. Like they brought you in and you had so much poison in your system your heart stopped."

Damien choked on the water he sipped. "What?"

"Yeah. Millie had to shock you back to life. And then Celine freaked out. Told Millie to keep you alive, whatever it took. She disappeared and came back with Northcott. He created some anti-venom to save your life."

"Seriously?"

"Seriously. He's still here. He's checked on you once already to make sure his creation is working like a charm. So, we should be able to talk to him easily."

"Do you think he'll do it?"

Michael shrugged. "I guess we'll find out."

Damien yawned.

"Tired?"

"Yeah, these painkillers are top grade, wow."

Michael chuckled. "Go back to sleep. It's the middle of the night anyway."

"You sure you don't want to track down the Duke and have this out?"

"While you struggle to stay awake? No way. I need you at the top of your game when we deal with him before we end up owing our souls to him."

"Fair enough," Damien said. "Tomorrow then."

"First chance we get."

Damien nodded before he settled back into his pillows

and let his eyes slide shut. Michael studied the monitors for a few seconds before he eased back in his chair.

As he kicked his feet up on the bed again, his phone chimed. He pulled it from his pocket and toggled it on.

The message on his screen furrowed his brow. "Celeste?" he whispered.

He read the lengthy text before he replied. *Michael - I'm sorry to come to you like this and I don't even know if you're awake but I have no one else. I need help. Are you still willing to help me? There's no one else I can trust. Not even Teddy. He is insistent that I follow through on Dominique's request. I can't do it. But I don't know what to do now. I have nowhere to turn. Please, Michael. Will you help me?*

He replied with an affirmative then stared at his phone as he awaited a response. Damien wasn't willing to send him out into the war zone, but he may be heading out there anyway. He sincerely hoped there were no more Dracopires prowling the skies.

CHAPTER 20

Michael knocked at the double doors leading to Celine and Gray's suite. Within seconds, Celine swung the door open and poked her head out.

"What is it? Is it Damien? Is he okay?"

"He's fine. He woke up in a little bit of pain. Millie saw him and gave him another dose of meds. He's sleeping it off now."

Celine nodded, slipping into the hall. "How is he otherwise?"

"He's okay. He's in pretty good spirits. He's a little concerned about losing his leg."

"Marcus assures me he won't."

Michael rubbed the back of his neck. "I told him everything that happened, including the part about Northcott."

Celine winced. "How'd he take it?"

"Like a champ. You know Damien."

The corners of her mouth turned up. "Yeah, I do." She reached out and grabbed his forearm. "How are you? Do you need a break?"

"I'm fine. But if you don't mind sitting with him–"

Celine pulled the door shut to her suite. "I don't mind. But first I'd like to make sure you're really fine."

"Yeah, I'm good. I fell asleep earlier. I was asleep when Damien woke up. Only for a few minutes though."

"That's not what I mean. You had a pretty rough experience, too, on the cliffs."

Michael shoved his hands into his pockets and shrugged. "I'm okay."

"It's okay not to be okay."

He offered her a tight-lipped smile. "I'm okay. Really."

She nodded as they wandered down the hall toward Damien's room. "Get some rest," Celine said as she eased the door open.

"Will do."

Michael waited as Celine slipped into Damien's room. The door slid shut behind her. He stood for a few moments before he wandered to his door, opening and closing it. He paused, still standing in the dimly lit hallway.

Silence surrounded him. After a second, he crept further down the hall. As he turned the corner, he picked up his pace and hurried to the main staircase and down to the foyer. He pulled on a windbreaker and slipped out through the front door into the cool night air.

Michael strolled along the path toward the gazebo, keeping an eye on the skies above. His ears strained for shrieks alerting him to an impending attack. His shoulders rose to his ears as he hurried along the way, suddenly nervous about meeting Celeste outdoors.

He ducked out of the moonlight and under the gazebo's roof, finding Celeste already under the protective cover. She leaned onto the banister, eyeing the ocean in the distance.

The sound of his footsteps on the floorboards alerted her to his presence. She spun to face him. "I was worried you wouldn't come."

"I always keep my word."

She nodded, concern etched in her features. "Thank you."

Michael strode toward her, eyeing the horizon. Celeste collapsed back against the wooden banister with a sigh.

"Oh, what am I going to do?"

"I know what you're *not* going to do," Michael countered. "And that's kill Gray."

Celeste crossed her arms over her chest. "No, you're likely right."

"I'd better be more than likely, Celeste. If you want my help, you've got to promise me that."

Celeste let her gaze fall to her feet.

"Seriously?" Michael questioned. "You dragged me all the way out here after you begged for my help and you're still considering killing him?"

Celeste flung her arms out, her eyes pleading. "You have to understand. I have nothing if I don't do it. I lose everything."

"That's not true."

"It is! Dominique will not be forgiving. And neither will Teddy. This choice costs me everything I've held dear for centuries."

"But it doesn't cost you everything."

"How do you figure that?"

"You'll have me, Celine, and every person up at that house behind you."

"So, I will survive on my sister's good graces."

"What are you doing now with Teddy? You only exist if you play by his rules."

Celeste stalked a few steps away. "He is my husband."

"That's not saying much when you can't even depend on him in a crisis."

"That's not true."

"Isn't it? Then why are you meeting me in the middle of

the night for help?"

Celeste considered his statement, tightening her arms around her midriff. "Celine will never accept this."

"Let me worry about Celine."

Celeste whipped around to face him, her eyebrows arched. "You're that certain?"

"Yep."

Celeste narrowed her eyes at him. "Is this your typical Carlyle bravado speaking or the truth?"

"I'm positive I can explain this to Celine. You did the right thing, Celeste. She'll understand that."

"I'm not certain she'll understand that I kept it from her. Nor that I considered it."

"We don't have to tell her all the gritty details. I'll explain it to her. It'll be fine."

Celeste clutched at her torso again, rubbing her upper arms. "I hope so. Once this is done, there is no going back for me."

Michael sauntered toward her, putting his hands on her arms and rubbing them. "You'll be fine. We Slayers protect our own."

"I hope to be counted among you."

"You will be. Trust me, Celeste. I've got this under control."

Celeste offered him a weak smile and a flutter of her eyelashes as she gripped one of his hands and squeezed. "Thank you. I am glad to have you on my side." She glanced up at him for a moment. "I really should go."

He sucked in a deep breath and eyed her. "Before you go, there's a favor I need to ask."

Celeste raised her eyebrows at him.

"I need your help with something."

* * *

Dominique fell through the atmosphere, barreling through the clouds toward Earth. She landed in a crouch on the rocky beach. She rose to stand, tossing her hair over her shoulder. After a few moments of staring out over the rocky ocean, she turned toward the cliffs behind her.

She glanced at the sheer climb before she threaded her fingers together and pushed her hands out in front of her, palms facing away from her body. With a roll of her neck, she approached the rock face.

Her night vision scanned the cliff, identifying a few key spots. With a half-smirk, she crouched in a lunge before she leapt upward. Her toes glanced off an outcropping and she used it to spring to another. She crisscrossed, hopping from rock to rock until she made one final leap to the top. She balanced herself with flailing arms as she glanced back at the rocky shore below her.

"Not bad, old girl," she said as she dusted off her jacket and grinned to herself.

She turned her attention forward, her eyes focused on the lights glowing from the hilltop. The Buckley house was lit like a beacon. The town didn't need a lighthouse with that monstrosity on the hill glowing like a jack-o-lantern at Halloween.

Was the house lit for a reason? She imagined people scurrying about inside. What were they doing? She hoped they were mourning the loss of Grayson Buckley.

Had Celeste accomplished her task? Had she robbed Celine of the man she called her husband for over two centuries? If she hadn't it would be soon coming. She'd given Celeste a deadline. And she had better deliver results. Or else.

Her cell phone chimed in her pocket. She slid it out and checked the display. She let her gaze float upward as she puckered her lips and sighed.

The one word printed on the screen annoyed her. *Report.*

With a grimace, her thumbs flew across the keyboard. *Celine has made a mess of things and I had to clean it up. As usual. Just returned from Sangmond. Thanks to me, our plans are still on track. Now to find out if Celeste completed her task.*

A message appeared before she could shove the phone back into her pocket. *If she hasn't, I expect you to do it. This time we need results.*

With a roll of her eyes, Dominique clicked the display off and shoved the phone into her pocket without responding.

"Of course you do," she murmured under her breath as she strode away from the Buckley house.

She considered going to the vanWoodsen residence now but decided against it. She'd wait a few more hours until she was certain Celeste would be finished. She had no desire to hear her cousin whine about her arriving too soon.

Instead, she turned onto another path, heading for a different seaside home. The house of Marcus Northcott rose in the distance. Few lights glowed from within.

Dominique sauntered toward it, climbing the front steps and pushing through the front door. Silence met her as she stepped inside.

"Marcus?" she called.

She received no answer. She glanced into the sitting room, finding it empty.

"Marcus?" she called again.

Her eyes rose to the ceiling. Was he asleep? Doubtful, she thought, as she poured herself a bourbon. Where was he?

* * *

Celeste paced the gazebo floor, her cell phone clutched in her hand. She glanced at the screen several times, finding no new messages.

With a huff, she spun to complete her journey back across the octagonal space. Perhaps he had betrayed her and spoken with Dominique. Had her cousin returned from the Sangmond realm yet? She wasn't certain, but if she had and Marcus Northcott had gone to her–

Her thoughts were interrupted by the sound of footsteps. Marcus stepped from the moonlight outside onto the gazebo's platform.

Celeste sighed. "There you are. I was beginning to think you weren't coming."

"I said I would," he answered. "Perhaps now you can explain why you summoned me to an urgent meeting in the wee hours of the morning."

"You have no doubt discovered the fact that Dominique has arrived in Bucksville."

Marcus arched an eyebrow as he stalked toward the gazebo's edge. "I am aware."

"Her presence has understandably set Celine on edge."

"It always does."

"Dominique has threatened both Michael and Damien. Being human, they are obviously vulnerable."

"Have you called me here to list statements of general fact, Celeste, or is there a point to this?"

Celeste grimaced at him before continuing. "If anything should happen to them, Celine will likely fall apart."

"I'm certain this is what Dominique aspires to."

"And is it what you aspire to?"

Marcus twisted to face her, offering her a shrug. "Why?"

"You are Dominique's ally, are you not?"

He twisted back toward the ocean. "Ally is a stretch."

Celeste raised her eyebrows at the statement. "Really?"

"You should be more than aware of the fact that Dominique and I do not see eye to eye on most things."

"Then perhaps you would be interested in a proposition?"

Marcus glanced over his shoulder with his eyebrow arched high.

"It wouldn't necessarily thwart any plans you have with Dominique, though she may not be pleased until she can see the logic behind it."

"I'm listening."

Celeste licked her lips and hesitated for a moment before she floated the idea.

"Would you consider turning Michael and Damien into immortals?"

Marcus spun to face her fully as she made her request. "Forcibly?" he inquired.

"I do not believe that will be necessary."

Marcus raised his eyebrows at her.

Celeste shrugged, flinging her hands out. "It's my understanding they both want to be turned."

He narrowed his eyes at Celeste. "Why are you coming to me with this?"

"You have the ability to handle these matters. Easily."

"And what makes you think I will handle it? As you pointed out, Dominique may not be pleased. Celine certainly will not be. So, why would I do this?"

"In the long run, it helps Celine. She will no longer fret over their well-being." Celeste tilted her head, clasping her hands in front of her. "Well, she will not fret as much."

Marcus stalked across the gazebo, staring out at the rolling ocean, a finger pressed to his lips.

Celeste approached him, leaning against the railing. "Are you really concerned about displeasing Dominique?"

"I shall take the matter under consideration," Marcus said, stalking away.

"Marcus, wait. I need an answer."

"I do not have one."

"When will you?"

He stalked back toward her. "When I have considered all the angles. Celine will never forgive me for this."

"Does it matter? Isn't the goal to break her? To leave her no other option but submission?"

"Goals change."

Celeste pulled her chin back in surprise.

He offered a half-smile, half-smirk before he backed away. "Have a lovely night, Celeste."

* * *

Marcus strode down the path in the darkness, approaching the darkened form of his seaside home. He climbed to the porch and pushed into the foyer. As he strode into the sitting room, flicking on a lamp, he froze.

Dominique offered him a wicked smile from across the room, sitting in his favorite armchair, her feet propped on the nearby coffee table. She waved her almost-empty bourbon glass in the air.

"Welcome home, dear."

Marcus ignored her, crossing to the drink cart and pouring himself a brandy.

"Where have you been?" Dominique asked as she joined him.

"Out."

Dominique drizzled more bourbon into her glass. "You know," she said, pausing to take a sip, "I normally love a mysterious man, but I just can't stand when you're secretive."

"I owe you no explanations, Dominique." Marcus shuffled to the opposite side of the room, staring out his window at the lit Buckley house on the hill.

"That's where you're wrong."

"Is it?" Marcus pulled his lips to the side in mock consideration. "I fail to recall any reason why I need to explain myself to you."

Dominique stormed across the room. "You are ours, Marcus. You play by our rules."

"I still fail to see how I must account for my whereabouts to you."

"We have given you far too much leeway. Apparently, more tabs need to be kept on you so progress can be made."

Marcus sipped his brandy, his eyes narrowed over the rim of the glass as he stared into the night sky.

"So, where have you been? Making progress, I hope. Where are you on regaining your soul marker?"

Marcus spun and returned to refill his glass. "An opportunity has arisen that may lead to a resolution."

"In your favor?"

He twisted to face her. "Would I accept otherwise?"

She wrinkled her nose. "Hard to say. You've become soft over the years, Marcus. I'm surprised by the slaps to your face you have accepted."

Marcus's jaw flexed as he tolerated the insult. "Speaking of slaps to the face, you took quite a beating from Celine the other day. Enough to draw blood."

Dominique's nose wrinkled as her lips turned down in a frown. "That won't be happening again."

Marcus scoffed at the statement. "I wouldn't be so sure. Celine is not going to take this lying down."

"And I cannot wait to crush her."

"What is your plan?"

Dominique flicked her gaze to Marcus. "Wouldn't you like to know?"

"I very much would, yes."

"Get your soul marker back and I may feel like sharing a bit more."

CHAPTER 21

Celine yawned and stretched as she stood from the chair next to Damien's bed and sauntered to the window. The morning sun already peeked over the horizon, painting the sky and sea a deep shade of red.

Damien's monitors continued beeping on a regular basis. The sound brought a smile to her face. The machines reminded her of his continued progress. He grew stronger by the minute.

While the news warmed her heart, it worried her, too. When would Dominique strike again? She hoped not soon. Damien would not survive another attack.

A light knock sounded at Damien's door. Michael stuck his head inside.

"Hey," he whispered. "How is he?"

Celine crossed the room and slipped into the hall. "Good. He slept through the rest of the night."

"That's good," Michael said with a nod.

"Yeah. I hope to get good news from Millie and Marcus today about his recovery. Did you get any rest?"

"Yeah, some."

"Good." Celine bit her lower lip.

"You okay?" Michael asked.

"We came way too close to losing him."

Michael rubbed the back of his neck. "He's not the only one."

Celine's shoulders slumped and she cocked her head. "I'm sorry. I didn't mean to make this all about what happened to Damien." Celine reached out and squeezed Michael's forearm. "You went through a lot, too."

"Thanks, but that's not what I meant."

Celine squashed her eyebrows together, pulling her chin back. "What?"

"Look, umm, can we talk? Privately?"

"Of course. Let me see if Gray can sit with Damien. I don't want him waking up alone."

"Yeah, sure. I'll meet you in the sitting room." Michael ambled down the hall as Celine headed for the double doors at the end of the hall. Before she could twist the knob, Millie appeared in the hallway.

"Good morning, Celine," she called.

"Oh, Millie, good morning."

"How is our patient this morning?"

"Still sleeping, but I'm glad you're here," Celine said as she retraced her steps.

Millie paused, her fingertips lingering on the doorknob. "Is there something amiss?"

"No, but I need to step away for a moment and I didn't want to leave him alone."

"Perfect timing on my part, then. I'd like to give him a thorough exam after he wakes up. I'll stay with him."

"Thank you. I hope we'll have good news after you've seen him."

Millie disappeared through the doorway into Damien's room as Celine shoved her hands into her back pockets and continued down the hall. Her mind wandered over the conversation she'd had with Michael moments earlier. What did he mean and why did he request a private conversation with her?

Perhaps he regretted his decision to stay. Perhaps the latest round of battle proved too much for him. She'd soon find out, she thought, as she bounced down the steps toward the massive space below.

Her footsteps echoed in the empty foyer as she crossed to the sitting room. She found Michael inside, leaning against the mantle, staring at the flames leaping inside the fireplace.

"Thanks for coming," he said as she entered.

"Sure. What's up?"

Michael crossed the room and pushed the doors shut behind them. He spun to face her, sucking in a deep breath.

"We need to talk."

"Okay," Celine answered.

"You may want to sit down. And I'm going to ask that you hear me out entirely before you jump to any conclusions or take any action."

Celine flicked her eyes sideways, taking in the view of the front lawn as the sun rose higher in the sky. With a deep inhale, she cut her gaze back to Michael.

"That sounds ominous."

Michael motioned toward the couch and Celine circled around it, sinking onto the soft cushion.

She threw her hands in the air. "Okay, I'm sitting!"

Michael followed her, pacing the floor in front of the armchair. "It's come to my attention that Damien and I are not Dominique's only targets."

"Well, that's no surprise. She's threatened everyone. She's trying to destroy my family in a desperate attempt to force me to her side."

Michael nodded as he tapped his chin with his index

finger. "Yeah, well, she's got a pretty decent plan for it, too. Specifically, she's after Gray."

Celine scrunched her face. "How do you know this?"

Michael bit the inside of his cheek as he formulated his response. "She asked Celeste to kill him."

Celine's eyes widened and she drew her chin back. "And Celeste told you?"

Michael spun for his trek back toward Celine. "Yeah, Celeste came to me."

"Why didn't she just come to me?" Celine inquired.

Michael winced and cocked his head. "It's complicated."

"How?"

"She's pretty afraid of Dominique and what she'll do when she realizes she's *not* going to kill Gray."

"Fair enough but I still don't get it."

Michael perched on the edge of the armchair. "The thing is… I think she came here last night to do it."

Celine's jaw dropped at his admission.

"But," Michael continued, "when she saw how upset you were over Damien… I guess she lost her nerve."

Celine leapt from her seat, running her palm across her forehead. "Unbelievable."

"Celine," Michael said, bouncing from his seat and approaching her. "Please don't blame Celeste just yet."

Celine whipped around to face him. "Don't blame Celeste? Are you kidding? She walked into this house last night to kill my husband."

"But she didn't," Michael countered.

Celine flung her arms in the air. "Oh, perfect. Let's give her an award for that. As my cousin lay dying, my sister didn't kill my husband because I was upset."

"I don't think she ever wanted to do it."

"Yet she walked into this house prepared to."

"Because she's terrified of Dominique *and* Teddy. She felt she had nowhere to turn. She was afraid to come to you."

Celine scoffed as she shook her head.

"She was really upset. She said she was in terrible trouble with nowhere to turn. She was in tears and then she confessed everything to me."

Celine wrinkled her nose and bit the inside of her lower lip as she flicked her gaze away from him. "My sister is an incredible actress. She always has been."

"I don't think she's acting. I think she's scared."

Celine crossed her arms over her chest.

"Come on, Celine. She helped you escape from Northcott when he had you trapped. Would she really do that and then kill Gray?"

"Apparently, yes, since you're telling me she walked into this house last night ready to kill my husband then chickened out."

Michael pressed his lips into a thin line, running his fingers through his hair. "Dominique seems pretty persuasive."

Celine flicked her gaze out the window again.

"Look, just meet with her, talk to her and go from there. Okay? That's all I'm asking. I think she's genuine. I think she feels alone, and I think she's on your side. She just needs to know that you're on hers. According to her, even Teddy turned on her. Maybe it's been him all along!"

Celine sighed and her jaw flexed as she considered his request.

"Fine. I'll talk to her."

"I'll let her know."

Celine stalked toward the door. Michael twisted as she tugged open the doors.

"Hey, Celine," he called over his shoulder. "Thanks."

She offered him a nod before disappearing into the foyer.

* * *

Celeste stared out over the sparkling ocean water as the sun rose overhead. She wrung her hands and checked her phone again. No messages awaited her. She sighed, squeezing her eyes closed.

Everything seemed to come together last night. She'd left both of her conversations with some sense of peace. But now as the sun rose higher in the sky, she questioned everything.

What if Michael could not convince her sister? What if Teddy insisted she kill Gray before she heard back from him? What if Marcus turned on her and reported her request to Dominique?

Celeste's shoulders slumped as she buried her face in her hands. The hours ticked by and she came ever closer to her doom.

Warm hands wrapped around her shoulders. "Did you get any sleep?" Teddy inquired.

She spun to face him, her features twisted into a mask of anguish. "None. Oh, Teddy. What am I going to do?"

"Now, now," Teddy answered, placing his hands on her shoulders and steadying her. "Let's not fall to pieces."

Celeste sniffled and dabbed at the few tears that had fallen to her cheeks.

"All is not lost. You will simply go to the house this morning and take care of your business. When you return, we will move on. Dominique will be appeased, we will be back in her good graces and we can rest on our laurels. And once the whole thing is over, you'll be there for your sister when she will need you the most."

"And I will be the cause of her upset."

"Only initially."

"Teddy, I would be robbing her of her husband."

"Well, you know we have never agreed with that

marriage to start with. So you are robbing her of the mistake she made centuries ago. In a way, we're righting a wrong. Think of it that way. It may make the task easier for you to complete."

Celeste turned away from him, stalking back to the railing of their ocean-facing deck and stretching her fingers around the weathered wood.

"You're still feeling reluctant?" Teddy questioned.

Celeste tightened her grip on the wood. "Yes. Of course, I am. I've been asked to kill my sister's husband. It should be more cause for concern if I was not reluctant."

"A husband she never should have had. Remember that. A husband she's been told time and again to leave. A husband who has been spared countless times before. She's been warned."

Celeste lifted her gaze from her feet to the rolling ocean, offering no response. Teddy stalked back toward the house.

Before he disappeared through the French doors, he eyed her again. "You aren't considering not following through, are you? That would be very unwise."

With the warning, he disappeared into the house, leaving Celeste alone with her thoughts. She squeezed her eyes closed, emotions threatening to overcome her.

Chimes sounded, drawing her attention away from her own thoughts. She popped her eyes open and reached into her pocket for her phone. A new message awaited her: *Come to the house when you can. Celine's willing to talk.*

Her heart lifted at the message. She'd go right away. Soon this whole nightmare would be over. At least she hoped so.

* * *

Marcus strode through the door and into Damien's bedroom. Damien sat in bed, a nearly-empty plate of break-

223

fast in front of him. Michael lounged in the armchair, a discarded plate on the nightstand nearby.

Millie stood at the foot of the bed. Her pen flew across the paper as she made notes on Damien's current condition.

"And how is the patient?" Marcus inquired as he joined Millie.

"Doing much better," she admitted. "Pulse is strong, no signs of fever or infection and a healthy appetite."

Marcus's lips twisted into a half-smile, half-smirk. "I am unsurprised. Have you processed a blood sample yet?"

"Not yet, though I was about to. Would you care to come with me?"

"I'll follow in a moment, doctor. First, I would like to inspect the wound myself. My eyes are more trained than yours."

"I shall begin preparing the sample," Millie said as she stowed the pen under the board's clip and set the chart on the dresser.

She disappeared from the room, pulling the door closed behind her. Marcus peeled back the bandage on Damien's leg and assessed the wound.

"How's it look?" Michael questioned.

"Fine. As I expected."

Michael held back rolling his eyes at the arrogant statement.

"I guess your serum or whatever did the trick," Damien said. "I suppose thanks are in order."

Marcus clasped his hands behind his back. "I understand you gentlemen are seeking more assistance of a different type."

Michael straightened in his chair. "You spoke with Celeste?"

"I did."

Damien set his plate aside, leaning forward. "And?"

The corners of Marcus's mouth turned down into a frown. "Do you understand what it is you ask?"

Michael and Damien exchanged a glance. "We do," Michael answered as Damien nodded.

Marcus raised his eyebrows as he paced the floor at the foot of the bed. "And you realize Celine will not be pleased if I grant your request."

"Yeah, we get that," Michael said.

"But it's for the best in the long run," Damien added.

"I am inclined to agree," Marcus said. "Therefore, I am willing to grant your request. You should arrive at my home at midnight tonight. Good day, gentlemen." Marcus strode from the room.

"Whoa, whoa, wait just a minute," Michael said, leaping from his chair. "There're a few things that need to be discussed."

"Such as?" Marcus inquired, twisting to face him.

"Such as how this is going to happen and what's going to happen afterward."

Marcus narrowed his eyes at Michael. "I am going to perform the ceremony to turn you from a human to an immortal. Afterward, you will be immortal."

"That's not what I meant, and you know it," Michael shot back with narrowed eyes. "We need to discuss what we'll owe you."

"Consider it a favor."

"I'm not so sure I want to owe you for the favor."

"Do you want my help or not?"

"We do," Damien said, leaning forward with a nod.

"Then I suggest you arrive at my home at midnight. Good day, gentleman." Marcus spun, whipping the door open and disappearing into the hallway. The door slammed shut behind him.

Michael lowered himself to the armchair and shot a glance at Damien.

"What do you think?" Michael asked.

"I think if we want this done, we'd better get to his house by midnight."

Michael pursed his lips and nodded.

"You having second thoughts?"

Michael considered it a moment. With a sigh, he answered, "No. I just hate owing that guy anything."

"More than that, I'm afraid of Celine's reaction to this."

Michael tented his fingers as he slouched in the chair. "Which will likely be terrible."

"Yeah, although, we won't be such easy prey for Dominique, so maybe she'll be okay with it."

"Celine okay with Northcott turning us into immortals as a 'favor?'"

Damien wrinkled his nose. "You're right. But what other choice do we have?"

"None," Michael admitted.

Damien raised his eyebrows and drew in a deep breath. "Then we head over to the Duke's at midnight."

Michael nodded. "For better or worse."

CHAPTER 22

Celine pushed through the door of her bedroom suite and stormed across the room. She flopped onto her chaise, her blonde hair splaying out onto the velvet fabric behind her. She covered her face with her hands.

"Is Damien worse?" Gray asked as he strode into the room, tugging on his blazer.

Celine pulled her hands away and flung them at her sides, blowing lip bubbles as she shook her head.

"No, he seems to be improving."

Gray perched on the chaise next to her. "So, why the long face?"

Celine stared into his stormy blue eyes. He'd spoken with Celeste last night. He'd been in the same room with her. She reached out to caress his hand, realizing how close she'd come to losing him.

"You need to avoid Celeste for a while. If you see her coming, go the other way."

Gray screwed up his face. "What? Why? Has something happened?"

"Something happened all right," Celine answered with a sigh. "Dominique has tasked Celeste with killing you."

Gray's eyebrows shot up. "Oh. Well, I guess she didn't do it."

"I don't trust her and I'm not willing to risk your life until we're certain."

"Surely, she didn't tell you she's planning to kill me," Gray answered.

"No. But she didn't tell me anything at all. She went to Michael."

Gray blinked rapidly at the statement. "She told Michael?"

"Yeah. Apparently, she came here last night to do the job and chickened out after seeing me so upset over Damien. When Michael pushed her as to why she was acting strangely, she told him everything."

"So, she still could be looking to kill me," Gray concluded as he flicked his gaze to the floor.

"Michael says no, but I'm not willing to risk your life on what Celeste told Michael. She's a practiced liar and a fantastic actress."

Gray wrinkled his nose. "Your sister isn't exactly trustworthy, no. And I would prefer not to gamble my life on Michael's word."

"I told him I'd speak with her. We'll revise our strategy after that. Until then, avoid her."

Gray nodded and squeezed her hand. "I will."

"I suppose this is the silver lining to Damien's attack," Celine said, her lips forming a pout. "If he'd not been so bad off, she may have killed you last night."

Gray shook his head and sighed. "We really need to deal with Dominique."

"I'm trying to, but she's a larger problem than even Marcus."

Gray barked a laugh as he leapt from the chaise and stalked around the room. "Never thought we'd see the day when Marcus Northcott was the least of our problems."

"I'll admit I'm surprised, too, but Dominique always was a wild card."

"And getting wilder, apparently," Gray said as he settled in front of the large window overlooking the grounds. "We've never dealt with this level of aggression from her in the past."

Celine sighed. "No. She is on a new kind of rampage, that's for sure. What is driving it, I'm not certain, but she's going all out to attack anyone close to me."

Celine rubbed at her face again. Gray twisted to eye her, then wandered over, massaging her shoulders.

She dropped her hands down and stared up at him as he hovered behind her. "I'm sorry, Gray."

"It's not your fault. She's crazy."

Celine sighed. "I can't help but feel that it is. And if anyone dies because of it–"

"It's not your fault. And I have every faith that we'll stand strong and protect our own. But you have to realize that anything that happens–"

"No!" Celine shouted as she leapt from the chaise and stalked across the room to the window. She shook her head and planted her hands on her hips. "No, nothing can happen."

"Celine," Gray said, wrapping her in his arms and tugging her back toward him.

Celine broke free of his grasp and collapsed on the window seat. "No, Gray. *Nothing* can happen. I'm not willing to lose any of you. Not you, or Damien, or Alexander, or Michael. No one."

"You're putting too much pressure on yourself to be responsible for every person in this house."

"I *am* responsible, Gray. She's here because of me. This falls on no one but me."

"She's here because she's crazy. And if you had given in to her and Northcott's demands at any point in the past, she'd just be tormenting some other innocent person, if not still tormenting you just for fun."

Celine stared down at her hands in her lap. "I refuse to lose any of you. No matter what it takes."

"I'll certainly support you in fighting her. Whatever it takes."

Celine reached for his hand, grasping it and squeezing. "Thanks."

"When is Celeste coming to speak with you?"

"I'm not sure. Michael's setting it up." With a groan, Celine pulled herself to stand. "I should check with him about it."

"All right. In the meantime, I suppose I'll hide in the office with the door locked." He winked at her.

"Mmm, you should get lots of work done that way." She stood on her tiptoes to give him a peck on the cheek before she strode to the door, spinning to offer him a coy smile. "I'll let you know when it's safe to come out."

Celine snaked through the halls to the main stairs. She descended them and crossed toward the sitting room. A knock on the door stopped her before she made it.

She tugged open the large front door, finding a courier waiting outside.

"For Michael Carlyle," the man said.

"Thank you. I can sign for it."

She scrawled her signature across the paper tethered to his clipboard and accepted the envelope. A note on the front referenced Carlyle Industries Northeast Branch opening. Celine smiled at it, realizing the envelope contained the executed contracts for the new branch. It also meant

Michael's stay in Bucksville would be permanent. For better or worse.

Michael bounced down the steps, drawing her attention away from the envelope.

"This came for you," she said, handing it over.

"Thanks." Michael pulled the tab to open the sealed envelope, pulling the papers out and shuffling through them.

"Contracts?"

"Yep," Michael said tossing them on the table.

Celine raised her eyebrows. "Regretting that decision?"

"Not at all," Michael said. "Hey, I talked to Celeste. She's heading up here as soon as she can. Thanks for talking to her."

Celine nodded. "No problem. I guess I'll wait in the sitting room."

"Yeah, she should be here any minute, I'd guess."

Celine smiled and nodded.

"I'm going to head up and hang out with Damien for a little while. Unless you want me to stay and join the conversation with Celeste."

"No, I think that's probably best between us. And don't worry, I'll keep an open mind."

He tapped her on the forearm as he gave her a tight-lipped smile. "Thanks."

Michael spun on his heel and retreated up the stairs, leaving his paperwork sprawled on the foyer's large wooden table. Celine's eyes fell to them as he departed.

She swiped the legal-length papers off the table and let her eyes slide over the bold, black letters announcing the Northeast division of the international conglomerate. She flipped through, smiling at Michael's signature as the new Vice-President.

Her gaze focused on the name above his, her brow pinching as she read it. Her posture stiffened and she drew her chin back. Her arm fell to her side as the gears in her mind spun. She set the paper down and hurried up the stairs in search of two very specific items.

* * *

Celeste read the message three more times before clicking off her display. Her sister would speak with her. They'd won half the battle. The other half would come when she had to convince Celine she hadn't betrayed her. Not really. She'd considered it only because she felt she had no other choice.

Celeste shook her head as she chewed her lower lip. That wouldn't fly. She imagined the conversation in her head.

"Hi, Celine, thanks for speaking with me. I only considered killing Gray because I had no other choices."

"Death is never a choice, Celeste. I hate you!"

Celeste winced at the imagined conversation. She'd have to find some other way to explain to Celine. Perhaps she'd say that she'd never intended to do it, but didn't know how to explain it in order to seek help. She cocked her head and puckered her full lips. That might work.

With an emphatic head nod, she hurried through the French doors and into the house's dining room.

"Teddy, I'm going out!" she shouted into the kitchen.

Teddy emerged as she tugged her trench coat over her red dress. "Out?"

Celeste swallowed hard and nodded, having hoped to avoid him before she ducked out the door.

Teddy's gaze wandered to the coffee table. "Aren't you forgetting something?"

Celeste's eyes flicked to the dagger before flicking back to his. A fleeting smile crossed her lips as she prepared to lie to her husband. A knock at their front door interrupted her.

Celeste whipped her head in the direction of the foyer.

"I'll get it," Teddy said, pushing past her and disappearing around the corner. He returned moments later with Dominique in tow.

She sauntered into the room and locked eyes with Celeste.

"Dominique!" Celeste exclaimed, her eyes wide. "What are you doing here?"

"Checking on you," Dominique said coolly.

"Well, I appreciate that, though we are fine."

"Are you?" Dominique responded as she stalked around the room, glancing out the window before returning to the center.

She gave Celeste one final glance before her eyes fell to the dagger on the coffee table. With a sniff, she flicked her gaze back to Celeste.

"This looks unused."

"Well–" Celeste began.

Dominique waved her hand in the air, cutting off Celeste's speech. "Is Gray dead or not?"

Celeste settled her gaze on her shoes and licked her lips. "No."

Dominique frowned at the statement.

"With all due respect, Dominique," Teddy said, "you're early. And if I'm not mistaken, Celeste was on her way to complete the deed now."

"Oh, heavens, yes. I'm early. By a few hours."

Teddy grinned and nodded at her.

Dominique grasped the knife and wandered to Teddy, standing inches from his face. "That's not going to fly. You've had centuries to solve this problem and you've done nothing."

"The thing is, Celeste went to the house last night to complete the task," Teddy said.

"Yet she failed."

"Celine was incredibly upset by Damien's rather precarious condition after the Dracopire attack. And Celeste felt it best–"

"Best to what?" Dominique barked. "Best to give her a few hours to rally before killing her husband? Best to allow her to recover instead of striking when it could do the most damage? No, see, I'm tired of these excuses. You screwed up, again. And this time someone's going to pay for it."

Celeste squeezed her eyes shut and swallowed hard, preparing for the onslaught of pain Dominique would soon bring to her. A single tear rolled down her cheek as she bit into her lower lip wishing she'd had the opportunity to tell her sister one last time that she loved her.

"Dominique, please, if you'd just–" Teddy tried.

"Enough!" Dominique shouted. "No more! There is a consequence to every action and it's time you faced them."

Celeste opened her eyes and laid a hand on Teddy's arm.

Dominique tossed the dagger into the air and caught it, blade pointing down. With one swift motion, she plunged the cold steel into Teddy's chest.

CHAPTER 23

Teddy gasped, his face twisting into a mask of betrayal and confusion as his eyes fell to the hilt of the knife stuck in his chest. His jaw fell open as he gaped at his crisp white shirt. A thick wet stain of crimson blood blossomed.

Celeste stumbled back a step, gasping. Her hand flew to her mouth which hung open.

Teddy puffed out a sharp breath as his eyes turned glassy. He flicked his gaze upward to Dominique.

She lifted her hand to shoulder-height and cupped her fingers, offering a prissy wave. "Bye-bye." She reached forward with one finger and pushed him over.

He thudded to the floor, landing on his back. The hilt of the knife stuck into the air as he gasped his last.

A raspy breath rattled through the air before his head lolled to the side, his glassy eyes staring blankly ahead.

Celeste trembled as she clutched her arms around her torso. A sob escaped her, and a tear ran down her cheek.

Dominique stuck her hands on her hips and sighed. She made a clicking sound with her tongue.

She leaned forward, setting a high-heeled boot against his chest, and wrenched the knife from his body. With a groan, she straightened and studied the bloody object. She frowned and shook her head.

"This dagger is known as the Immortal Killer, but really, it isn't guaranteed to kill. Not unless it's dipped in a specific poison." She pulled a handkerchief from her pocket and swiped it across one side of the blade. "It's not easy to get a hold of that poison, but I did. Kind of a waste that this didn't kill Gray, but what can you do."

She wiped the second side of the knife clean before she stowed it in the waistband of her leather pants. She made a face at Celeste.

Celeste's lower lip trembled, and she shot an incredulous glance at Dominique.

Dominique flung her arms out to her sides. "Oh, calm down, Celeste. You're off the hook!"

"Why?" Celeste breathed. "Why did you do this?"

Dominique's eyes slid from side to side. "I thought I did a fairly good job of explaining that."

Celeste's forehead creased. Dominique tossed her arms in the air again. "You're kidding. Okay, I'll try again. You didn't do your job. Someone had to pay."

"But why Teddy? He wanted me to do it. He agreed with you. He–"

"Isn't my flesh and blood. And also, why are you complaining?" She ticked off reasons on her fingers. "You're still alive. He sold you out to me. Multiple times, I might add. He was unsupportive. And he'd really reached the end of his usefulness." She flung her arms in the air. "Come on, Celeste, I did you a favor!"

Celeste let out another shaky sob as she stared down at her husband's body. Dominique wiggled her eyebrows as she set her lips in an unimpressed frown.

"You're so dramatic. You're even worse than Celine! Get yourself together. We have more work to do."

Dominique stepped over Teddy's body and stamped across the floorboards with her high heels. "I'll be back later."

With the warning called over her shoulder, she proceeded out of the house. Celeste jumped as the front door slammed. She fell to her knees next to her husband's body, already turning cold, and wept.

She gently closed his eyes before wiping at her tears. Shock set in as she tugged her trench coat tighter around her and shuffled to the front door.

Ominous gray clouds raced across the sky, threatening more rain. Celeste marched along the path to the main house. Her feet plodded along on automatic pilot. She'd been so concerned about what she'd say to her sister when they met. Now, she could think of nothing.

Images of Teddy's unmoving body danced in her mind. She replayed over and over Dominique's savage stabbing. Her eyes barely took in her surroundings as she trudged along the path.

The house rose in the distance, its sprawling gray stones spreading across the property. Celeste continued along toward it, oblivious to the rain that had begun to fall. Large drops pelted her as she walked in the open expanse leading to the house.

The clouds let loose, and a deluge poured from the sky. It did not quicken her pace. She barely felt the water soaking her as she closed the gap to the front door.

Celeste slogged through the front door. Her wet hair dripped onto her beige coat, staining it a shade darker. The belt, tied behind her, dribbled a trail of water as she stepped into the expansive foyer.

She stood, unmoving, with her hands in her pockets, staring blankly ahead.

Celine strode into the foyer from a back hall. Her eyes narrowed at her sister's drenched form across the space. Something seemed off. Though perhaps her sister had designed this presentation to make her more sympathetic.

With a deep inhale, Celine approached her, ready to get the conversation finished. Celeste stared straight ahead as though in a trance. Had Dominique done something to her?

"Celeste?" Celine questioned. "Are you all right?"

Celine closed the gap between the two women. The edges of her sister's trench coat dripped, forming a puddle at her feet. Her normally rosy skin appeared gray and clammy. Her pale lips moved but no sound came out. Her sparkling blue eyes lacked their sparkle. Even her champagne blonde hair seemed to have lost its luster.

Celine reached out toward her sister, lightly touching her hand. "Celeste?"

As if suddenly realizing someone stood in front of her, Celeste jumped. She snapped her gaze to her sister's face. Her blue eyes turned glassy, and her forehead crinkled. Her lips set in a frown.

"What is it?" Celine asked her.

Her lower lip trembled, and she swallowed hard. She fell forward, leaning against her sister as sobs wracked her body.

Celine's jaw dropped as her sister thudded against her. Her forehead crinkled as she considered the statement. Her arms wrapped around Celeste's shoulders as her sister continued to sob.

Michael bounded down the stairs. "Celeste?" he questioned as he took in the scene below him.

He hurried down the last few steps, closing the gap between them. "What happened?"

"I don't know," Celine answered. "She hasn't said a word since she came in. She just started crying after I touched her. She seems to be in some kind of shock."

Michael rubbed Celeste's shoulders, easing her away from Celine. "Celeste? Hey, what's going on?"

Celeste glanced up at him before she collapsed against him in tears. Michael wrapped his arms around her as she clung to him, her shoulders shaking.

"It's okay," he said, rubbing her back. "Let's head into the sitting room and sit down, okay?"

Celeste didn't respond. Michael guided her toward the room, his arms still wrapped tightly around her.

Gray stepped into the foyer as Michael led Celeste away. His eyebrows shot up at the scene. Celine shoved her hands into her back pockets and strode across the foyer toward him.

"She's really putting on a show, huh?" Gray inquired.

Celine shook her head, her forehead still pinched. "Something's wrong with her."

"Yes, and it's called she's afraid she's gone too far with her betrayals."

Celine pursed her lips, shaking her head again. "No. Celeste is a phenomenal actress, but this is something else."

"What?" Gray asked.

"I guess I'll try to find out. She hasn't said a word yet. She's just been crying since I found her here." Celine shrugged. "Maybe she feels that bad about what happened."

"Or she's one hell of an actress."

"I guess we'll find out."

"Good luck. I'll be in the study if you need me."

"Thanks."

Gray gave her a kiss on the cheek before returning to the hallway behind him. Celine crossed the foyer and hovered at the doorway to the sitting room. Celeste perched on the couch. Michael handed her a brandy, rubbing her arm as he offered it to her.

"Take a sip of this," he said, his tone even and calm.

Celine eased the doors shut behind her and crossed to the couch, lowering herself down to the cushion next to her sister.

"Feeling any better?" she asked.

Celeste squeezed her eyes shut as she took another sip of brandy.

Celine flicked her gaze to Michael. He offered her a shrug. She returned her focus to her sister. "Celeste, if this is about what almost happened with Gray–"

Celeste's head drooped forward toward her knees. Celine and Michael exchanged a surprised glance at the reaction. Michael sank onto the couch on her other side, his hand rubbing her back.

"Look, Celeste, it's okay. I mean, it's not okay," Celine said, "but we'll get through this. The important thing is you didn't do it."

Celeste's hand trembled. The brandy inside her glass sloshed. She gave a slight shake of her head.

Michael tugged the glass from her grasp and set it on the coffee table. "Celeste, what's going on?"

Celine tucked a lock of her sister's damp hair behind her ear. "Talk to us."

Michael rubbed her shoulders. "We want to help you. I told you that. But you've gotta tell us what's going on."

"He's dead," Celeste sobbed, before burying her face in her hands. She doubled over as she wept.

Celine and Michael shared a puzzled look.

"Who's dead?" Celine questioned, leaning forward in an attempt to catch her sister's gaze.

Celeste straightened and sniffled. She pressed her lips together in a desperate attempt to stop her crying. "Teddy."

Celine's eyes widened and her jaw dropped. "What?"

"Teddy's dead," Celeste's voice repeated, low and gravelly.

"How? What happened?"

Celeste's forehead crinkled and her lip trembled again. "She killed him. Because I didn't kill Gray. She stabbed him with the poisoned blade."

Celine searched for words but came up with none for a moment. She rubbed Celeste's back as she struggled to find something consoling to say.

"Celeste, I'm so sorry," was all she managed.

"She did it right in front of me," Celeste answered, her voice wavering again as she squeezed her eyes shut, causing fresh tears to flow.

Celine squeezed her eyes closed, loathing for her cousin building within her. If she couldn't rob her of her husband, she'd rob her sister. Celeste had been faced with an impossible choice.

"You're in shock," Michael said.

Celine nodded. "Yes, Michael's right. You should lie down. Maybe try to get some sleep."

"I am alone now."

"No, you're not," Michael countered.

"He's right. We're all here with you. We're your family."

Celeste snapped her gaze to her sister's face. "Are you? Even after what I nearly did?"

Celine grasped her sister's hand. "You didn't do it, though. And you were facing an impossible choice."

"I thought it would be me who paid the price for my obstinance. Not Teddy."

"In either case, you were facing something dire."

"She'll come after you next, Celine," Celeste said, her eyes filled with worry. She grasped her sister's hands. "She won't stop until you're broken."

"I know," Celine said. "But we aren't going to let her win."

Celeste flicked her gaze across the room. "I don't know how you'll stop her. She is… undefeatable."

"No one is undefeatable," Celine assured her. "Now, I think you should lie down until the shock passes."

Celeste's breath caught in her throat, and she grabbed Celine's hands. "I don't want to be alone. Please."

"You won't be," Michael promised. "I'll stay with you."

Celeste twisted to face him, her fingers caressing his cheek. "Thank you."

Celine and Michael tugged her to stand, and Michael wrapped his arm around her shoulders.

"Thanks," Celine said. "I'll send Millie up with a sedative to help her rest."

He nodded. "Come on," he urged, guiding Celeste across the room. "You'll be okay. We're all here for you."

Celine collapsed onto the couch as she listened to Michael's voice continue in a soothing tone as they crossed the foyer. She blew out a long breath, clasping her hands in front of her as she tensed her muscles. It took her mind a moment to comprehend the news. She and Teddy had never seen eye to eye, but she hadn't wished him dead.

And in an irreversible way. Slowly, she rose and shuffled across the room. Her mind felt jumbled. She couldn't imagine how Celeste felt.

Celine wandered through the halls into the west wing in search of Millie.

"Ah, Celine, back so soon? I have no news yet," Millie said with a coy grin.

Celine's lips formed a fleeting smile. "I wish you had, but that's impossible, I understand. But there's something else."

"What is it? Is it Damien?"

Celine shook her head. "No, umm. It's Celeste. She… Teddy's dead."

Millie slumped onto her stool.

"Celeste is a mess. I sent her upstairs with Michael. Could you maybe give her something to help her rest?"

"Of course," Millie answered, hurrying to prepare a sedative-filled syringe.

"Thanks."

"I'll also give her a quick once over, though, I imagine she's still in shock. While that may be frightening to witness, it is a normal part of the grieving process."

Celine firmed her lower lip and nodded. "Thanks, Millie. I need to tell Gray and Alexander."

"Would you like me to go with you? Are you certain you're all right?"

"I'm okay. I'm also in shock, but I'm okay."

Millie offered her a consoling smile, squeezing her forearm as she passed. Celine followed her from the room and they parted ways in the foyer with Millie heading upstairs.

Celine snaked through another hall to the study. She pushed open the door as she blew out a breath.

Gray sat across the room at the desk while Alexander leaned over his shoulder. He straightened as Celine entered.

"Did you work it all out with Celeste or should I keep my door locked?" Gray asked.

Celine remained silent, her features pinching as she formulated the words to impart the news.

"Celine?" Gray inquired, rising from his seat.

"Is everything all right? Has something happened?" Alexander added.

Celine swallowed hard, her gaze flicking between the two men. She settled her eyes on Gray. "Teddy's dead."

Gray's features did little to hide his shock. "What?"

"Oh my word," Alexander gasped.

Celine lifted her hand to cover her mouth as she composed herself.

"How?"

"Dominique," Celine answered. "Apparently she used the

dagger meant for you to kill him since Celeste didn't follow through."

Gray pulled her into an embrace. "You okay?"

"I'm better than Celeste. She's a wreck."

"I can imagine."

"Michael took her upstairs to rest, and I sent Millie up with a sedative."

"Is there anything to be done?" Alexander inquired.

Celine pulled back from Gray. "I'm not sure. I was going to head over and find out."

"I don't think that's wise," Gray said.

Celine shrugged. "It has to be done, Gray."

"You should not go alone," Alexander said.

"He's right. I'll go with you."

Celine shot him a glance. "Actually, I'd prefer you stay here."

"You're joking."

"I'm not. Dominique is out for blood and she's not afraid to use whatever means necessary to shock me or anyone else into submission. I don't want you somewhere where you can run into her. She directly threatened you."

"I'll go with you," Alexander offered.

Celine flicked her gaze to him. "Thank you, though I really wish neither of you would go. Your both targets."

Gray shook his head as he gripped her arms. "You are her primary target. You can't go alone."

Celine bit her lower lip as she parsed through the situation in her mind. "I'll take Marcus."

Gray flung his arms in the air. "You can't be serious, Celine."

"She won't kill him!"

"No, I'm sure she wouldn't. He's in league with her. They'll just combine their powers to overtake you."

"I agree with Gray. This is a terrible idea. He may have

assisted us in the past, but I don't believe we should trust him entirely."

Celine sighed. "We can't all go. Someone needs to stay here to make sure nothing happens to Michael and Damien."

Gray sighed as he stalked to stare out the window, his arms crossed over his chest tightly. "I'll stay."

Alexander began, "If you prefer to go–"

Gray waved a hand in the air. "No, you're more knowledgeable in the event something can be done for him. And probably less of a target."

Celine put her arm on his forearm and glanced up at him. "I'm sorry, Gray."

"It's fine. It's not your fault. Just hurry back."

"We will."

Celine and Alexander hurried from the office, snaking through the halls.

Celine held up a finger. "Just give me a minute. I should tell Marcus the latest. Despite Gray's feelings on the matter, he and Teddy were very good friends."

Alexander nodded as Celine slipped into the library. Marcus stood at one of the massive windows taking in the sunrise.

"Good morning, Celine," he said, as he twisted to face her. "Have you seen Damien? He is doing quite well."

"I have, yes," she said with a sullen nod.

"You seem less than pleased."

Celine lowered her eyes and bit the inside of her lower lip. "Something's happened." She sucked in a deep breath.

Marcus furrowed his brow. "With Damien?"

Celine shook her head. She puffed out her cheeks and raised her gaze to meet his. "I'm really sorry to tell you this Marcus, but Dominique..." Her voice trailed off as she sought the words to finish the statement.

"Dominique what?"

Celine's lip quivered and her features pinched. "She killed Teddy this morning."

"What?" Marcus exclaimed, his eyes widening. "Why?"

Celine's chest heaved as she breathed in another long inhale. "Apparently, she had asked Celeste to kill Gray and she failed."

"Is it reversible?"

"I don't think so. She used an Immortal Killer dipped in poison."

"Are you certain?"

Celine shook her head. "No. Everything I know about the situation I learned from Celeste. Alexander and I were going to their home now."

"I'll come with you."

"Okay."

They departed from the library, collecting Alexander and heading into the cool, breezy morning. Nothing but the crashing ocean filled the air as they made their way silently to the wooded path.

Alexander broke the silence first. "I have to admit, I'm still quite in shock."

Celine nodded. "As am I. I can't believe she did this."

"I can understand coming after us. But she's murdered her own ally."

"Dominique is a wild card," Marcus answered. "Though, to be honest, I did not anticipate her ever doing this."

"She must believe she doesn't need him." Celine shook her head and pursed her lips as tears stung her eyes. "Poor Celeste. Poor Teddy."

"How is your sister?" Marcus inquired.

"A wreck as you can imagine. Michael is with her, and Millie is giving her something to help her sleep."

They crossed the open field and approached the seaside home. Celine swung the front door open. It squeaked on its hinges as they stepped inside the quiet space. No sounds came from within. Nothing but still, dead air.

Celine took a few steps into the foyer, her eyes scanning the space. "Here." She pointed toward the sitting room.

She hurried toward Teddy's still body. A scarlet red stain surrounded the gaping wound on his chest. She knelt next to his body, placing the back of her hand against his cheek. Clammy coldness radiated from his gray skin.

Marcus circled around him and knelt at his other side. He tugged open an eyelid on the corpse before he studied the wound after pulling Teddy's shirt away.

"Is there anything that can be done?" Celine inquired.

He puckered his lips as he stared down at the wound, black on the edges. "No."

Celine chewed the inside of her cheek as she resigned herself to the reality of his death.

"She's definitely used the poison, causing the wound from the dagger to be permanently fatal. See the darkening here where the skin has turned necrotic?"

Celine nodded. "I was afraid of that."

"I'm sorry, Celine," Alexander said, squeezing her shoulder.

"Goodbye, old friend," Marcus said.

"We'll need to deal with his body. I can't believe she did this. How can she be so cruel?" She flicked a tear away that had rolled down her cheek.

A slow clapping sounded from their left. They snapped their gaze to the foyer, finding Dominique leaning against the doorway.

"Bravo, Celine."

Celine leapt to her feet, her palms balling into fists. Marcus rose to stand, and Alexander placed himself between Dominique and Celine.

"Oh, please, don't stop on my account," Dominique said

with a chuckle. "If you'd like to shed a few more tears over the body of a man you hated, go ahead."

"I didn't hate him," Celine countered.

"What do you want, Dominique?" Marcus inquired.

Dominique stalked further into the room with her arms crossed over her chest and shrugged. "Just checking in. I can see everyone here is going to be as melodramatic about this as Celeste."

Celine's eyes went wide, and her jaw dropped. "You killed her husband!"

Dominique flicked her hand upward. "It was kind of a favor, though, right? I mean, I didn't kill *her*, and he wasn't all *that* supportive toward her. In fact, it may surprise you to know that he pushed her to kill Gray. Yet here you stand, cousin, shedding your tears over a man who chose me over you."

Celine cocked her head, setting her jaw and squeezing her fists tighter.

"I think you both should go," Marcus said to her and Alexander. "I'll handle things from here."

"Are you sure?" Celine inquired.

"Awww, isn't that so sweet?" Dominique cooed. "Celine and Marcus getting along and all over a dead Ted. Maybe his death will work out to my advantage."

Marcus nodded at Celine. "Go, before you two start at it again."

"Why stop us? I'm more than happy to oblige Celine with round two of our fight."

"I wouldn't object either," Celine answered through gritted teeth. She lifted her hand to summon a fireball.

"She's goading you. Do not fall for it," Marcus said.

Alexander caught her arm. "We should go."

"You should listen to Al," Dominique said with a wink to him, "he always was smart."

"One day, Dominique, you're not going to be so flip," Celine shouted, jabbing her finger toward the woman as Alexander tugged her from the room.

"Mmm, maybe, but I doubt it," she answered.

Celine lunged for her, but Alexander wrestled her back and through the open front door. She stormed down the steps to the path below.

"That woman!" she fumed. "One day, Alex, she's going to get what's coming to her."

"But that day is not today, unfortunately."

Celine shot a fiery glance back at the house. "How does she always come out on top?"

"She has no morals or principles, that's how. She twists and manipulates the scenario to fit her agenda, regardless of who it harms or what she's stated previously."

"This has to end. She's getting more and more dangerous by the day."

"We need a strategy, I agree. We'll need to start brainstorming immediately. And we've got to find a way to keep Michael and Damien safe. She'll come after them first."

Celine nodded. "Yes, they must be protected no matter the cost."

Alexander offered her a weak smile. "Let's head back." He tugged her arm toward the wooded path. Begrudgingly, she shuffled away from the house with one final heated glance back at it.

CHAPTER 24

Dominique circled around Teddy's body, flicking her gaze toward it before she stared back up at Marcus.

"What an interesting scene to walk in on. You and Celine were practically civil. What's next? Holding hands?"

"You should not have interrupted," Marcus countered.

She narrowed her eyes at him. "You know, if this little charade of caring on your part actually got you anywhere, I wouldn't have, but it doesn't. It just makes Celine more emboldened in the choices she's made. She thinks you support her."

"And she's beginning to trust me."

Dominique shook her head. "Not enough."

"That remains to be seen."

"She's not leaving her husband for you, Marcus. Get over yourself. She doesn't like you *that* much. She just doesn't mind having you as an ally to keep her precious family safe."

"Sometimes, Dominique, it pays to take the less aggressive approach."

She closed the gap between them, staring up into his dark

eyes, fire flashing in hers. "And sometimes it pays to crush your enemy and leave them with nothing."

"I have tried that approach–"

"You haven't. You've *threatened* that approach, but you've never followed through. And now you're even weaker than you were centuries ago."

He flexed his jaw. "My powers have not diminished."

"No, but your drive has." She narrowed her eyes again as she studied him. "Something's going on with you. You're different."

"So are you," he countered. "Care to share just how that came about?"

Dominique wrinkled her nose and stalked away from him, focusing her gaze out the window. "I don't know what you're talking about. Outside of a burning desire to wrap up centuries of chasing Celine Devereaux, I am no different."

"I beg to differ."

She twisted to shoot him a glare. "I'm not much interested in your opinions, Marcus."

"Ah, but this is not my opinion, Dominique. It is fact. You've changed. Celine may not have noticed, but I did. The purple blood on your lip during your fight carlicr this wcck gave you away." Marcus stalked toward her, stepping between her and the window. "What have you done?"

She flicked her gaze to him, arching an eyebrow. "I made a few modifications."

"Such as?"

She offered him a wicked smile. "Some very interesting ones."

* * *

Celine slid into the darkened room, easing the door shut behind her. Michael lifted his gaze from the woman lying on the bed to her. He pressed a finger to his lips.

Celine nodded and crept toward them. Her sister's hand clutched Michael's as she slept, her face still tear-stained.

"How is she?" Celine whispered.

Michael motioned toward the door as he slid his hand carefully from Celeste's grasp. Celine retreated across the room, meeting him outside in the hallway.

"She cried herself to sleep," Michael said as he pulled the door shut.

Celine pressed her lips together.

"She just kept saying 'what am I going to do now?' and that kind of thing."

"We went to the house. Unfortunately, there's nothing to be done."

"You can't bring him back the way you did with Celeste?"

Celine shook her head. "No. She used a special poison paired with a specific dagger that means certain death even for an immortal. Not even Marcus could do anything."

Michael rubbed the back of his neck. "Wow. This is unbelievable."

"Dominique's dangerous. We need to figure out a way to stop her before this gets any worse. Teddy's loss was bad enough. I can't lose anyone in this house."

Michael nodded. "Yeah, I get it."

"We're going to have to do whatever it takes, even if it means sacrificing."

He nodded in silent response.

Celine squeezed his arm. "I'll sit with her if you want a break."

"Actually, I was just going to visit Damien if you're going to stay with her."

"Okay, good. No one's told him yet. I can go break the news–"

Michael turned his lips down as he shook his head. "No, I'll tell him."

"Are you sure?"

"Yeah. I'm sure you don't want to rehash it all again. I'll tell him."

Celine squeezed her lips together and patted his arm. "Okay, thanks."

"Let me know if she wakes up."

"I will," Celine said, giving his arm another squeeze.

She slid back inside the darkened room as Michael spun away, continuing around the corner into the hall containing their bedrooms. He pushed into Damien's room.

Damien sat with his laptop on his lap, pounding away at the keys.

"Hey," he said as Michael stalked inside. "Where you been, buddy? I thought you forgot about me."

"No, things got a little…crazy."

"Crazy?" Damien asked, setting his laptop aside as he stared at Michael.

Michael slogged across the room and collapsed into the empty armchair at Damien's bedside. He ran his fingers through his sandy blonde hair as he blew out a long breath.

"Yeah, crazy."

"Care to elaborate."

Michael's head bobbed up and down for a moment before he flicked his gaze to Damien. "Dominique killed Teddy."

Damien's head fell forward as his jaw gaped open. "What? Are you serious?"

"Yeah," Michael said, his head still bouncing up and down. "Celeste is a mess."

"Well, can't Celine just bring him back to life like she did with Celeste when we first got here?"

Michael's head bobbing finally ceased and turned into a shake. "No. Apparently, she used some special weapon that means they can't. Celine already went and checked it out. Even Marcus Northcott can't do anything."

Damien slouched back in his pillows as he contemplated the news. "Wow. That's... crazy."

"Told you."

"So, now what? Why would she kill Teddy? Aren't they technically on her side?"

"I mean, I thought so, but I guess not really. Dominique asked Celeste to kill Gray and when she didn't, she killed Teddy with the knife meant for Gray."

Damien raised his eyebrows. "Whoa."

"Yeah, super twisted, right? Celeste thought Dominique would go after her. But apparently not."

"Why didn't she?"

Michael shrugged, his hands clasped in front of him as he leaned forward on his knees staring blankly ahead. "No idea."

"I'm surprised Celeste didn't do it."

"I'm not," Michael said, leaping from the chair and pacing the floor.

Damien furrowed his brow. "Really? She's not exactly our ally."

"She's changed."

"I mean, she did help us rescue Celine, but–"

"And she didn't want to kill Gray. Even though she thought she had no choice, she didn't want to do it."

"How do you know?"

"When she came here with the knife, she didn't do it. Instead, she confessed to me what was happening and asked for my help." Michael paused in his pacing, his hands on his hips as he shook his head. "If only I had been able to help her more."

"I'm sure you did the best you could. How could you have

prevented Dominique from killing Teddy with her special knife or whatever."

"I could have gone to Celine sooner. I could have made Celeste stay here."

"None of that would have helped, unless Celine would have brought Teddy here, right?"

Michael sighed, his arms clasped around his neck. "I guess." He shook his head again. "I just… I can't believe this is happening."

Silence filled the room for several moments before Damien spoke. "Do you think we shouldn't go through with our plans tonight?"

"It's even more important that we do, whether we like it or not. We can't take a chance with that crazy woman here. Even immortality is a risk, but at least we're way better off than if we are human."

Damien nodded. "Okay, good. I'd prefer to go through with it, too." He paused for a moment, his eyes searching the blanket in front of him. "Wow, I can't believe I just said that. I can't believe I'd rather trust Marcus Northcott to solve our problems."

"That's how messed up this situation is."

"I feel super uncomfortable keeping it from Celine, but–"

"But we have to," Michael cautioned. "She'll never go for this."

"Yeah, you're right. But it just feels weird," Damien answered with a shrug.

"She'll know soon enough."

"Yeah, and then we can listen to her holler at us."

"Which I'm sure she will for days," Michael said.

"Maybe decades in our newfound immortal lives," Damien said.

"Possibly, but I'm planning on reminding her that this actually helped the situation."

"Hopefully she'll see it that way given the circumstances."

"Don't worry, we'll convince her."

"I sure hope so."

* * *

Celeste opened her swollen eyes, finding an unfamiliar room surrounding her. Celine squeezed her hand and patted it, drawing her attention toward her.

"Hey, sis," she said with a broad smile, "how are you feeling?"

Celeste sniffled and squeezed her sore eyes closed. "Awful."

Celine rubbed her arm. "I'm sorry."

Celeste kept her eyes closed, emotions coursing through her. After a moment, she fluttered her eyelashes. "I should go." She pushed herself up to sit.

"No," Celine said, bracing her hands against her sister's shoulders. "No, you don't have to go."

"There are things–"

"We're handling everything. It's fine. Just relax."

Fresh tears streamed down Celeste's face and she buried her head in her hands as she sobbed again.

Celine swung around to sit next to her, wrapping her arm around her sister's shaking shoulders and pulling her close. Celeste sniffled again, wiping at her face with her fingers as she brought her weeping under control.

"I'm sorry to go to pieces like this again."

"Don't apologize, Celeste. You've been through a major trauma. And you're grieving. You can go to pieces as much as you'd like."

Celeste nodded as she sniffled. "Did Michael leave?"

Celine wrinkled her forehead. "Uh, he just went to spend some time with Damien. I can get him if you'd like?"

"Please. If you and he wouldn't mind."

"Okay, sure," Celine said, climbing from the bed. The door popped open before she took a step.

Marcus strode into the room. "You're awake, good."

"Hello, Marcus," Celeste said.

Celine froze, uncertain if she should leave her sister.

"I am very sorry for your loss, dear," Marcus said.

Celeste lowered her eyes to the blanket covering her and nodded. "Thank you."

"May I have a word with you regarding what is to be done next?"

Celine perched on the edge of the bed, intending to stay for the conversation.

Celeste flicked her gaze to her sister. "You were going for Michael?"

"Oh, I can stay–"

"No, I'd prefer you to retrieve Michael if you wouldn't mind."

"Oh," Celine murmured as she slid her feet onto the floor, "of course. I'll be right back."

Celine slipped out the door after a final glance between the two of them. Celeste waited a moment before she flicked her gaze to Marcus.

"How are you taking it?" he inquired.

Celeste shrugged. "I assume you are here to discuss something other than the next steps with Teddy's body."

"No. You forget, he was my friend."

"Then you will be happy to know he did not betray you in his final moments. He stuck with your side. Yours and Dominique's."

"But you did not?"

"Obviously I did not do what was asked of me. Which is half the reason Teddy is dead and I am hiding in the Buckleys' mansion."

"And the other half?"

Celeste averted her gaze, finding something to stare at across the room. "Never mind."

Marcus arched an eyebrow at her. "Are your tears over Teddy's demise?"

She flicked her gaze back to him, her features pinched with anger. "What else would they be over?"

"Teddy's betrayal."

Celeste did not answer, rubbing her finger along the blanket as she studied it.

"Dominique mentioned that he pushed you to kill Gray. You obviously did not agree, yet you found no solace in Teddy."

"Loyalty to the cause was always his strong suit."

"A fact that you now lament."

"Loyalty to me would have been appreciated, yes," Celeste said.

Marcus strode to the window and stared over the woods outside.

"I suppose you are here to exact Dominique's revenge on me?"

"Dominique will not harm you, Celeste," Marcus said.

"I find that hard to believe."

"You shouldn't."

She flicked her blues eyes to his form. "Is there some reason you believe Dominique will be so merciful to me?"

He twisted to face her. "Let's just say I have a strong reason to believe it. Now, about Teddy's body…"

CHAPTER 25

$\mathcal{D}$ominique stared down at the decaying body of her former ally. She raised her eyebrows at him. "Too bad Celeste had to be so stupid. I didn't mind you so much." She stretched and sighed. "But things must be done. See you around, old man."

She kicked at his foot before she stepped over his body and stomped from the room. Bright sunshine shone through the parted clouds as she stalked down the steps to the pathway below.

She shielded her eyes against it, staring up at the sprawling form of the Buckley house. She wondered what the landscape would look like without it. She imagined smoke billowing into the sky, walls blackened and crumbling. A new house rose in its place. Along with a new dynasty. One that she'd be key in creating.

Her cell phone chimed, and she slid it from her pocket, checking the display. The smile building on her lips at the thought of the crumbling Buckley estate faded quickly as she spotted the text message. *Is everything prepared for my arrival?*

She sent back an affirmative before she returned to her

daydreaming. Suddenly, the excitement building had soured. She'd be key in creating the new dynasty, but would she be key in benefitting from it? Or would Celine reap those rewards?

With a sigh and a set jaw, she turned away from the estate, selecting a different path. It snaked along the coast. The ocean lapped at the rocks below, not angry today as it was on so many other occasions when she'd watched it.

Perhaps Maine wasn't all that terrible of a place, she thought, as she strolled along. She enjoyed the many thunderstorms that occurred in the area and the anger of the ocean. It matched the emotions that boiled under her surface on most occasions.

As she turned inland, leaving the coast behind, her thoughts turned to another with anger boiling under the surface. Marcus Northcott. Engaged to Celine centuries ago, he'd lost her to Grayson Buckley. The man had spent hundreds of years chasing her, but she'd slipped through his grasp on every occasion. He'd even managed to contain her to an enchanted cell, and she'd still slipped the noose.

Dominique kicked a stone down the path at the thought. Thanks to Celine's meddling friends which she now kept under lock and key in the massive gothic mansion. They would need to be eliminated. And soon.

Marcus had come so close to having her and still lost. Her forehead pinched. Since then, something seemed different about him. Some change had tempered the anger that used to fuel him. What, she wondered? What had changed Marcus Northcott? And more importantly, could they still depend on him?

Another house rose on the hill ahead of her. Smaller than the Buckleys' monstrosity, but still grand enough to welcome her earthly master. At least she hoped. She'd not hear the end of it if it wasn't.

Dominique pressed forward, entering into the silence of the large home. Marble floors echoed her footsteps as she crossed to the stairs and climbed them. Her cell phone chirped as she reached the top and she tugged it from her pocket.

What of Celeste and her task?

Dominique wrinkled her nose as she typed her response. *She failed.*

The response was nearly immediate. *And?*

Dominique sucked in a deep breath through her nose. "And I took care of it like I always do," she murmured aloud as she typed the same response.

After one step down the wide hall, her phone chimed again. *What do you mean? Is Gray dead? What of Celeste?*

With a shake of her head, her thumbs flew across the virtual keyboard. *No, Gray is not dead yet. Celeste needed to be dealt with. We can't continue to have this insolence. I taught her a lesson. Which leaves me with Gray to deal with...if I can ever get near him. Celine has her entire crew under lock and key in that horrid house.*

She stormed down the hall and burst into her bedroom, peeling off her leather jacket and tossing it on a nearby chair before she crossed the room and flung herself onto the blood-red duvet. The phone chimed again. With a roll of her eyes, she grabbed it, lifting it above her as she lay sprawled.

Explain yourself. What have you done to Celeste?

She puckered her lips as she pounded out her response. *Celeste is fine. I killed Teddy.*

Within seconds, her phone rang. "Ugh," she moaned as she swiped to accept the call. "Calm down, the precious Devereaux sisters are unharmed."

"Why did you kill Theodore? He was an ally," the woman's voice answered.

Dominique closed her eyes for a moment as she formulated her response. "Not much of one. He's always talking about how loyal he is, but he does nothing. What has he done for us all these years? Celine manages to elude us at every turn."

The woman on the other end huffed and paused for a moment before continuing. "He isn't much of a loss, but you wasted the opportunity to end Gray's life on a definite note."

Dominique wrapped her fingers around the hilt of the dagger still stuffed in her waistband. "Sometimes, you have to take a step back to take a step forward."

"And did this so-called step back satisfy your urge for bloodshed?"

Dominique considered it with a shrug. "More or less, yeah. It felt good."

"I'm so pleased," the woman answered, her voice thick with sarcasm.

Dominique rolled onto her belly, propped up by her elbows. "What's that supposed to mean."

The woman paused a moment before responding. "Nothing. You've done well and you've always been loyal."

"I always take action, too."

"Appropriate or not," the woman added. "But you are my biggest asset. So, I will allow you this… odd choice. However, I hope it does not set us back too many steps."

"Don't worry, I won't let it."

"You're a good girl, Dominique. Now make sure everything is prepared for my arrival."

"Already done."

"Good. I will see you soon."

"Wait, just a second," Dominique said before the woman ended the call. She pushed herself up to sit.

"Yes?"

"We need to talk about Marcus when you get here."

"Why?"

Dominique scrunched up her face and shook her head. "Something's off with him. And we need to find out what before it sets us back more steps than my so-called 'odd choice.'"

"Fine. We'll discuss it when I arrive." The line clicked on the other end as the caller ended the call.

Dominique clicked off her phone's display and tossed it down on the duvet. With a huff, she slid off the bed and pulled the dagger from her pants. She crossed the room, stopping in front of a large painting of the English countryside. She eased it to the floor after pulling it from the wall, revealing a hidden wall safe.

She spun the dial back and forth before pulling on the lever. The door swung open with a creak of hinges in need of oil. Inside, a display case with a velvet lining sat empty.

Dominique slid off the glass top and set it aside. Reverently, she placed the dagger on the display stand before returning its glass cover.

With another creak, she swung the safe door closed and locked it before hiding it behind the painting again.

She'd need that dagger again soon. Could she locate the poison to ensure a clean and final kill? Perhaps it wasn't necessary. Maybe it was better to watch Gray suffer. And by extension, Celine.

Either way, she thought with a villainous grin, it would be fun to watch.

* * *

Michael stalked into the bedroom, a cup of tea balanced on a saucer. Celeste perched on the edge of the bed. Marcus lifted his gaze from her to the new arrival as he entered the room.

He flicked his gaze back to her. "We'll talk later." Marcus

strode toward the door. He paused as he passed Michael. "See you later."

Michael offered him a slight nod before he slipped from the room. He turned his attention to Celeste, who twisted to face him.

"Thank you for coming."

He crossed to her and eased onto the bed next to her, wrapping his arm around her shoulders. She laid her cheek on his shoulder.

He offered her the teacup. "I brought you some tea. How are you doing?"

She pulled her head up and sniffled as she accepted the cup. "Can I be honest?"

"Absolutely," he said, rubbing her back.

"Marcus asked me the same, though he seemed convinced my tears were not over Teddy's death."

Michael shook his head. "The guy's a jerk. If he bothers you again–"

Celeste pressed a finger against his lips. "He isn't entirely incorrect."

Michael screwed up his face as Celeste sipped at her tea.

"Teddy betrayed me in those final hours," she said, staring blankly ahead as she lowered the teacup. It clattered against the saucer, the liquid sloshing inside. "A man I'd spent centuries with."

"Celeste, I'm sure he was doing his best to deal with Dominique."

Celeste scoffed at the statement. "I asked him to do it for me."

"And he refused?"

"Not outright, but he may as well have. He made a point of asking Dominique if he could do it for me."

"I assume she said no."

"Of course she did. The point is, had he not even brought it up, she'd never have been the wiser."

Michael rubbed her shoulder again. "Yeah, but Gray may be dead, and Celine would be less than forgiving even if you didn't stab him yourself. You know that, right?"

Celeste took another sip of her tea. "I chose the right side," she said as she set the cup down again.

Michael gave her a cocky grin. "I'd like to think so."

"This will not be the easy side," Celeste warned.

"Yeah, Celine has basically said the same thing. I guess Dominique is unlike anything we've encountered before."

"And then some," Celeste agreed. "She does not back down. She does not like to lose. And she will do *anything*, and I do mean anything to achieve her goal."

"Even murder."

Celeste bit her lower lip. "And who knows what else."

* * *

Celine stalked into the empty library. After Marcus's arrival to discuss Teddy's body with her sister, she'd retreated here, unwilling to go to Damien's room. She bit her lower lip as she stared out the towering window at the landscape.

She wasn't sure she could face her cousin at the moment. She'd wait until she had more news about what she suspected. Celine crossed her arms over her chest and drummed her fingers against her forearm. The waiting was slowly killing her.

There was nothing she could do but wait, though.

As the sun lowered in the sky, turning the daylight to dusk, she threaded through the halls and headed out into the cool evening air. She stalked away from the house to the cliffs overlooking the ocean.

With her arms wrapped around her torso, she stared out

over the ocean and the growing darkness on the horizon. Another storm blew up the coast. Black clouds raced toward her. Lightning lit them and thunder rumbled in the distance.

A scuff sounded to her side. Celine glanced over her shoulder at the path. She returned her gaze forward with a huff as she spotted Dominique approaching.

"Oh, hey, Celine," Dominique said, fake friendliness dripping from her voice. She sidled up next to her, crossing her arms and staring out at the ocean.

After a few moments, Dominique side-eyed Celine. "So, how are things?"

Celine shot her an angry glance. "You can't be serious."

"Something happen?"

Celine wrinkled her nose and shook her head as thunder rumbled in the distance again.

"Looks like it's going to storm," Dominique said. "You know, when I first came here, I didn't think I would like it, but it's really grown on me. The constant thunderstorms, the angry sea. It's really got quite a gothic ambiance. I can see the appeal. I'm thinking about sticking around for a while. How crazy is that?"

"You are crazy," Celine snapped.

Dominique offered an unimpressed glance. "Why do you have to be so rude? I mean, we're cousins. It would be nice to have my family close. You, Celeste."

Celine spun to face her. "You're kidding, right?"

Dominique flung her arms out. "Nope. Bought a house and everything. You should see it. Now, it's not as big as what you're used to but I'm sure I'll be very comfy there. I'll have you over some time. We can do lunch."

"I wouldn't step foot in any house you're living in."

Dominique shook her head. "Why must you always be so serious? Lighten up, Celine."

Celine glanced at the black clouds filling in over the

ocean before flicking her gaze back to Dominique. "Maybe it's because you're always trying to destroy my family."

"I really wasn't planning on getting into this, but," she answered, wrinkling her nose, leaning forward, and whispering, "it's a family you never should have had to begin with."

"I would pick them any day over you."

Dominique winced and pressed her hand to her heart. "Youch! Going right for the heart on that one."

Celine tensed her jaw, holding her finger out in front of her in warning. "Leave my family alone. This is your last warning."

Celine spun on her heel as thunder boomed overhead and stalked toward the Buckley house. Dominique doubled over in laughter, her howling cackle reverberating off the surrounding trees and rocky landscape.

"Oh, that's rich." She flung her arms out. "What're you gonna do to me, Celine?"

Celine spun to face her, her face set and her eyes narrowed. She cocked her head and spat out," Don't test me."

Dominique arched an eyebrow as she leaned forward. "Why not?"

"I will not back down. And there's no one stopping me this time."

"Bring it on," Dominique said, electricity crackling between her fingers.

Celine flung her arms out, two lightning bolts flinging from her hands, striking nearby trees and charring them. "Let's go."

"I'm ready any time."

Celine flung her hands to her front, blasting arcs of energy from both palms. Quick to react, Dominique leaned backward, hovering with bent knees as the energy beam passed over her. She held one hand up, deflecting it as she rose to stand. With a shove, she pushed Celine's attack beam off to a nearby rock. It smashed into the boulder before dissipating into the air.

"Good try," she snarked. "But not good enough."

Dominique blasted a stream of fire toward Celine. Celine dove to the side and the beam collided with a tree. It exploded into a fiery ball. Dominique's shoulders slumped at the miss.

Celine tossed a fire orb at it, knocking it into the ocean below before scrambling to her feet.

"You want to keep going?" Celine shouted.

Dominique returned to her aggressive stance, lunging forward with her arms spread. "Hell yeah."

With a shriek, Celine launched two lightning bolts in rapid succession. Dominique dodged the first, but the second smacked her in the thigh.

She stumbled but managed to stay upright. Lightning burst from the sky as thunder boomed as she recovered. Celine launched another attack before her cousin could right her posture.

Large drops of rain splotched down on the ground around them, darkening the dirt. Celine kept up her assault, tossing bolt after bolt at her adversary. Her shrill scream continued as she hurled one after another, crippling her enemy.

Dominique collapsed to one knee, shielding her head with her arm as she sustained one blow after another. Celine closed the gap between them, her assault nonstop.

Dominique curled into a ball for a moment before a shriek emerged from her. She tossed her arms back. A powerful blast knocked Celine backward. Dominique rose to stand, red flames radiating around her.

Celine lifted her head, her eyes going wide at the sight. Dominique stalked toward her, flames leaping from her body and her eyes blazing red. She threw her hand in front of her, a red flame shooting from it at Celine.

Celine rolled to the side and fired an ethereal blue fireball of her own. It struck Dominique in the upper arm. She absorbed the blow, her red flame turning purple as the blue light melded with it.

"What the hell?" Celine murmured to herself as rain fell in a heavier stream.

Dominique lifted her hand to the sky before she let out another battle cry, slamming her hand down onto the earth. The ground shook and splintered underneath her. The crack raced toward Celine. She backpedaled away from the developing fissure.

A purple-red flame sailed toward her. She rolled away from it. Another blasted the ground next to where she came to a stop. Celine rolled in the opposite direction.

Rain began to pelt the ground harder. Another giant fireball flew at her. Celine held both hands out, blowing it back toward Dominique. It struck her square in the chest, knocking her backward.

She smacked into the dirt on her back, sliding to a stop feet from where she landed. The flames leaping from her skin died down.

The skies let loose. Rain pounded them both, drenching them. Thunder boomed and lightning tore across the darkened sky.

Celine climbed to her feet as Dominique leapt to hers.

"Give it up, Celine," she called over the thumping rain. "You can't win."

"I'll never stop trying to defend my family."

Dominique's dark hair clung to her skin as she lowered her chin, glaring at her cousin. "Then you will suffer."

ichael paced the floor of Damien's room. The sun had already set. Dark clouds pushed up the coast and thunder rumbled in the night sky.

"Of course," Damien lamented, his hand smacking against his blanket. "We couldn't get through the creepy ceremony *without* a storm."

"Par for the course around here," Michael said.

Damien traced the edge of the blanket as thunder rumbled again. He glanced at the clock before throwing his head back into the pillow behind him. "Why did it have to be midnight? Couldn't he do a reasonable hour like nine?"

Michael scoffed at the statement as he rubbed his chin and spun to pace in the opposite direction. "You don't think–" He turned his lips upside down and shook his head. "Nah."

"What?"

Michael ceased his pacing and flicked his gaze to Damien. He shrugged. "He asked Celine to kill somebody."

Damien's eyes went wide, and he stared up at the ceiling as he considered it. "Ohhhh," he mumbled. "That's… wait, what should we do if that happens?"

"I'm not killing anyone!" Michael shouted.

"Me either!"

"Okay, so if we have to kill someone, we both agree not to do it and just stay human, right?"

Damien nodded before flicking his gaze to Michael. "But wait, that solves none of our problems."

"Are you seriously suggesting we kill someone?"

"No," Damien said. "Man, I hope we don't have to kill someone."

"Well, okay, Celine didn't actually have to kill anyone. She just stabbed the Duke."

A smile lit up Damien's face. "Right. So, if he does the ceremony and gives you or me a knife and tells us to kill someone, we just stab him instead. Easy! Problem solved."

"Yeah, and then run. I seriously do not want to be around him after I stab him."

"Right," Damien said. "Stab him and run."

Michael blew out a long breath and resumed his pacing. "I really hope we don't have to stab someone."

"Me either." Silence passed between them for several moments as lightning lit the sky and thunder pounded over them. "Hey, have you seen Celine?"

"Yeah, earlier, why?"

Damien shook his head. "Millie said she asked about me, but she hasn't been by at all today."

"That's weird." Michael thumbed toward the door. "Do you want me to go find her?"

"Nooooo," Damien said, his eyes going wide. He waved his hands frantically in front of him. "I'm not complaining. I just think it's weird."

"It is kind of weird," Michael said. "She was all about being here before."

"Well, I'm not dying anymore."

Michael nodded.

"And like I said, I'm not complaining. With this whole Marcus is turning us immortal at the stroke of midnight thing hanging over my head, I am terrified I'll let it slip to her."

"You can't do that, under any circumstances. Not until this is over."

"Yeah, no kidding! That's why I don't want to see her. The second she looks at me she's going to know I'm hiding something, and you know how bad I am at lying."

"Yeah, I know," Michael said. "Really bad."

Damien nodded. "Really, really bad."

Damien pulled his laptop onto his lap and tapped around on the keyboard. He clicked around on his trackpad a few places before he winced and slammed the laptop shut.

"What?"

"Nothing," Damien claimed, tossing the laptop aside.

"You're lying."

"See!" Damien shouted. "Even you can tell when I'm lying."

"What did you look up?"

Damien squashed his lips together. "I looked up ceremonies to turn people immortal."

"And?"

Damien lowered his gaze to his blanket and grimaced, shaking his head. "Nothing good."

"Great," Michael lamented with a sigh, collapsing into the armchair.

Michael's leg bobbed up and down. "Okay, now I can't stop thinking about what you read. What did it say?"

Damien wrinkled his nose. "Probably shouldn't–"

"Damien! Just answer. The stuff I'm making up in my head is way worse, probably."

"It ranged," Damien said, tracing the fabric of the blanket

over him. "From drinking the blood of an animal to bathing in it to, you know, murdering babies and stuff."

Michael's head banged into the chair's high back as he squeezed his eyes shut. "That was so much worse than what I made up."

"What did you make up that you thought was so terrible?"

"You know, just stuff like stabbing someone or, I dunno, taking drugs."

"Taking drugs? Seriously, *that's* all you could come up with. It's not even that terrible."

"Well, it could be a hallucinogen and you have horrible hallucinations about really scary stuff or whatever."

Damien's brows furrowed as he considered Michael's version of terrible. He shook his head after a moment. "Either way, we're committed. Let's just hope it's none of those horrible things–"

"Including drugs," Michael said, pointing at him.

"Including drugs," Damien answered with a nod. "And in less than four hours, we're official members of the immortal club."

* * *

Marcus strode along the path toward the vanWoodsen seaside home. The body of his friend and former ally needed to be taken care of before his other task for the night.

Thunder punctuated his final thought. His mind turned to the odd request. He wondered if Michael and Damien would follow through. It would be a tragedy if they didn't. Damien, in particular, was a waste as a mere human.

Rain pelted the canopy of leaves above him and lightning flashed through the sky.

How would Dominique react to the situation? He hoped

the plan worked the way he expected and the gains he'd make with the compromise would offset any perceived loss.

A shriek from near the cliffs drew his attention away from his own wandering mind.

"I won't be the only one suffering," Celine's voice screamed.

Marcus's eyes slid closed for a moment as he shook his head, slowing his pace and reorienting his footsteps toward the noise.

"We'll see about that," Dominique shrieked.

Marcus threaded through the thick brush, leaving the path in favor of the most direct route to the cliffs. He stepped from within the thick woods into the pouring rain.

Dominique and Celine tumbled in a knot of limbs toward the cliffs. Marcus shook his head at the tangle of women. They toppled over the sheer rock, disappearing from his sight.

A sickening smack sounded as they landed on the rocks below. Marcus hurried to the edge, peering over it.

Celine grimaced as she pulled herself from the surface of a rock. She rolled her neck and huffed as she climbed to standing.

Dominique slowly rose to her feet. Purple-red blood dripped from an already healing gash on the back of her hand. She swiped at her full lips with her other hand as she scowled at her cousin.

"This is getting old, Celine."

Celine responded by whipping a fireball at her cousin. Dominique deflected it, knocking it into the ocean. It splashed into the waves with a zapping sound and dissipated, the water around it glowing blue for a few moments.

"It's not old for me." Celine lobbed another blue orb at her cousin. "I'm just getting warmed up."

"Oh, I can go all day," Dominique responded, tossing a flaming orb at Celine.

With a huff, Marcus launched himself off the cliff, landing on a rock in a crouched position between the two women.

"Ladies, I see we are having another spirited conversation."

"Stay out of it, Marcus," Celine snapped.

"Yeah," Dominique said, "for once, I agree with Celine. You really should step aside and let us have this out."

Marcus flicked his gaze to Dominique. "You cannot kill her even if you wanted to and had the ability."

"Oh, I think I can dig deep," Dominique said.

She whipped her arm back and swung it forward, lobbing a purple-red fireball Celine's way. Marcus smacked it away with a lightning bolt.

"Have you forgotten your objective, Dominique?"

Dominique sneered at him.

"Well, have you? Because if Celine is harmed and you are responsible, well–" He paused, shrugging as the rain continued to pelt down on them. "–I can only imagine the punishment would be swift and severe."

Dominique's nose wrinkled as she gritted her teeth. Water dripped from her dark hair as she sucked in deep breaths.

"He's right, Dominique. Am I not vital to 'the cause?'" Celine inquired. "More vital than whatever petty grudge you're harboring."

Dominique shrieked and blasted a red arc toward Celine, blowing her backward into the cliffside.

Celine gasped as she landed on the rocky ground and gulped in a deep breath before climbing to her feet.

"Your vitalness is relative," Dominique shouted over the pounding rain.

"Not really," Marcus insisted. "Though yours is."

Celine hopped across the massive boulders, closing the gap between them. "For once, I agree with Marcus. No one would care if I ended you. If you managed to take me out, though, well, I cannot imagine that would go over with whoever is pulling your strings."

Dominique tossed her head back as she huffed, peeling a dripping lock of hair from her cheek. She bit the inside of her cheek. After a moment, she jabbed a finger toward Celine.

"This isn't over, Celine. You've only just begun to pay. And I am going to take immense pleasure in destroying every one of your so-called family."

"I'll never give you the chance."

"You can't protect them all, Celine. And whichever one you leave dangling, I will rip them away from you and tear them apart limb by limb until they beg me to kill them."

"Leave my family alone."

"Spare me your warnings. Submit or watch as I destroy them one by one."

"I'll never join you."

Dominique flung her arms out. "Then their blood is on your hands." She flicked her gaze to Marcus. "We need to talk."

"I'm quite busy."

"Make the time." She spun on the rock, leaping to another then another before she launched herself to the cliffs above and stalked away.

Thunder rumbled overhead and lightning ripped across the sky.

Marcus twisted to face Celine. "Another squabble? Really, Celine?"

She wrapped her arms around her torso as the rain continued to drench her. "You know I'll defend what's mine."

"I also know Dominique has the ability to goad you into a fight at any moment."

"So what?"

"So, despite your impressive powers, she is dangerous. You are immortal, yes. That does not mean you cannot be harmed."

"Thanks for caring, Marcus. I really appreciate it." Celine leapt from her rock down to the pebbles of the beach below.

"Do not underestimate her, Celine!" Marcus shouted as she made her way up the beach.

She waved his comment away and continued on her path.

Marcus shook his head at her as she wandered away. With a sigh, he stepped down to the beach and headed in the opposite direction.

He climbed through the cave and back to the path above, veering off to the vanWoodsen's seaside cottage. The rain slowed as he ambled up the path to the seaside home. He pushed through the door, his clothes and hair dripping, and stalked into the sitting room off the foyer. Teddy's body still lay sprawled on the area rug.

Marcus stared down at him for a moment before he removed the vial of blue liquid from his interior pocket. With a few words uttered in Latin, he knelt next to Teddy's body and parted his lips.

He pressed the vial to Teddy's gray lips and tipped it. Liquid slid into his mouth. A gurgling noise emanated from deep inside the body. Marcus stood and backed several steps away. Smoke puffed from Teddy's lips, turning into a steady stream after a few moments.

A spark flashed from Teddy's chest, then another from his mouth. A searing flash emanated from the body. Marcus shielded his eyes with his arm as the brilliant beam blinded him.

As the light faded, he lowered his arm. His eyes fell to the spot where the body had laid moments earlier. A small gemstone spun on the floor in its place.

Marcus stalked over toward it and snatched it from the ground. He held it up to the light and peered at it. The perfect obsidian crystal gleamed in the light.

"Just in case, old friend," he said and slid the crystal into his pocket before stalking from the house.

* * *

Dominique thundered down the path toward the dark house. With a grimace, she swiped at her bloody hand, already healed, but still stained with blood.

Anger coursed through every inch of her body. Not only had she failed to conquer Celine, she'd not even inflicted a wound worthy of mention.

The thought frustrated her, particularly given what she'd gone through to ensure victory.

The doors to the house blew open in front of her as she approached, and she stormed into the entryway. The sound of her pounding footsteps resounded through the massive empty space as she stormed across the patterned marble floor and mounted the stairs.

With two hops, she landed on the top stair and continued down the darkened hall to her bedroom. She crossed to the painting hiding the wall safe and ripped it from the wall.

With a few twists of her wrist, she input the combination and wrenched the safe open. She eyed the Immortal Killer for a moment before she raised her gaze to the shelf above. Vials filled with purple-red liquid lined the felted ledge.

She huffed heavy breaths through her nose as she grabbed one along with the metal syringe sitting underneath it.

She loaded the vial into the needle and slipped two

fingers through the finger grips and her thumb through the thumb ring. She placed the tip of the needle against the skin of her inner elbow.

She squeezed her eyes closed for a moment, pursing her lips as the cold metal brushed against her skin and the needle threatened to pierce it. A warning rang in her mind.

"You shouldn't do this too quickly, as tempting as it may be. It may weaken you rather than strengthen you," the doctor's voice said as it echoed through her mind.

She paused, her hand wavering as she reconsidered her injection. The conversation continued in her mind.

"I need to strengthen as quickly as possible," she answered.

"I'd still urge caution. This has never been attempted before. We have no idea what may happen."

The warning faded from her mind as she stared down at the thick liquid.

"I don't have time for caution, doc," she murmured before depressing the plunger and injecting the liquid into her system.

The needle pierced her skin with a pinch. As the liquid rushed into her system, she squeezed her eyes closed, and gritted her teeth against the intense burn.

She forced out a pained breath, ripping the needle from her arm with a trembling hand. It clattered to the floor as she stumbled forward toward the bed. She doubled over, her hands finding the silky soft duvet as the fire burned through her entire arm.

The burning pain entered her chest and spread out from there as her heart pumped the new formula through the veins all over her body. It mixed with her blood, creating a war on the cellular level. One that threatened to destroy her. But if she overcame it, she would not die, but instead, become more powerful than she'd ever been.

As the searing sensation spread throughout her entire body, she clenched her jaw. A low scream mixed with a growl emanated from her slightly parted lips. Her flesh reddened and her irises yellowed, the pupils distending into an oval. Her teeth transformed, two large fangs forming that extended past her lips. Scales appeared, rippling along her skin before melting into her flesh. Her ears extended to points, before morphing back to human form.

The wicked effects of the serum caused her body to shudder. Her neck craned at odd angles as the transformation ripped through her. She gripped the duvet with the long, yellowed claws that grew and shrank from the tips of her fingers.

An uncontrollable shriek emerged from her as her vision clouded. The fabric of the duvet ripped as she tore at it with a hulk-like strength.

The fiery pain intensified until her vision went black. Sounds dulled. The musty smell of the closed-up manor home disappeared as her nose burned. Her fingertips lost sensitivity and she could no longer determine if she held the duvet or not.

She collapsed to the floor in a heap. The world slipped away, replaced with only one thing: scorching pain.

CHAPTER 27

*C*eline continued up the hill as the rain slowed. She rolled her neck and wiggled her shoulders as she pushed into the foyer of the great house. The fall from the cliffs hadn't done much damage, but she still felt it.

Gray crossed the foyer as she entered. Her blonde hair hung limply around her face, still dripping. A smudge of dirt across her cheek hadn't been washed away by the pouring rain.

"Celine!" he called as he saw her dripping form enter. "What the hell happened?"

Alexander emerged from the sitting room as Gray's panicked voice carried across the large space.

"Celine!" he exclaimed. "Are you all right?"

"I'm fine," she murmured, wiping at her cheek and staring at the grainy particles that covered her fingers.

"What happened?" Gray reiterated.

"I got into it with Dominique again."

"Celine–" Gray began, his voice low with warning.

Celine waved her hand at him as she stalked into the

sitting room to pour herself a brandy. "Save it. I've already gotten the lecture from Marcus, of all people."

"For once I agree with the man," Alexander said.

"So do I," Gray added.

Celine sipped the amber liquid and squeezed her eyes closed. "I can't help it. She's really pushing it this time. She's at me every chance she gets."

"Fighting with her in an all-out battle isn't going to solve anything, Celine," Gray said as he joined her, pouring himself a drink.

She sighed and let her head fall back between her shoulders. "I know, I know."

"Are you certain you're unharmed?" Alexander inquired.

Celine twisted to face him, nodding. "Yeah, I'm fine."

"You're sure? You look a little worse for wear," Gray said, rubbing the smudge off her cheek.

She offered a half-hearted chuckle. "Yeah, we got caught in the thunderstorm."

"And the dirt?" Gray asked.

Celine studied the amber liquid as she swirled it in her glass. "And we fell over the cliff."

Gray's head sunk to his chest and Alexander's eyes widened.

"Celine!" Alexander exclaimed. "Are you certain you're all right?"

She glanced up, flicking her gaze between them. "I'm fine. Really. She took the worst of it."

"Not worst enough if she's still alive," Gray lamented before downing his brandy and pouring another.

"Yes, she is," Celine admitted.

He stalked across the room, his lips forming a deep grimace. "And probably because Northcott saved her. When is he going to stop attacking this family!"

"His intervention may be for the best in this case. They

cannot continue fighting like this," Alexander said, flicking his gaze to Celine.

She raised her hands in surrender. "I know. She just gets to me every time. I need to stop letting her bait me."

"What was it this time?" Gray asked. "Whose life did she threaten to end."

"Well, she wasn't specific. But the first thing that set me off was her announcement that she's bought a house here and plans to stay. It just got under my skin because she's basically saying she's here until she kills all of us."

"Well," Gray said as he studied the flames leaping in the fireplace, "all of *us*. You will be kept alive for whatever disgusting purposes they have in mind."

"Not if I can help it," Celine said.

"Gray brings up a good point," Alexander said as he eased into an armchair. "We need to discuss what to do about keeping this family safe. In particular, we need immediate action regarding Michael and Damien. They are the most vulnerable among us. She will go after them first."

Celine chewed her lower lip as she lowered her eyes to her drink. Her fingernails tapped the side of the glass as her mind raced.

"Celine?" Alexander prodded.

She drew in a deep breath and raised her eyes to him. "Yeah, I know. I just–I'm still deciding what's best."

"They need to go. They're too vulnerable here," Gray said, his eyes never leaving the fireplace.

"It's not that simple with Damien's injury," Celine retorted. "Let's just wait until morning. Millie will check his wound again and we'll go from there."

Gray shook his head and sighed. "Start searching for a hiding place for them. We'll need it."

* * *

Damien zipped his hoodie as he stared at his reflection in the mirror. His heart thudded against his ribs loud enough that he wondered if Michael would hear it. He ran a trembling hand through his brown hair as he studied his blue eyes. He blew out a long breath, his mind racing, second-guessing the decision.

Too late now, he decided. He winced as he stepped away from the mirror. The calf-length gash on his leg still smarted when he twisted the wrong way. With a grimace, he limped his way to the bed and collapsed on it, rubbing at the thick bandage through his pant leg.

The door opened and Michael slipped into his room, similarly clad.

"Hey, you ready?" he inquired.

"Yeah," Damien said, flinching as he rose to stand.

Michael raised his eyebrows and pointed to his leg. "You gonna make it?"

"Yeah, I'll make it. Just gets a little achy sometimes."

"You sure?"

"I'll make it," Damien assured him. "Wouldn't miss it."

"Really?" Michael questioned. "You're that ready?"

Damien swallowed hard and bit his lower lip. "I–" He shook his head and rubbed the back of his neck. "No, I feel like I'll never be ready for this. But it has to be done."

"Same. I'm having some serious misgivings at this moment."

Damien's eyes widened. "Do you want to call it off?"

"No," Michael said with a quick shake of his head. "No. It needs to be done."

"I agree."

"But that doesn't make me any more comfortable with it."

"Right." Damien bobbled his head around before he added, "Let's just get it over with."

Michael firmed his bottom lip and nodded. "Come on,

man. Together."

With a nod, they stepped into the hallway. Damien lowered his voice to just above a whisper. "We gotta be careful not to get caught sneaking out."

Michael nodded as he scanned the hallway. "No sign of anyone in this hall."

"Should we try for the front?"

"Yeah, we'll try for it. It's the most direct route."

Damien nodded. "I'll need it."

"Is your leg bothering you?" Michael asked as they snaked into another empty hallway.

Damien shook his head. "No, it's fine. I just–any delays make me less sure I'll actually make it to go through with this."

They rounded another corner. No one in sight. "Let's make a deal. If you start to chicken out, I'll stop you. If I start to chicken out, you stop me."

"Deal," Damien said. "Hopefully we don't chicken out at the same time."

They strode out of the hall and into the gallery over-looking the foyer. Damien recoiled, stumbling backward and pulling Michael with him.

Celine entered through the front door, dripping wet and filthy.

"Yikes, go back!" Damien hissed.

"Whoa, close call. What happened to her?" Michael questioned.

"No idea. But it doesn't look good."

"Great, she'll be in a crappy mood when we admit what we did."

They circled back through the halls to a back stairway and descended it, navigating to a side door. They spilled into the damp night. The rain had ceased, but the heaviness still clung to the air.

Dark clouds sailed past the moon, obscuring it from view at times. Michael blew out a long breath as they started down the path to Marcus's seaside home.

Despite the warmth still in the air, Damien shivered. His pulse quickened with every step. He tried to imagine the conversation with Celine afterward. His mind conjured images of her face: disappointed, shocked, hurt, and maybe more.

An image of an angry Celine formed in his mind. It melded with the Celine from 1812 Alterra and became terrifying. She slammed him against a wall and rendered him mute in the vision.

Heat washed through his body and his eyes widened. He gulped as he hoped an angry Celine was not what his future held.

His foot fell on a twig, snapping it, drawing his attention back to reality. His ankle twisted as he pulled it away and he flinched as the wound on his leg pulled. A deep ache shot up his calf.

Another shudder ran up his spine as he recalled his last experience in these woods and the source of the large wound. The shrieks of the Dracopire reverberated in his mind. He could still feel the hot breath of the beast breathing over him as he ripped into his flesh.

Damien suppressed another tremor. He needed to go through with this transformation. No matter what.

* * *

The lights of Marcus Northcott's seaside home glowed through the night. Michael and Damien headed toward it as they emerged from the wooded path. Damien's legs wobbled as they reached the stairs and climbed up to the covered porch.

He swallowed hard as Michael banged against the door. He considered running, but the door popped open seconds after Michael knocked.

Dembe's dark face stared out at them. He pulled the door open wider and motioned for them to enter the foyer.

Damien's heart thudded in his chest again and his throat parched. His shallow breathing made him feel unsteady, bordering on dizzy. He blew out a long breath and shoved his trembling hands into his pockets.

What were they doing, he questioned? Making themselves less of a target, he reasoned. He raised his chin, repeating the mantra to himself as Dembe signaled for them to enter the sitting room.

They both stalked inside, finding it empty. Damien paced around the floor before perching on the edge of the couch.

"Easy, man, we're almost through," Michael said from the armchair he'd plopped into.

Damien nodded, leaping from his seat as Marcus strode into the room.

Marcus clasped his hands behind his back, a smirk on his lips as his gaze flicked between Michael and Damien. "Gentlemen, are we ready?"

"Yes," Michael said as he rose to stand in a slow and deliberate manner.

"No," Damien said, his voice breathy and high-pitched.

Marcus's eyes widened, and he raised his eyebrows at Damien's statement. "Am I to understand you wish to cancel the plans we've made?"

"Damien—" Michael began when Damien waved him away.

"I—I just want to get a few things straight."

Marcus sighed and crossed the room, pouring three drinks. He offered one to Michael who accepted. He held a glass out to Damien.

"No," Damien said with a wave of his hand.

"Take it, Damien. It appears you need it."

"What I need to do is get a few things straight."

Marcus waved the brandy at Damien again. "Such as?"

Damien snatched the proffered glass from his hand. "Such as what this is going to cost us. And what we have to do."

"Consider this… a gift. I always maintained you were a waste as a mere human."

"A gift?" Damien questioned. "You're kidding, right?"

"Yeah, how long before you call the marker in?" Michael questioned.

Marcus sipped his brandy and stalked to stare out the window. The glow of the Buckley house on the hill shone back. "You both are really being quite theatrical, particularly when it is you who requested this from me."

"Yeah, well, now we're just requesting a few more details," Michael said.

Marcus sighed and spun to face them. "I already told you, there is no price. No strings attached."

"Why would you do that?" Damien inquired.

Marcus offered him an amused grin. "An excellent question. I suppose you expect me to say that I'd somehow own you or that you'd owe me a favor in the future."

"That's exactly what I think you'll say."

"Yet that is not my answer. Consider it less of a gift for yourselves and more of a gift for Celine. She worries over you."

Damien scrunched his features, his eyes narrowing. "So, you want us to believe that you're doing this out of the kindness of your heart for Celine?"

"Wait, I thought you didn't have a heart?" Michael said.

"What you believe is entirely up to you. I can assure you there is no cost. And I will also remind you that you sought me out and requested this of me. If you choose not to continue with the arrangement, that is entirely up to you."

Silence fell between them. Damien studied the brandy in his glass before shooting a glance at Michael. Michael offered a slight shrug.

Marcus took another sip of his brandy before he set the glass on the mantle. "It is clear you have some misgivings. Consider our arrangement canceled. Good night, gentlemen."

He strode across the room toward the foyer when Damien spoke up. "Wait."

Marcus slowed and twisted to face him, his eyebrows raised in question.

"We still want to do it."

Marcus turned fully, his lips puckered. "An excellent decision. Follow me."

Damien downed the rest of his brandy in one gulp and set his glass aside, raking the back of his hand against his lips.

He and Michael followed Marcus as he led them down the hall. "You okay, man?" Michael whispered.

"We have to, right?"

"Yep," Michael said. He clapped a hand around Damien's shoulder. "It'll all be over soon."

Damien blew out a long breath as Marcus opened the door leading down to the basement. Damien recalled being stuck in the same basement as they sought Celine's stolen portrait. The rush of memories did little to ease his mind.

Marcus gestured toward the stairs. "After you, gentlemen."

Candlelight glowed from the dark space below. Damien swallowed hard and offered a nervous half-chuckle, half-murmur. He placed his foot on the first stair leading down. It creaked under his weight. He squeezed his eyes closed as the room below wobbled.

Damien clutched at the handrail to steady himself. Sweat beaded on his forehead as he clambered down the stairs. As his feet touched the floor below, he spun to find Michael close on his heels.

His friend's presence gave him some measure of comfort, but not nearly enough. His gaze darted around the space. Dark shadows filled the corners. Flickering candlelight cast eerie glows off the rest of the room.

Marcus and Dembe joined them. Damien glanced up the stairs, noticing the door was now closed. Was it locked, too, he wondered? His throat went dry as he worried his fate was sealed. He stiffened his muscles, trying to prevent himself from shaking all over.

"I don't see any animals," Michael whispered.

"Me either. Or any… victims," Damien hissed back. "Unless it's under that sheet."

"Nah, it's not big enough for a body."

"Unless it's a kid." Damien's eyes widened and he gulped.

"What are you two babbling about?" Marcus questioned as he donned a black-hooded robe.

"Nothing," Damien squeaked.

Marcus pulled a black sheet off a make-shift altar. Damien cringed as the fabric fell away. He squeezed his eyes closed, risking a peek from one slit.

Marcus screwed up his face. "What are you doing?"

"Sorry," Damien answered as he found only a chalice and a knife underneath. "I thought it would be like a kid or something crazy."

"Do you really believe I'd ask you to sacrifice a child?"

Damien shrugged. "Seemed plausible."

"I may take back my statement about you being a waste as a human, Damien."

Damien shot a side-ways glance to Michael who winced.

Dembe handed each of them a black robe then clad himself in one and joined Marcus at the makeshift altar.

"Gentlemen, you have come here tonight with the purpose of extending your lives indefinitely. You seek immortality and all the benefits it brings," Marcus said. "Come closer."

He lifted the chalice and mumbled a few Latin words over it. He held it out to Damien. "Drink this."

Damien gulped and stared into the chalice with a horrified expression. "What is it?"

"Wine."

"Really?" Damien asked, accepting the proffered goblet and staring into it in the dim light.

"Just drink it," Marcus said with a shake of his head.

Damien's lower lip trembled as he lifted it to his lips and tilted the cup back. The bitter wine hit his tongue and he swallowed, relieved. "Just wine!" he announced as he offered the cup to Michael.

Michael took a sip and passed it back to Marcus. After another few muttered words in a language Damien did not recognize, Marcus lifted the ornate dagger from the table. He held the hilt toward Damien. "Take it."

Damien grimaced as he accepted the dagger, wrapping his trembling fingers around the bejeweled handle. His breathing turned shallow again as he stared down at the sharpened blade in his hand. His mouth went dry, and his heart pounded against his ribs.

Marcus stepped back and motioned to Dembe. "Draw his blood."

"What?" Damien exclaimed. "Uh-uh, no way."

Marcus huffed at him, pressing his lips into a thin line. "Do you wish to complete the transformation or not?"

"Yeah, but–"

"Then draw his blood."

Damien shot a panicked glance to Michael, then flicked his gaze to Marcus. "I'm not stabbing Dembe."

Marcus rolled his eyes at him. "For Bazios's sake, you do not need to gut the man, simply make a small slice on his finger."

Damien's expression turned sheepish. "Oh! Oh, right, okay." He offered another nervous laugh as Dembe extended his hand. "Sorry ahead of time, buddy." Damien girded himself, holding his breath and squeezing his eyes shut as he made a small slice across Dembe's index finger.

When he finished, he blew out a sharp breath and swiped his forearm across his sweaty forehead. Marcus stepped forward and relieved him of the knife. "Congratulations, Damien, you are finished."

"Really? That's it?" A relieved grin crossed his face, and he stepped back as Marcus transferred the knife to Michael. He tilted his head toward Dembe who extended his hand.

"You got this, buddy," Damien encouraged.

Michael gave him a nod and made a slice in Dembe's middle finger, though the wound on his index finger had already healed.

"Am I done?" Michael asked.

"Yes," Marcus said, sliding the knife from his hands and wiping it clean. "You are both finished."

Michael held his hands out and stared down at them. He turned them over and studied his palms, then flipped them back and examined them. "Really? I don't feel any different."

"Yes, really," Marcus said as Dembe lifted the chalice from the altar and disappeared into a back room.

"Are you sure something didn't go wrong? Because I don't feel any different at all. I just–"

Marcus palmed the knife and buried it in Michael's gut. Blood blossomed on his t-shirt, dripping to the floor below. Michael fell to his knees with a gasp.

CHAPTER 28

"Michael!" Damien shrieked as he stumbled back a step, his jaw hanging agape. He raced toward his wounded friend, his face pinching with concern.

Michael pulled the knife from his gut with a groan.

"Easy, buddy, just take it easy. We've got to stop the bleeding." Damien pushed his hands against Michael's abdomen.

"Ow!" Michael screamed.

Damien winced. "Sorry, buddy, sorry. But we've got to stop the bleeding until we can get help."

Michael nodded then shook his head. "Wait, wait." He pulled Damien's hands away and tugged up his shirt. His eyes went wide as he swiped across his abs, devoid of any wound.

Damien's eyes widened, too, as he stared at Michael's unblemished skin.

"And if you're still not satisfied," Marcus said, looming over them, "check the wound on your own leg."

Damien's eyebrows squashed together as his eyes fell to his leg. He tugged up the pant leg and peeled back the tape and gauze covering the long gash. He ran his fingertips over his skin where the wound had once been.

"It worked!" he exclaimed, a grin forming on his face.

"Of course, it worked. I am no amateur."

Damien rose to stand and pulled Michael up next to him. "You could have just said something, man," Michael said.

"Yeah, you didn't have to stab him."

Marcus shrugged, staring down his nose at them. "You remained unconvinced. I felt it the best way to prove it to you."

"Of course, you did," Michael groused.

Marcus offered an unimpressed stare. "You may go."

"Right," Michael said. He turned to Damien. "Ready?"

Damien nodded and they hurried up the stairs. Damien breathed a sigh of relief as he turned the doorknob, finding it open. They strode down the hall and let themselves out the front door and into the warm evening air.

Damien blew out a long breath as their feet hit the path to the woods. He doubled over, lacing his fingers together and tugging on his neck. "Ohhh, I'm so glad that's over."

"Yeah, man, me too. I mean, that was way easier than I expected. But I'm so glad it's done."

"We did it!" Damien exclaimed.

Michael clapped him on the back as they started down the path. "We did it! We're immortals!"

"This is super cool," Damien said. "I wonder if we have any super cool powers like fireballs and stuff."

Michael bit his lower lip as he considered the question. "I don't know. Northcott didn't say anything about it."

Damien cupped his hand in front of him. He wound it back and tossed it forward. He flicked his wrist around. "Nothing."

"Maybe you're doing something wrong."

"Like a wrist flick thing?" Damien twisted his wrist a few different ways. "I don't know. Maybe Celine will know. Or Alexander."

"In either case, she can't kill us over this since we're immortal."

Damien chuckled at the statement. "Hey, when he stabbed you, did it hurt?"

"Hell yes, it hurt. I thought I was dying."

"Huh. I thought it wouldn't hurt at all."

"Oh, it hurt."

Damien nodded. "Okay, note to self, we should still try not to get hurt."

"Right," Michael said as they approached the glowing lights of the Buckley house.

"I'm getting nervous all over again," Damien said.

"The worst is behind us."

"Remind me of that when Celine is chasing us around the house throwing fireballs at us for being so stupid as to have asked Marcus Northcott to do this."

"She'll get over it," Michael said. "I mean, I think so."

"Or we can war for centuries like she did with Celeste."

Michael rubbed the back of his neck as they closed the gap to the house. "We didn't betray her, though, so we have that going for us."

"Okay, I'm going with framing this as helping her by removing the worry she had over us."

"Good call," Michael said, pushing through the front door and into the foyer.

Lights still blazed in several rooms but no trace of anyone existed.

"Maybe they're all asleep," Michael said. "We could get off scot-free until morning."

"Could we be so lucky?" Damien asked. "Though that just postpones it and then I'll lay awake, tossing and turning, going over the conversation in my head a thousand times, coming up with answers to questions she'll never ask so I can stand stunned into silence by something I never saw coming when the conversation actually occurs."

"Wow," Michael said, clapping Damien on the shoulder, "you really overthink things."

"Don't I know it."

"How about a drink?" Michael said, stalking into the sitting room. "I couldn't sleep if I tried."

"Sure," Damien said as he plopped onto the couch. Michael passed him a brandy before pouring himself one and taking a sip.

Gray stalked into the room a moment later. His eyes went wide, and he did a double-take. "There you are. Where have you been? We've been searching everywhere for you."

"Oh, uh," Michael stammered, "yeah, we were around. Hey, is Celine still awake?"

"Still awake? She's combing through the halls for you ever since Millie went to check on you and found your room empty."

"Yeah, I needed to walk around. My leg was just bothersome laying there. Thought it would be good to get some weight on it. So, we took a walk."

"I'll get Celine," Gray said.

He disappeared from the room and Damien shot Michael a pained glance. "Here it comes."

"Yep. For better or worse. Best part is she can't kill us." Michael bobbed his head up and down. "Or wait, can she?"

"I don't know, and I hope we don't have to find out."

They waited for several minutes, falling into an uncomfortable silence. Damien's leg bobbed up and down as he sipped nervously at his drink. Michael paced the floor.

Gray returned within ten minutes with Celine, Alexander, and Millie in tow. Damien winced as he snuck a glance at Celine, expecting her face to be a mask of worry. He returned his gaze to his brandy, his mind pondering why she seemed relatively calm.

"There you are," Millie said. "I thought we had an escapee!"

"Nope, no escapee here," Damien said with a chuckle.

"Did some walking I hear. How did the leg hold up? Mind if I check the wound?"

"Uh, it's fine." Damien pressed his hand against his pant leg to stop her from raising it. "Actually, I do mind. Could we have a minute alone with Celine?"

"Why?" Gray asked.

"Obviously, it's private," Michael snarked. "So, telling you why would kind of defeat the purpose, wouldn't it?"

"Did something happen?" Celine inquired. "Is it your leg? Is it worse?"

"No," Damien said, tracing the rim of his brandy glass with his finger.

"Anything you have to say, you can say in front of all of us," Celine answered. "Is this about you two leaving?"

"In a way, yes," Damien said, shooting a glance at Michael. Michael nodded at him.

"About that," Gray said, stalking to the drink cart and pouring himself a brandy. "We've found a fcw locations that may be safe while we deal with this."

Damien puckered his lips at the statement.

"And it is imperative that you go immediately," Alexander said. "We cannot take the chance with Dominique. She and Celine had another battle earlier this evening and we–"

"The thing is," Damien said, interrupting Alexander. Alexander's face pinched with confusion as Damien cut him off. Damien swallowed hard before he continued. "Sorry, the thing is, we don't need to leave."

Michael crossed his arms over his chest and nodded at the statement.

Gray scoffed at them. "I'm not interested in your opinion on whether or not you feel inclined to stay. The option is off the table. There is no discussion here. You are too vulnerable to stay."

"What if we weren't?" Damien said.

"Yet you are. So, there is no discussion. Tomorrow morning, you'll–"

"But we aren't," Damien interrupted.

Celine narrowed her eyes at him. "D, did something happen?"

Damien swallowed hard, eyeing her as his stomach somersaulted. He flushed as he formulated the words to explain the situation to her.

He nodded, his eyes crinkling with concern. "Yeah," he squeaked.

"What?" Gray barked. "What could have possibly happened to make you less vulnerable?"

All eyes turned to Damien. He stared at Celine and offered a one-shouldered shrug, his face melting into a mask of distress.

Celine's head lolled to the side and her forehead crinkled. "Are you saying what I think you're saying?"

Gray snapped his gaze to her. "Did I miss something? He's not saying anything at all!"

Damien licked his lips and offered a weak smile. "We're not so vulnerable anymore."

Alexander furrowed his brow, glancing sideways as he parsed through the statement. He wiggled his finger between Michael and Damien. "Are you implying that you're both–"

"Immortals, yeah," Michael answered.

"What?" Gray exclaimed. "How the hell did that happen? There's no one here who could perform that ceremony. The only person who could is–"

"Marcus Northcott," Celine answered, her eyes never leaving Damien's.

Damien winced again and swallowed hard, his eyes silently apologizing to her.

"You're not serious," Gray said, slamming his glass onto the drink cart. "You're joking."

Damien lowered his gaze to the brandy in his glass.

"Oh, Damien," Celine said, squeezing her eyes shut for a moment.

Damien snapped his gaze up to her. "But we're fixed now. No more fretting over how to protect us!"

"You are both still vulnerable," Alexander said.

"But much less so," Michael argued.

"Yes, much less so, I agree," Alexander answered.

"I'd argue you are more vulnerable," Gray spat as he stalked to the fireplace and slammed his hands against the mantle.

"How do you figure that?" Michael shot back.

"Because you two buffoons just sold your souls to the devil, that's how!"

"We protected ourselves!" Michael hollered back. "The best way we could! This is ridiculous! The perils we face normally are bad enough, but the latest round showed us that our human existence was unsustainable."

"We could have protected you. Hid you," Alexander said.

Michael shook his head. "I don't hide from problems, I face them."

Gray scoffed as he twisted to face Michael. "Your pride has just led you to the stupidest decision of your life."

"Not really. We're immortal and we're in the clear."

"How do you figure that? You owe Northcott."

Michael flicked a finger toward Gray. "That's where you're wrong."

Gray's features formed an incredulous expression. "Oh, is it?"

"Yeah," Michael said with a shrug. "He said it was a gift. No strings attached."

"And you believed him? The man is a known liar."

"Who is aligned with Dominique, I might add," Alexander said.

"I don't see how this was stupid?" Damien squeaked out, his leg bobbing up and down as he listened to the arguments.

Gray turned to face him, his face pinched with anger. "Don't you?"

Damien shook his head. "No, sorry, I don't."

Gray scoffed and fixed his eyes on Damien. "I don't suppose either of you has your soul stone? I don't imagine he transformed you and then handed that off for you for safe-keeping?"

A sinking feeling filled the pit of Damien's stomach, and he shot a worried glance to Michael, his face wrinkled with concern.

"Umm," he murmured, his leg bobbing faster and his hands shaking as he ran one through his hair.

"Oh, Damien," Celine murmured. She shot a glance to Gray. "I need to fix this."

"Celine, wait," Gray shouted as she hurried to the door.

"I have to deal with this, Gray," she called over her shoulder.

"Celine, don't do this. Don't go to him."

"I have to!"

"Celine!" Gray shouted as the front door slammed shut.

He whipped around to face the room, shooting a glaring stare at Michael and then Damien. "Are you two happy now? She's walking straight into the enemy's clutches. Heaven knows what she'll have to trade to keep you safe."

* * *

Dominique gasped as her eyes shot open. She glanced around before she pushed herself up to sit. Her head ached and she clutched at her temples as the room spun for a moment. She puffed out her cheeks and blew out a long breath as her arms flopped into her lap.

Her head lolled to the side, and she grasped at the ribbons of scarlet fabric scattered around her. With a sour expression, she shook her head and climbed to her feet.

She'd shredded the duvet during her latest injection. Each dose brought an increasingly violent reaction. She hoped it translated to an increased stamina and fortitude.

She slipped a pocketknife from her pocket and flicked it open. With a quick motion, she swiped at her forearm. Purple-red blood poured from the temporary wound before it closed.

"Damn it!" she shrieked, hurling the knife across the room.

She leaned over the bed, gripping the mattress as she gritted her teeth and flexed her muscles. A muffled scream emanated from her clenched jaw. Anger flashed through her, and she slid her arms under the bed's thick wooden frame. With a grunt, she heaved it upward. It toppled over like a feather blowing in a breeze.

She stormed across the room toward the six-foot-tall wooden wardrobe. Her fingers closed around either side and she hefted it over her head, tossing it across the room. With one hand, she overturned the loveseat.

With her eyes narrowed, she stood with her chin pressed against her chest, scanning the space. A slow smile spread across her face. She may not yet be impervious to injury, however, her strength had increased.

She strode to the doorway and whistled into the hall. A

repeated smacking sound reverberated moments later. Dominique tugged on her leather jacket and crossed her arms as she eyed the destruction in the room. The smacking sound continued, growing louder until it was nearly on top of her.

She spun to face the new arrival. Brendan limped into the room, his gray skin sagging from his cheekbones.

"Took you long enough." Dominique stared down at his leg, cocked at an odd angle. "Still having trouble with that leg, huh?"

He nodded at her, his jaw creaking as he moved his head.

"You look like hell," she said with a grimace. "Ugh. We're really going to have to fix that if you're going to stick around."

"Die," the man whispered.

"What?" Dominique said, her eyebrows raising. Her leather jacket creaked as she leaned forward. "Did you say something?"

"Die," he whimpered again.

Dominique sighed, burying her head in her hands. "Not only do you look awful, you're stupid, too. Let me explain this again. You're already dead, idiot. Remember that?"

He stared ahead blankly. "Yeah, I thought you did. I think what you're asking for is for me to let you rest."

A whine escaped him. "Rest," he breathed.

"Fat chance, dumbo," Dominique said. "I need you around. Although the way you're moving, you're not much good to me. We're going to have to fix that, otherwise, you're useless."

Dominique narrowed her eyes at the man and tapped her chin. She raised a finger in the air. "Do you want to feel better than you've ever felt in your life?"

He flicked his bloodshot eyes toward her. "You'll be back to normal, only better. No more broken leg, no more flapping jaw. Just Brendan back to the way he was when he stupidly hit on me in the dive bar."

He slowly nodded at her, a rasping noise emanating from his cracked lips.

"Cool. Okay. I just need one thing from you." She approached him and whispered in his ear. "Your soul."

She stepped back and eyed him. He shook his head, his lips forming a grimace. Dominique lifted one side of her upper lip in a sneer. "Fine. Your loss. Guess you'll stay like this."

She pushed past him, knocking him back a few steps as she strode into the hall.

"W-w-wait," Brendan murmured.

Dominique stopped short, a smile forming on her lips. She spun and sauntered back into her destroyed bedroom. She pressed a finger toward her ear. "What's that?"

"Okay," he breathed.

"I'm sorry, I'm not sure I heard you. Did you say you'll give me your soul?"

He nodded. "Okay."

She pulled one side of her mouth back in a wicked smile. "Well, okay, then."

* * *

Dominique eyed the man standing in front of her. "How do you feel?"

Brendan held his hands out in front of him, turning them over as he stared at his restored body. He stepped on one leg, then hopped to the other. His fingertips felt the skin around his face before he stepped to the mirror, miraculously still standing in the wrecked room.

He smiled at his reflection. His tanned cheeks with his carefully trimmed stubble framed his smiling eyes. His dark hair, full and thick, topped his chiseled features. The top button of his flannel shirt pulled open as his muscles tugged at the material.

He barked out a laugh and clapped his hands together. "Haha! Fantastic! I'm back, baby!"

Dominique chuckled. "I told you. And better than ever."

He spun to face her, arching an eyebrow. "Yes, you did." He eyed her like a wolf eyeing a wayward lamb. He stalked toward her, slipping an arm around her waist.

She spread her fingers and clamped them onto his face, shoving him back. "Don't flatter yourself. I have higher aspirations than a local sailor."

"What did you bring me back for?"

Dominique rolled her eyes. "Not that, moron. Have this mess cleaned up by the time I get back. And buy a new duvet. Expensive, not that cheap crap they sell in the middle-class stores. Get something European."

She stalked from the room.

"How am I supposed to pay for it?" he shouted after her.

She pulled a credit card from her pocket and flung it over her shoulder. "I expect this to be taken care of by the time I get back."

"When will that be?"

"None of your business," she called as she bounced down the stairs.

She flung the doors open as she crossed the foyer and stalked through them into the warm night air. She strode down the path, snaking through the woods until the lights of Marcus's house glowed in front of her.

She skipped up the stairs and blew open the door, thundering into the foyer. "Marcus!" she called.

Marcus appeared at the end of the hallway. He slammed the door closed from which he'd emerged, narrowing his eyes at her. "Dominique. What are you doing here?"

"Nice to see you, too," she answered. She meandered into the sitting room and poured herself a bourbon, taking a long sip before she faced him. "Did you handle Teddy's body?"

"I did," he said as he stood in the doorway.

"Good. That's good." She sipped at her bourbon again. "And what about your other task?"

"I expect that to be resolved soon."

"Really?" Dominique said, raising her eyebrows and taking another sip of her bourbon.

"Did you doubt me?"

Dominique pressed a finger to her lips and strode to the fireplace. "Actually, yeah, I did."

Marcus huffed as he strode across the room and poured himself a drink. "You should know better than that, Dominique. I always win."

"Except when it comes to Celine."

"Some games take longer to play than others."

Dominique shot him a sideways glance. "You're setting a world record with this one, Marcus."

Marcus sipped at his brandy. "Good things take time."

"It's time to wrap this up."

Marcus strode to her and clinked his glass against hers. "And I have taken the first steps toward that earlier this evening."

CHAPTER 29

Michael and Damien strode in silence through the halls. Damien pushed open his door, stalking into his room with Michael on his heels. He slammed the door shut and meandered to his bed, sinking onto the edge.

Michael blew out a long breath as he paced the floor, rubbing his neck.

"Well, we've made a nice mess," Damien said, kicking the tassels on his area rug with his foot.

"We didn't mean to."

"No, but we still did it. As usual, stuck our foot right in it without even realizing because we're too green like Gray says."

"Gray's just a jerk."

"He's right though," Damien said with a sigh.

"Is he? No matter what we do, he thinks it's the wrong thing."

Damien flopped back on the mattress, flinging his arms out. "I guess we'll find out when Celine gets back."

Michael eased into the armchair with a sigh and a "yeah."

"If Celine gets back."

"What do you mean?"

"Gray seemed to think she'd have to trade herself for our souls and now that's all I can think about."

"Gray is an… never mind."

"I know what he is, but the fact is if he demands it of her, she'll do it. I know Celine. She'll trade herself for us and I hate that we put her in that position."

"Hopefully, that's not the case."

Damien scrubbed his face with his hands. "I can't believe we were so stupid not to even think of the soul thing."

"He said no charge!"

"Yeah, and then he conveniently kept our soul marker things." Damien tossed his hands onto the gray duvet in frustration.

"Maybe he forgot."

Damien craned his neck to stare upside down at Michael. "Marcus Northcott forgetful? Are you serious?"

Michael shrugged. "Could be. Or maybe they aren't instantaneously available."

Damien crinkled his brow as he crossed his arms. "Two-day shipping?"

"Only if he's a Soul Marker Prime member," Michael said.

The comment elicited chuckles from both men. As their laughter died down, Damien eased his head back to normal with a sigh. "I hope it's something as simple as that. Otherwise, I'm afraid of the consequences we just thrust on everyone."

* * *

Celine stepped from under the canopy of the trees and stared at the house at the cliff's edge overlooking the sea. Lights still glowed from within despite the early morning hour. Her stomach twisted and her knees wobbled a bit as she considered the task ahead.

After a moment, she drew in a deep breath and raised her chin. She allowed the anger to well inside her, drawing on the years of torment to fuel her fire. She stormed toward the house and burst through the front door. A startled Dembe stood with one foot on the stairs leading up, his jaw hanging open as she thundered past him and into the sitting room. Marcus stared out of the window facing the Buckley house, a brandy in his hand.

He twisted to face her, giving her a nod. "Celine! To what do I owe this unexpected pleasure?"

"How could you?" she cried, her voice raw and shrill.

"How could I what, dear?" he questioned.

Her features twisted into a mask of anger, her lips pinching and her nose crinkling. She raced toward him, her hands balled into fists, and raised her right arm.

Marcus caught her wrist mid-swing. "Now, Celine, let's not do anything we may regret."

"I wouldn't regret it," she spat, wrenching her arm from his grip.

"Perhaps you'd care to inform me of the source of your newfound rage."

She lowered her chin, glaring up at him. "You know damn well the source."

He cocked his head as he casually sipped his brandy. "I assume you've spoken with Damien and Michael. I assure you I did only what they asked of me."

"You manipulated them into trusting you."

"I did nothing of the sort. They freely participated. They approached me."

"Undo it," she demanded, curling her fingers into fists again.

Marcus sauntered across the room to refresh his drink. "Really, Celine, I did it for you!"

"Undo it, Marcus," she insisted, following him across the room. "I know you can. You did it with Celeste."

Marcus puckered his lips as if considering it. "But I made the deal with Damien and Michael, not you. So, it would have to be Damien and Michael who requested it."

"You don't need a request! Celeste didn't request it of you."

"A deal is a deal, as they say. And I am a man of my word."

Celine's lower lip trembled with rage as she glared at him.

"Oh, come now, Celine. All is not lost! Dear Damien can spend eternity with you now. As can his dimwitted companion, Michael."

"I assume they paid the usual price," she inquired, lowering her voice to a steady growl.

"Yes, they did."

"So, their souls are lost to you."

"Technically, yes. I hold their soul markers." He flashed two stones, one white, one blue before he closed his fist around them. "Though I do not intend to use them. Not yet anyway."

He shot her a sideways glance. "I could be persuaded to give them to you. For a price."

Celine's voice turned shrill again as she lifted her fists to pound his chest. "You bastard!"

He caught her wrists, ceasing any of her flailings. "Vulgarity really does not become you, dear. You should calm yourself. May I offer you a brandy?"

Celine twisted free, flicking away a tear that had fallen to her cheek. She shoved a lock of hair away from her face and swallowed hard. "What's the price?"

Marcus smirked at her over his brandy glass. "My soul."

* * *

Dominique leaned over the banister as a commotion erupted downstairs. An amused grin played across her features as she crept down a few more steps, peering between the balustrades and into the sitting room.

A soft chuckle emanated from her throat as she listened to the argument between her cousin and Marcus.

"Oh, what did you do this time, Marcus?"

She shot a glance to Dembe who still stood motionless on the bottom stair. With a raise of her chin, she wiggled her eyebrows at him. "Celine's all hot and bothered again, huh?" she whispered.

Dembe climbed the stairs noiselessly, putting an arm on her shoulder. "We should leave them to talk," he breathed.

Dominique shook off his hand. "No way, Dembe, we've got a ringside seat to the fight. Wonder what he did?"

Dembe stared down at her as she grasped the balustrades and pressed her head against them, shifting her angle to follow their movement.

"He turned Michael and Damien."

Dominique snapped her eyes to Dembe, her brow furrowed. She narrowed her eyes as she processed the statement. After a moment she shrugged. She'd find out his reasoning for the interesting move later. For now, she wanted to enjoy the show. Clearly, he'd struck a nerve with Celine.

"Interesting. Well, if he meant to tick her off, he's done a fabulous job. She's pretty mad."

"We should go."

She flicked her hand at him. "Go if you want. I'm sticking around for the show."

He climbed past her to the upper level.

"Should have brought popcorn," she murmured as she watched Celine's fists pummel Marcus.

* * *

Celine glared at him as she realized his end game. He'd taken control of Michael and Damien's souls to bargain for his. She spent a moment weighing the decision. If she traded his soul back, she had no hold over him. However, if she didn't, he had power over Michael and Damien.

Her shoulders slumped as she let out the breath she'd been holding. Defeated, she said, "Fine." She dug into her pocket and produced the black stone.

She held it up between her thumb and forefinger before she slammed it onto the drink cart and held out her hand, palm up.

He smirked at her as he opened his fist, revealing the two soul stones. He dropped the blue one into her hand. Pinching the white with his thumb, he held it up to the light.

"Perhaps, I shall hang on to Damien's. It may be useful."

"Give it to me."

"I've given you Michael's. That seems more than a fair bargain. A soul for a soul."

"You said both. And you're a man of your word, aren't you?"

Marcus tapped the stone in the air and smirked at her again. "So I am. You've gotten quite a bargain, I'd say." He dropped the white stone next to the blue.

Celine closed her fingers around the stones and poked a finger at him. "Leave my family alone."

She spun on her heel and stalked from the room.

"Pleasure doing business with you!" Marcus shouted after her.

The slamming door was the only response. He glanced

down at the drink cart. The smooth, black stone glinted in the light. He grabbed it, studying it as he sipped his brandy.

A slow round of applause sounded, and he snapped his gaze toward the foyer. Dominique leaned against the opening. She grinned at him, shoving her hands into her back pockets.

"Well, well, well, what an interesting show."

"Are you still here?"

"Yes, and I'm so glad I stayed," she said as she stalked into the room and poured herself a drink. She clinked her glass against his. "I got to witness the genius at work. Congratulations, Marcus. I was beginning to think you didn't have it in you."

"As usual, you underestimate subtlety." He stalked toward the window, staring at Celine as she disappeared into the thicket of trees across the field.

"I'll admit, I'm partial to glitzier moves, but whatever works." She joined him at the window, her eyes set on the Buckley house.

After a moment, she twisted to face him. "There is one thing I'm confused about."

Marcus shifted his gaze sideways. "Are you going to ask or play coy?"

"Why did you turn Michael and Damien? Now they're ten times harder for me to kill!"

"That is untrue."

"It's not. Literally, I could have snapped their necks, tossed them off a cliff, stabbed them, shot them, poison, drowning. There were any number of ways, all of which I have already imagined many times, for me to have ended their delicate little lives before you turned them immortal. Now, I've got to work at it. It almost seems like you've done her a favor."

Marcus stalked away from her. "As usual, you are short-sighted."

"How so?"

Marcus spun to face her. "As humans, Celine is obviously aware of their fragility. She will take whatever steps are necessary to shield them from you. Including hiding them from your reach."

"Which she didn't do yet."

"Yet being the keyword. After the Dracopire attack, I am positive Celine would have removed them from the situation."

"They can be tracked."

"But that takes time, Dominique. Time you do not have if you want to strike at her immediately."

Dominique ground her teeth as she considered his words.

"As immortals, they are in plain sight. Yes, you may have to flex your muscles a bit more, but I have every confidence that you'll find a way to destroy them in their present state."

Dominique narrowed her eyes as she sipped her bourbon.

"In short, Dominique, I have removed the need for Celine to spirit them away and make them untouchable. I have lulled her into a false sense of security. And now, we may strike at will."

Dominique flicked her gaze to him. "And you recovered your soul."

His lips curled into a satisfied smile. He approached her and stared down at her blue eyes. "Perhaps now you can share your plan for destroying every member of Celine's family."

Dominique lowered her chin her features twisted into an evil grin. "You're never going to believe what I've got planned."

CHAPTER 30

$\mathcal{C}$eline wrapped her arms around her midriff as she stared out over the horizon. The salty morning breeze that swept off the sea chilled her. She nestled into her hoodie as the sky lightened and pink streaks kissed the ocean.

Her hand still clutched the two soul stones she'd just recovered. As the sea rolled, splashing against the rocky shore, she pondered their next move.

Movement behind her caught her eye. She shot a sideways glance over her shoulder before returning her gaze to the undulating waves.

"Did it work?" she asked.

Marcus Northcott sidled up to her, his focus on the horizon as he came to a stop. "Brilliantly."

The corners of her mouth turned up slightly and she spun to face him, dropping the soul stones into her pocket. "So, Dominique fell for it."

"Your performance was superb. Even I almost believed you were angry. You may have missed your calling in life, Celine."

"And you've been welcomed back into the dark fold?"

"It seems so."

"Has she shared her plans yet?"

"She's hinted at something big. She asked me to meet her at her new base of operations. I shall find out more there."

Celine nodded and puckered her lips in thought. "Was she putting you off or do you think she'll tell you?"

"She was nearly giddy with anticipation. She will tell me."

One corner of Celine's mouth pulled up in a smirk. "And you will tell me."

He raised his eyebrows at her.

"I'll gather the troops," Celine said as she stepped away from him.

"Gray will never accept this," he called to her.

"Gray will have to. We need each other, Marcus. We can't defeat Dominique alone. Neither of us."

"Then I leave you to summon your army and explain this to them. Au revoir, Celine."

They stalked in opposite directions. Celine spun back after a few steps, raking a wayward piece of hair from blowing across her face.

"Hey, Marcus," she called to him.

He twisted to face her.

"Welcome to the Slayers." She offered him an amused grin before she continued on her path back to the house.

Celine climbed to the cliffs above, recalling the discussion they'd had in the library days earlier. "There's something we need to discuss," she said.

Marcus spun to face her. "Oh?"

"Michael and Damien are going to ask you to turn them into immortals."

He strode back to her, his hands clasped behind his back. "And I suppose you want me to deny them."

Celine flicked her gaze up to his dark eyes. "No, I want you to turn them."

It was one of the few occasions she'd seen genuine surprise cross Marcus's chiseled features. "I'm quite shocked, Celine."

"They can't continue in this world as humans. It's far too dangerous."

"And you trust me with this?"

"I'm not sure trust is an accurate word, but this is to your advantage."

"How?"

Celine waved his soul stone at him. "Dominique wants you to retrieve this. Once you turn Michael and Damien, I'll trade it back to you for their souls. Dominique will think you've won. And I will have what I want."

"You lose your power over my soul, though."

"It was never mine to begin with."

"How do you know they will ask?"

"They've mentioned it already. You're the closest person who can perform the ceremony. Damien will have worked this out already. He'll realize you're the only option. And he will ask you."

"You're confident. Though I cannot see him being short-sighted enough to put you in this position."

"That's where I'll need you to work your magic. Tell him it's a gift. He's naive enough to believe you."

"Michael is savvier."

"He won't abandon Damien. And Damien will believe you. Let Damien convince Michael. You focus on convincing Damien."

Marcus arched an eyebrow.

"You want to defeat Dominique, don't you?" Celine questioned.

He flicked his gaze out the window before he answered. "Yes."

"Once you get your soul stone back, she'll accept you right back into the fold. Which is where we'll need you to be."

"Intriguing, Celine. You wish me to play double agent."

"Subterfuge is your strong suit. It's a perfect role for you."

"I must admit I'm somewhat surprised by the deceptive nature of your plan. Were you not always an advocate of everything above board?"

"Fight fire with fire, right?"

"Why not tell everyone the plan?"

"Because this needs to appear to Dominique that it's happened organically. She can't even catch a whiff of this being contrived or she'll never trust you."

"And you believe those close to you cannot pull that off?"

"I know they can't. I also know the uphill battle I'd face with Gray."

"He would not approve. You know this, yet you ask me to do it anyway."

"Better to ask for forgiveness than permission."

He smirked at her. "Careful, Celine, your dark side is showing."

"Do we have a deal or not?"

"Yes, we have a deal. When dear Damien asks me for the favor, I shall grant it. I always said the boy's talents were a waste as a human."

"And then we'll have a major argument over it."

"And I shall achieve what Dominique asks of me."

Celine stuck out her hand and Marcus accepted it. "To working together for the common good."

"To working together to achieve our goals."

The memory faded from her mind as the Buckley house filled her vision. She pushed through the doors and into the quiet house. Everyone must have disbanded, probably tired of arguing with each other over the state of affairs. Everything would be made clear soon.

Her gaze rose to the second floor as she slicked her hair behind her ears. She'd seek out Michael and Damien first to assure them their souls were safe. She took a step toward the stairs when Millie appeared from a back hall.

"Celine, good morning," she called.

"Good morning, Millie."

"Were you able to settle everything to your satisfaction?" she asked as she shoved her glasses on top of her head and closed the distance between them.

"Yes, thanks," Celine answered.

She offered a tight-lipped smile and wiggled a folder in her hands. "I have the results of the analysis you requested I run."

Celine's eyebrows shot up. "And?"

Millie pushed the folder forward. "It is as you suspected."

Celine grabbed it and flicked it open, scanning the results inside. A smile crossed her lips, and she glanced up at Millie. "Thanks, Millie. I appreciate you doing this so quickly."

"You're welcome. If you need anything else, please let me know."

"I will. You should get some rest. I didn't mean for you to stay up all night for this."

"I'll rest later. First, I'd like to examine the blood samples from Michael and Damien. I'm fascinated to study someone so newly transformed!"

"Have fun," Celine said with a chuckle. Millie tottered off toward her lab while Celine hurried up the stairs.

She wound through the halls, heading for Damien's door. A voice called out seconds after she knocked. She slipped inside the room.

Damien and Michael leapt from the armchairs near the

window. Worry creased both of their features. She glanced between them both.

"Well?" Michael asked.

"Yeah, how bad is it?" Damien said.

Celine dug into her pocket and produced both soul stones. "I got them."

Damien approached and stared at them. "Which is which?" he asked.

"Yours is the white one. Michael's is blue." Damien leaned closer to study them. "Go ahead, take it."

Damien picked his up and stared into it. "Is there a reason they're different colors?"

"Because you've lived different lives. Everyone's is unique. Like a fingerprint."

Damien flicked his gaze to Celine. "What color is yours?"

Celine pulled hers from her pocket and flashed it at him. "Iridescent rainbow."

"Wow, yours is way cooler than mine."

Celine chuckled at his assessment.

"What'd it cost to get these back?" Michael questioned.

"Don't worry about it," Celine answered.

"That bad, huh?"

She shook her head. "I gave Marcus his soul stone back in exchange for them."

Damien's shoulders slumped and he lowered his gaze to the floor. "Oh, man. I'm really sorry, Celine. We didn't mean to–"

"It's fine. It was an easy trade. His soul wasn't mine to keep anyway. It's most likely the adjudicator would have returned it to him when it comes back from its repose."

"Yeah, but until then we may have had some peace."

"There won't be any peace until Dominique is gone. That's where our focus needs to be."

Damien's features pinched. "I still feel really bad about this. I feel so stupid."

Celine wrapped her fingers around his hand and squeezed. "D, don't feel bad. It's fine. And it's better this way, you're right. You're safer now." She grabbed Michael's hand. "Both of you."

"I'm glad you see it that way," Michael said. "Gray's pretty sore about it."

"What's done is done. He'll live."

Michael nodded and Damien offered another contrite glance. "Besides," she continued, releasing their hands and grabbing the folded paper she'd stuffed into her pocket, "we have something else to discuss."

"Oh, man, now what?" Michael questioned.

"Yeah, how much worse is this? Werewolves?" Damien asked.

"Evil elves?"

"That all-seeing eye thing from Lord of the Rings?"

Celine chuckled at them. "None of that," she promised. "I had Millie do an analysis. Just a hunch I had."

Damien's face paled and he sobered quickly. "On me, right?"

Celine nodded.

"Am I sick? Did that Dracopire thing poison me for life? Will I grow scales? Or die a slow painful death?"

"None of that. It wasn't that kind of analysis. And besides, Marcus's magic potion should have stopped any ill effects from the Dracopire, and now that you're immortal, your body will flush any toxins from your system without an issue."

Damien ran his fingers through his hair as he blew out a sigh of relief. "Oh, whew. Thank goodness."

"So, what did you analyze?" Michael asked.

Celine flicked her gaze to Michael and then back to Damien. "I found your father, D."

Damien stopped dead and stared at her. "Really? You know who my dad is?"

"Oh, ah, I should go," Michael said. "Let you talk."

"No, you can stay," Damien said.

"Nah, you can tell me later, man. It's private."

"Actually, you should stay, Michael."

Michael ground to a halt as he crossed the room and turned to face them.

"It involves you, too."

His gaze darted around the room, and he cocked his head. "What?"

"When the paperwork came for the new branch, I glanced at it. I spotted your father's name on the signature page."

"Okay?"

"Monica said Damien was named after his father, but not really, right?"

"Yeah, which means next to nothing," Damien said.

"Not really. She meant you didn't have your father's first name. But maybe your name was the same as your father's middle name."

Realization dawned on Michael. "My father's name is Winston Carlyle. Winston Damien Carlyle."

Celine's lips curved upward.

"So, what are you saying?" Damien questioned.

"I'm saying Winston Carlyle is your father, D. Michael is your half-brother."

Damien's jaw dropped and he flicked his gaze to Michael then back to Celine. "Are you sure?"

"Positive. Millie ran the analysis twice and she never makes mistakes."

Damien fluttered his eyelashes, his gaze falling to the floor. He raised his eyebrows as he stood in stunned silence.

Michael let out a quiet laugh before he stalked toward Damien. Damien lifted his eyes to Michael and the two men stared at each other for a moment before Michael broke into a grin. He pulled Damien into a hug and clapped him on the back.

"We're brothers, man. This is amazing."

"Unbelievable," Damien agreed.

Celine smiled at the brotherly display, allowing them the moment to bond.

As they split apart, Damien asked, "Are you okay with this?"

"Okay with it?" Michael said with a laugh. "Are you kidding me? This is the best news I've gotten in a while."

"Really?" Damien asked, his voice wavering with emotion.

"Yeah. I mean, are you okay with it?"

"I couldn't have picked a better brother. We're a team. And now... we're family."

Michael clapped him on the back again. "Best friends and blood brothers." He locked his hand around Damien's.

Damien nodded with a grin. "Best friends and blood brothers."

He flicked his gaze to Celine and held an arm out. "Get on over here."

Celine smiled and approached them, wrapping her arms around them both. "I'm really glad this worked out this way. I didn't say anything when I asked Millie to run the DNA analysis in case it didn't pan out."

"But it did," Michael said.

Damien turned pensive for a moment. "Hey, if your dad is my dad... do you think there's any chance he could help us find my mom?"

Michael shrugged. "Uh, I can ask, but–"

"But it's probably not the best idea since we're only half-brothers and that may be a tricky question."

Michael laughed as he dropped his arms to his sides. "My dad's infidelity is no secret. What I mean is, I'm not sure he's going to remember twenty-five years ago. I mean, it's not like it happened once with him. So, it'd be a toss-up on whether or not he remembers this particular affair. And, of course, there could be more than one to consider."

Damien winced.

"Maybe we should take a moment to take the win on finding your dad, D."

Damien nodded as Michael shook his head. "No, I'll ask."

"Let's just leave it for the moment," Damien said. "Celine's right. I'm thrilled we found my dad and we can take a moment to celebrate that. We'll ask about my mom when we get a free minute. There's no rush."

"I know you want to know, man," Michael said. "I'll text him as soon as I can."

"Thanks, buddy."

Celine's cell phone chimed, and she pulled it from her pocket and glanced at the screen.

"And on that note, with two problems solved, we really need to discuss how we'll handle Dominique moving forward."

"Right," Damien said. "And how we can help now that we're not just dead weight."

"You were never dead weight, D," Celine said. "Meet me in the private sitting room. I'll find Gray and Alexander."

"Private one? In the back?"

"I'd prefer to keep our meeting away from prying eyes."

"Good plan," Michael said.

They parted ways with Michael and Damien heading to the sitting room near the rear of the house and Celine stalking toward her suite.

She pushed through the doors, finding Gray inside, staring out the window. He breathed a sigh of relief as she stepped inside, hastening to her and wrapping her in his arms. "Oh, thank God, you're safe."

She squeezed him tightly. "I'm fine, Gray. And the problem is solved."

He leaned back, cupping her face in his hands. "What did it cost?"

She sucked in a deep breath. "I traded his soul for theirs."

Gray let his arms drop from around her waist and stalked toward the large, bay window. "Unbelievable. I hope they realize what they've done."

"It's over, Gray. We need to talk about what's going to happen now."

"I suppose we don't need to send them away, so we can skip that discussion."

"And move on to the more important one: what we're going to do about Dominique."

Gray sighed and nodded.

"Can you find Alexander and Celeste? We're meeting in the back sitting room to discuss it."

"Sure. Back sitting room?"

"Away from prying eyes," Celine said as she stalked toward the bedroom. "I'll be down in a second."

The door to their suite closed as Celine dug a change of clothes from her drawer and tugged her hoodie over her head, replacing it with a sweater. She freed her blonde curls from under it and finger-combed them.

She considered the task ahead. She'd need all of them to defeat Dominique. The problem would be convincing them to work together.

With a deep sigh, she strode from the room, determined. She wound through the halls and down to the sitting room tucked in the back of the house. Decorated in dark woods and muted tones, it provided the perfect meeting spot for them.

She scanned the room as she stepped inside. Silence pervaded the space. Alexander sat pensively in a leather armchair. Michael and Damien sat near each other on the sofa. Gray stared out the window. Celeste perched on the armchair opposite Alexander.

"Good to see you back, Celine. Gray filled us in on the news," Alexander said.

"That problem is solved, but Dominique is still a major issue."

"Shall we begin to discuss it?" Gray asked, spinning to face them and leaning against the windowsill.

Celine checked her phone. "We're still waiting on someone."

"Who?" Gray barked.

"Millie?" Alexander posed, rising from his chair. "I can fetch her."

"No, not Millie," Celine answered.

"Then who?" Gray asked again.

"Me," a voice announced from the doorway. All eyes turned to the open door. Marcus Northcott stood inside, a smirk on his lips.

Gray leapt from his seat against the sill. "Get out of here! Haven't you taken enough from this family?"

"Take it easy, Gray," Celine said.

"Celine?" Alexander questioned. "You seem unsurprised."

"She is not," Marcus said as he strode into the room.

Gray focused his attention on Celine. "You can't be serious. You invited him?"

"Yes, I did."

"After what he just did to Michael and Damien?"

An amused grin lit up Marcus's features. "Oh, you haven't told them yet. I am so pleased I arrived in time to witness their faces as you tell the tale."

Gray waved an angry finger at Marcus. "We know the

tale. You transformed Michael and Damien and she had to bargain your soul for theirs."

Marcus smirked at him. "I did nothing to Michael and Damien that was not requested."

"You took advantage of them, plain and simple. And all to get your hands on your soul stone."

"Enough!" Celine shouted. "Marcus didn't take advantage of anyone. Not really."

"The hell he didn't, Celine!" Gray argued. "He used the situation to force your hand."

"Oh, but I didn't," Marcus gloated.

"Marcus, please," Celine said. She turned to the others in the room. "Marcus didn't take advantage of them. I asked him to do it."

Gray's eyebrows raised and his chin lowered to his chest. "What?"

"Yeah, I second that," Michael said, his brow crinkled. "We asked him. Actually, we asked Celeste to ask him." Michael glanced at her and flicked his hands up in apology. "Sorry, Celeste."

She waved his apology away.

"And then we discussed it with him," Damien said.

Marcus pointed a finger to Celine. "After she discussed it with me."

Celine nodded. "It's true. Before you spoke with him, we had a conversation about it. I knew you'd ask him. You're a problem solver, D, and this was the only way to solve the problem. I told him to do it."

"Why would you do that, Celine?" Alexander questioned.

"We needed Michael and Damien safe. And we needed to stage a believable argument that would get Dominique to believe Marcus was still on her side."

"Aren't you?" Gray inquired, shooting him a glaring look.

"She believes I am, which is what matters."

Damien rose and paced the floor. "So, you knew we would ask him, and you were okay with it?"

"Yeah. Sorry, D. I couldn't risk you letting anything slip that would tip Dominique off."

"And the whole time we were sneaking around–"

"I knew. I was fine with it and there's no harm done. Marcus has his soul stone back, which was all part of the plan."

"And I have been welcomed back into the fold."

"This is unbelievable," Gray groused. "We can't trust him! Celine, please."

"We can't defeat her on our own."

"No, you cannot," Marcus agreed. "Particularly after what she just confided to me."

"What does that mean?" Alexander asked.

"It means things are much worse than we could have ever imagined."

All eyes turned to Marcus as he continued his tale. "Her tentative alliance with the Dracopires is stronger than we imagined. By week's end, she will welcome an army of them to this realm."

"Impossible," Gray barked.

"I agree," Alexander said. "The adjudicators would never allow it."

"I'm not certain she cares," Marcus answered. He flicked his gaze to Celine. "There's more."

"More than an army of Dracopires?" Celine questioned.

"Yes," Marcus answered. "Have you noticed anything odd with Dominique during your battles with her?"

Celine considered it. "Her blood."

Marcus nodded. "Her blood is purple-red, not red."

"What does that mean?" Damien questioned.

"What it means exactly, I'm still not entirely certain. But what I do know is that she has been injecting herself with some sort of serum designed to modify her immortality."

"I'm assuming you're not talking about modifying it for the worse," Michael said.

Marcus shook his head. "I do not know the specifics of what is in it, but it is designed to make her invincible."

"Invincible?" Alexander repeated.

"Yes," Marcus said. "Unable to be harmed. Unable to be killed. And insanely powerful. Invincible."

Celine sank into the armchair next to Alexander, her jaw hanging open. Thunder boomed overhead as silence fell over the room.

"What are you thinking, Celine?" Gray questioned.

She pinched her eyebrows together and tensed her jaw, flicking a worried gaze toward him. "That the question may not be how we can beat her, but rather if we can."

EPILOGUE

ominique flung open the French doors and stepped onto the stone balcony attached to her bedroom. Black clouds gathered on the horizon and lightning ripped through the sky. Thunder boomed, bringing a smile to her lips. She poured herself a glass of champagne and took a sip.

The wind whipped her dark hair around wildly. She flicked her head to remove it from her face. It blew back over her shoulders as a few drops of rain splatted to the ground.

Red flashes formed in the sky as creatures from another realm broke through the barrier and entered the earthly realm. Her smile broadened as creatures filled the sky, their hulking bodies sailed through the black clouds.

Screeches filled the air. Music to her ears. She flicked her gaze to the Buckley estate on the hill. She'd soon watch it burn, right along with this entire little town. They'd beg her for mercy before she was finished.

One of the dragon-like creatures dove from the sky, speeding toward her, teeth bared. The massive wings flung outward as he dove toward the balcony. With expert control, he slowed to a stop and flapped his wings to float down to the stone floor.

With a thud, he landed and stalked forward toward Dominique.

She sipped at her champagne again. "Leoric, I'm so pleased to see you and your army here."

"My people await your orders."

She smirked at him. "And you shall have them. Soon. Settle your people in. We shall discuss details in the morning."

The massive Dracopire bowed his head. He unfurled his wings, flapping hard to shoot skyward. The turbulence whipped her hair wildly again.

She took another sip of her champagne as she tore her eyes away from the hulking beast's rise and followed the approach of a black town car up the winding drive.

The car slid around the governor's circle, easing to stop outside the front door. After another sip, she set the flute on the stone railing and strode into the house.

Her heels clicked across the marble floor before pounding down the stairs. She stalked to the rosette inlaid on the foyer floor and stood straight.

The front doors burst open. A dark-haired woman, her hair pulled into a chic French twist, strode through them. Her porcelain skin was almost devoid of wrinkles. Her delicate features fit her small, oval face perfectly, giving her a regal appearance. Her capelet fluttered around her. Her emerald eyes scanned the space as she tugged her black leather gloves off, finger by finger.

"Welcome, Maitresse," Dominique said with a bow of her head. She raised her eyes to study the woman's reaction.

The woman puckered her lips and lifted her shoulder in a slight shrug. "It will do," she said, her French accent thick.

"I have given you a beautiful bedroom suite with—"

The woman flicked her hand in the air to silence her. "I care not. I prefer to know where our progress stands."

Dominique drew one side of her mouth back in a satisfied smile. "You will be even more pleased with that."

The woman arched a dark eyebrow. Dominique approached her, waving her hand toward the sky as she wrapped the other arm around the woman's shoulders.

"Come and witness the arrival of your army." She guided the woman out onto the stone stoop. Red flashes still broke through the sky.

"You have done well, Dominique."

Dominique raised her chin, a prideful smile spreading across her face. "Soon, we will achieve your goal. We will crush the Buckleys and force Celine to our side. Soon, we will rule the world."

* * *

Continue the series with Book 6 coming 2024. Until then, check out *Death of a Duchess*, a supernatural suspense mystery series!

OTHER SERIES BY NELLIE H. STEELE

<u>Cozy Mystery Series</u>

Cate Kensie Mysteries
Lily & Cassie by the Sea Mysteries
Pearl Party Mysteries
Middle Age is Murder Cozy Mysteries

<u>Supernatural Suspense/Urban Fantasy</u>

Shadow Slayers Stories
Duchess of Blackmoore Mysteries

<u>Adventure</u>

Maggie Edwards Adventures
Clif & Ri on the Sea